I0628948

An Emerald Abyss

A Gordan Hudde Novel

Mark Hudson

ISBN: 0999006630
ISBN 13: 9780999006634

Published by One Flyer Publishing.

My heartfelt thanks to all my fellow veterans past and present, and including those who will raise their hands and swear in the future. A special thank-you to all those who have seen combat and the family members who stand by them!

Table of Contents

1

Current Date, Tuesday. 0800hrs

THE TWO BLACKED-OUT GMC Yukons sped up the wooded road toward the CIA headquarters buildings, blue and white lights flashing from windshield-mounted equipment. At the gate, the uniformed men from the security protective services allowed them access with little fanfare but great interest.

The large concrete and steel buildings burst out into view, nestled between the peaceful-appearing woods and the Potomac River, where it had been built.

The drivers had no time to enjoy the view; both vehicles slid to a stop, with their front-right wheels hopping the bright, red-painted curbs. Five men, four enlisted and one officer, jogged to the main doors and ran straight at the security team near the metal detectors. The crisp uniforms of the Army urban fatigues were a stark contrast to the white and navy worn by the security staff of the CIA headquarters; only their sidearms were similar.

"What is this about the Colonel?" the leader of the CIA security team, a Captain, asked.

"Trust me, son, your Director is in danger. My CO called over to yours already; we must not delay!" Colonel Darby obviously wanted to hurry past this necessary nicety of explaining himself and was frankly shocked that he had to, as their bosses had already shared the info.

The security head glanced back over his shoulder at his coworkers with a dismissive look. "Look, sir, I think we would..."

He was interrupted by the *Whoop-Whoop!* of an alarm; red and white lights began flashing on a wall-mounted system; everyone but the Colonel seemed unable to resist looking at them.

The Colonel reached out and grabbed the security officer's shoulder. "We need to hurry."

"Follow me!" The security officer said, and three other uniformed men, along with the Army five, began to run the halls.

The CIA director's secretary was standing in the hall, with one hand held to his throat and the other pointing inside the office.

The men stacked quickly at the either side of the door; one was cracked open.

Impatient, the Colonel went through the large, oak double doors first. His Army men had un-holstered their firearms, training them ahead for whatever they were about to encounter.

CIA Director John Stevens was a big man; he looked like a giant standing over the man kneeling at his feet. A .45-caliber 1911 style handgun was trained at the head of the kneeling man, who held his hands up behind his head, exhibiting "no fight left." the Army four holstered their weapons and began to zip-cuff and search the kneeling suspect.

"Director Stevens, I'm Colonel Darby from Fort Belvoir, and I have been tasked to bring in the fugitive." He held out his hand.

Darby looked into the eyes of Stevens, who appeared a bit dazed. He reached out to take possession of the Kimber weapon from the Director. "Nice," he couldn't help but to say.

"Yeah — it's his; I think I'll keep it" Stevens replied, nodding at the now-prone detainee.

"Director your nose is bleeding. I'm sorry I haven't got anything to offer you." He paused. "Are you alright, sir?"

"Yes, yes." He wiped the blood from his near totally grey mustache with the back of his large black hand as best he could. He chuckled, a bit nervously, "I guess it's been a while since I tasted my own blood."

"Well, you did good work to disarm him. With your permission, we would like to remove him back to our base."

"I guess." Stevens still seemed a bit out of it. "Can someone contact me later?"

The Colonel figured getting attacked by one of your own men would be a rough way to start a Tuesday morning. He turned and grabbed the prone man by the back of his denim jacket, and, with the help of one of the sergeants, they yanked him to his feet.

He spun the fugitive around to face the Director. Grabbing him by the hair, he forced his face up so that they could lock eyes. The blazing green eyes of the fugitive locked onto the brown of the Director's. The black Spartan-looking beard still had some carpet fibers woven into it, and he appeared to also now have some blood seeping from his nose, most likely from being face-planted onto the floor by the rough Army men.

"I'll see you again," the fugitive said.

The Colonel thought he may have seen a wink. "Don't worry, Director. From what I hear, this is the last you will see of Gordan Hudde."

And with that, they all spun and left the Director alone, nursing a sore nose.

John Stevens ejected the magazine from the handgun and then slid the slide back to send the one round up into the air. He missed catching it with his left hand and had to bend down to pick it off the floor; a drop of blood from his nose fell onto the carpet at the same time.

He set the three parts of the weapon onto his desk and grabbed a napkin to dab his nose.

He pressed the buzzer for his secretary.

"Sir?"

"Yeah, I'm going to need Mykhaylychenko front and center...and I mean now."

2

Date: Ten years earlier, Time 0200hrs local Afghanistan time.

STAFF SERGEANT GORDAN Hudde kneeled between eight other men ranking from E-6 to private first class at Delaram Military Base, Afghanistan, finishing up the operation brief for his team.

"Remember this operation is speed plus surprise. Nothing more than day pack for extra ammo. We are expected to be back by first light — *hoohah*?"

"Hoohah" came the positive reply from his team.

"OK. Check your buddy for noise discipline, and let's be ready to move. Let's show these Delta guys that the Rangers don't sit behind anyone!"

His team members began taking turns hopping up and down and turning or twisting to see if anything needed to be taped up or tied down.

"We're good," a Sergeant called out, giving him a thumbs-up.

A lone figure emerged from the communication tent and shuffled off in his direction.

"What's the word, Bulldog?" Hudde asked the approaching CIA operative who was calling the shots for this mission. Hudde didn't know this agent's real name, but he had been coming and going for weeks with an assortment of Delta soldiers and local villagers. The compact-but-heavy man had an AK slung across his back and was wearing the standard camouflage top with solid black pants. With his *shemagh* in place, the only part of his face that Hudde could see were his eyes, and those eyes were burning black and bright. Hudde would never admit it, but the guy was fittingly spooky.

"Mount up" was all he said as he passed.

"Roger that." Hudde let out two low whistles; all his men turned to look. Hudde spun his finger in the air, and all his men began heading toward the assortment of vehicles.

Hudde waited until all his men had crammed into the back of the High Mobility Multi-Wheeled Vehicle, or "Humvee," before he handed his Scar-16 to one of his men to hold, and then he climbed in last so that he could be first out.

The Marines based here had been coming into more and more contact just west and south of the town of Farah. They had become accustomed to heading right through Farah, up the very center of the town, without any casualties. Then the contact began getting closer and more lethal to the town over the last few months. That's when "Bulldog" said he'd found the reason: It seemed that one of the Iranian spooks had moved into town and was now directing the local Taliban to more dangerous ends.

The brain trust had decided that Hudde's platoon and a few Delta guys should be brought in to assist "Bulldog" in a "snatch-and-grab" operation. The Marines were to drop off the Army guys near the objective and continue through the village, as normal. The platoon of Rangers would split up, and each squad would set up security at intersections around the objective.

Once the Rangers were in place, the Delta guys in a Humvee and a pickup truck would come screaming up to the front door, bust in, and grab the Iranian *haji*. The Rangers would "Escape & Evade" to the edge of town and return in their vehicles. As always, there were several rally points set up as possible casualty-airlift locations or emergency-evacuation locations. No air support was to be on standby, as they were so close to Delaram that no one felt that there was any need. No casualties had been taken by the Marines in almost a year now from the village of Farah; nobody was expecting any real excitement except right at the extraction point.

It always seemed easy when you were in a tent, far away from your target.

The caravan began moving — a MATV, a heavily armored Humvee, followed by a LAV, a wheeled tank with a 25mm gun, with five Humvees and another MATV bringing up the rear. One of the Humvees held Marines; the rest were full of Rangers. Hudde relaxed for the ride. He knew that the small number of Taliban would not risk taking on the amount of firepower they had assembled, and there was nothing you could do in the event of a roadside bomb. So he sat and looked out as the rocky desert landscape slipped by, lit by the bright three-quarter moon. There was going to be no need for night-vision equipment tonight.

Just after the caravan turned west, heading through the center of town, two Humvees and the trailing MATV continued north five blocks before they also headed west. Hudde figured that "Bulldog" and his Delta attachment would be leaving the base about that time.

The caravan slowed to a crawl, and Hudde and his men jumped out of the vehicle and slid to the wall on the north side of the street, waiting until they observed the Ranger Captain and his squad slip out of their vehicle. Then they began heading north, deeper into the village.

The only noises they heard were the occasional dog barking and the whine of the diesel engines off in the distance, as the Marines headed up and out of the village farther off to the west.

Hudde reached the intersection south and east of the target building, and he and his men took positions to defend against any enemy coming from those directions. They each, in turn, were depending on the other three teams to protect them from other directions, just as those teams depended on Hudde and his team.

Captain Schroeder called out on his mic, "All teams, all teams. This is Red Leader in position. Over."

Hudde keyed his radio. "Red Leader, this is Blue Leader: In position. Over."

Hudde heard Green Leader and then Yellow Leader each repeat the same. He instinctively knew that Red leader would have the radio man call "Bulldog" and give them the status and a "Go" sign.

They all sat in the relative open, feeling anxious and hoping that this would continue to be boring.

Hudde heard the vehicles before he saw the blackout lights heading quickly down the street at him. The pickup truck was first, with a delta member standing in the back using the bed-mounted .50 caliber as something to maintain his balance. Another man sat looking forward, probably gearing up to jump out the moment that the vehicle slid to a stop in front of one of the only two-story buildings on this street, which was the target.

The Humvee was so close to the back of the pickup, they appeared to be one. Gordan caught a glimpse of "Bulldog" in the back seat as it zipped past. Hudde closed his eyes and leaned against the wall of the building, knowing that the vehicle would be towing a bunch of dust that he didn't need screwing up his vision.

That's when an explosion caused him to fall forward onto his face. His ears were ringing so much that he momentarily could not hear the radio or the gunfire that began springing up from a rooftop directly east of the target building.

Some of his men began returning the sporadic gunfire; Hudde turned and observed the turned-over and burning Humvee. The pickup truck was unrecognizable.

Hudde realized that he was being ordered to fall back to Rally Point One by the Captain.

"I'm checking for survivors," Hudde called out into his mic, and the Captain's voice screamed in his ear

"Negative, Blue Leader. This is Red Leader, and I say again: Fall back to Rally Point One. That is an order!"

Hudde tapped his saw gunner on the Kevlar and pointed at the roof. "Fuck them up — I'm heading across the street!"

The saw gunner rolled and began sending three-to-five-round bursts about a foot lower than the actual roof.

Hudde pulled one of the two grenades from his web gear and pulled the pin before he sprinted across the street. Once behind the burning wrecks, he heaved the grenade at the roof, where the shooting had temporarily gone silent. He wasted no time looking for the results.

One of the Delta members was lying near the burning back wheel of the Humvee; Hudde pulled him to the south side of the bomb-damaged target house and checked for wounds.

From the light of the burning vehicles, Hudde made out that three enemy men were dragging a body across the street and into the building from where the assault appeared to have sprung.

Hudde could hear the other three teams calling out, as they were now coming under fire as well.

Hudde transmitted, "We have survivors at the target location. We have a hostage who was taken directly in front of me here. Suggest we fall back to target area and retake this block."

"Negative, negative, Blue Leader! I say again: Your orders are to fall back to Rally Point One. Red Leader out!"

The Delta soldier grabbed Hudde by the shoulder and screamed into his ear, "Where is Bulldog?"

"I think he just got dragged into the house across the street." Hudde looked down. "Can you go?"

"Hell, yeah."

Hudde called out to his team and gave the upside-down gun sign to point at the house across the street. Then he flashed the "Rally" sign and used the karate chop motion, again pointing at the same house.

His men were taken back a bit. If the enemy were in the house, why would they rally there?

Hudde didn't wait for anyone and charged the front door, where, moments before, three tangos had dragged a fellow American. Hudde didn't stop to rethink at the door. He just kicked the handle, and the door splintered.

He was standing inside a small room with five or six tangos standing over a prone "Bulldog."

Hudde kicked the closest man in the chest, sending him backwards, giving Hudde the room to fire three rounds point blank, taking that man out as he stumbled and fell into another tango that Hudde shot in the face.

Hudde smashed the next man in the head with the hot barrel of his rifle, dropping the now-empty weapon, and, drawing his K-bar, he drove his knife into the man's neck and pushed him into the wall. He temporarily held the man up until he knew he was no longer a threat; then he released him, allowing him to drop to the floor.

Behind him, he heard the familiar sound of the Delta soldiers' HK mp5 firing. Hudde turned to see the last enemy soldier inside drop.

Hudde's team began running into the door, cautious at first; the other eight men ultimately made it safely inside. Hudde pointed at two men and told them to clear the roof. Then he turned to check on "Bulldog," who was sitting and drinking from a canteen from the squad medic.

"Can you walk out of here?" Hudde asked.

"I'll fight my fucking way out of here," Bulldog yelled out too loud as the medic bandaged the burns that had removed the man's hair and part of an ear.

Hudde turned his attention to the calls coming across the platoon's radio. The Captain had been gravely injured, and the other teams had run into more enemy attempting to move to the Rally Point.

It was obvious to Hudde that their plans were known to the enemy. They had lain in wait after planting a road-side bomb in the direct path of the extraction team. Direct movement to the Rally Point would be booby trapped or baited for an ambush.

Hudde got on the radio and repeated that they could temporarily recoup in the house they currently held. He had his men drag the corpses off to the side of the room, and then he explored the back of the house. It opened up into a high-walled courtyard; his two men looked down from their prone positions on the roof and gave him an "All Clear." In fact, they were no longer taking fire, which made sense because the enemy seemed to know where the fallback positions were and appeared to be lying in wait along those routes.

Hudde asked the radioman if he could contact the Marine convoy to see if they could double back. He had them call for emergency air cover and was told that two A10s were twenty minutes from time on target. The Corps said they could be back in thirty to forty minutes.

Hudde called, and the other three teams were leap-frogging back to the location; Yellow Team had taken two injuries but was going to make it to this position first. Hudde had a man pop smoke just outside the front door.

Yellow Team Leader called out that he'd identified red smoke, and Hudde had two team members step out to offer cover if it was needed, as the other team leapt in pairs into the same dwelling.

Hudde asked for six-man groups of volunteers that he would lead out to the destroyed vehicles to see if they could recover bodies — *no man left behind.*

His plan was to wait for the A10s to drop whatever ordnance they had, and they would charge out to the wrecks to see what they could recover.

When the pilots arrived to the AO, they circled once while the final team, the Red Team, ran into the dwelling past Hudde as he stood at the door. The enemy had begun to realize that the soldiers had doubled back; now, the enemy began to move back as well.

Hudde directed the pilots that anything north and west of the burning wreckage was clear for engagement. The pilots were worried about collateral damage in the village and continued to circle.

The Marine Corps caravan called, saying that they would be in the area in ten minutes. Hudde directed them to the street directly behind the home they had taken over. He then directed his men to prepare a charge to blow a hole in the back wall so they could exit without giving any snipers a silhouette to shoot at while climbing over.

He screamed at his radioman, "Where the hell are the A10s!??

Just then the familiar sound of a supercharged chainsaw ripped through the momentary quiet, and Hudde knew it was the sound of the 30mm cannon firing from the aircraft somewhere overhead.

"Go, go, go!" he screamed as the team exited the smashed wooden door and ran to the wreckage of the two military vehicles. The driver on the pickup was found in two parts, which his team wrapped into a poncho and tied together; they would mourn later.

The second recovery team was frantically searching the grounds for a missing arm of the .50-caliber gunner Hudde had watched drive by just more than an hour ago.

The third team was working to free the body of the last Delta soldier, trapped and smoldering in the Humvee; they did so just as some enemy fire began clinking on the twisted metal around them.

Everyone made it back into the house, with the bodies of the dead being dragged unceremoniously in ponchos. They headed straight back into the courtyard, where the men were looking back at Hudde.

"Do it!" he yelled out and knelt over a casualty to shield the soldier from dust and debris.

Hudde was shocked when, just before the blast from the satchel charge went off, the soldier below him reached up and pulled him down, saying into his ear, "You disregarded a direct order!"

Hudde looked down just as the wall exploded into dust and sand. He was looking into the eyes of Captain Schroeder.

"What?"

"I won't forget," the Captain said before Hudde ran out to meet the incoming Marine Corps "cavalry," literally riding into their rescue.

3

Date: Three weeks ago; late afternoon in Otter, Georgia

GORDAN HUDDE STEPPED into Teddy's bar-beque, the most famous small BBQ within five hundred miles. He filled his barrel chest with the aroma and allowed his head to fall back while he exhaled and smiled.

"You wait," the owner of the establishment called out over the counter when he saw Hudde. "At some point, you're going to start putting on some weight, and my daughter may have to pay for her own school when you quit coming in here every day."

Teddy was almost a half a foot taller than Gordan and maybe about a dozen years or so older. He had been a promising linebacker from the town and later, at The University of Georgia with the Bulldogs before sustaining a career-ending knee injury. His family lived above the restaurant, and they all had worked there through-out the years. When Hudde sometimes couldn't sleep at night, he would often come to the smokehouse and share coffee or beer with the big man, telling war and sport stories and looking for reasons to laugh.

They fist-bumped over the counter. Hudde's fist was possibly larger than the big Black man's.

"I'm never getting fat or full, so you best keep cook-ing!" Hudde smiled and waved at Teddy's high school senior daughter Gabrielle, who was helping out today.

He turned back to Teddy. "How about two pulled-pork sandwiches and a big side of potato salad?"

"You got it. Hey — how come you haven't dropped by in a while?" Teddy asked while getting Gordan's food prepared.

"I've been tiring myself out clearing some trees and cutting up some wood for the stove this winter, I guess. I've been sleeping in till 0600hrs almost every morning since I started." Gordan started to pull out his cash. "You miss me?" He grinned.

"Well that last kind of beer you brought anyway." Teddy said. "Maybe you should buy a chainsaw — like any normal person in the twenty-first century."

"Yeah. OK. Whatever." Gordan carried his meal over to the only seats left in the small eating area, a two-chair table near the front window.

Just as he was sitting down, the small bell rang as the door opened. Valerie Baker came through the door looking a bit like a cowgirl: Blue jeans with a tight white-cotton-looking blouse with some shiny turquoise buttons, and her long, straight black and shiny ponytail coming out from under an Australian bush hat.

Teddy called out to her, "Miss Baker, I always appreciate seeing you here. Step up, step up."

Gordan couldn't hear what the conversation was but didn't start eating his own food until she had hers and turned looking for a seat.

Gordan patted his black mustache and beard with the paper napkin and stood, offering the other chair opposite him.

Her head turned as she took in the room and realized that she would have to wait for a seat or take Gordan up on his offer. Her lips turned up into a slight grin; she apologized to some people while she bumped some chairs as she picked through the tight area.

"I'd be happy to share my table with you if you can get past your uneasiness, Miss Baker," Gordan said as he waved a hand at the empty chair.

At about 5'6" tall and about two inches of cowboy boot heel, she was only three or four inches shorter than Gordan. Her Cherokee heritage was something she was proud of, and being an independent woman was another.

"Thank you," she said as they both sat. She began setting her food in the order that made her happy.

"Although I don't know what you're talking about, I'm not uneasy about anything." She took a forkful of potato salad and raised her eyebrows at Gordan, staring at him as she chewed.

"First." Gordan paused. "I'm very pleased to see that you eat meat," pointing at her sandwich. "I was worried you may be one of those New Age vegans or something." Gordan stopped and took a sip of his iced tea.

"Second, finding me physically attractive shouldn't keep us from being friends." He fought back a smile.

She batted her eyelashes a couple of extra times as she patted her lips with the paper napkin.

"First, let me assure you that I *am* a meat eater. Nothing like a good steak and a cold beer after a long day."

There was a pause as she seemed to really study Gordan, looking him up and down.

He ran his right hand over his Spartan-looking beard, waiting for whatever was going to come next.

"Second," she shook her head a bit sadly, "while you appear to be a very healthy specimen, your head is a bit too big, your arms a bit too long, and it's your legs, no, maybe it's your waist that is too short." She put a finger to her lips as she thought about what was to come next. "Some of the women have said you were roguishly hand-some, but I'm not sure I can agree."

Gordan smiled and opened his mouth to speak, but she cut him off.

"And third, I've always been attracted to 'bad boys,' and you seem to be a bit of a Boy Scout. I mean, you haven't even had the courage to ask me out yet." She now smiled a smile Gordan guessed she would give anyone that she'd just disemboweled, and she sat back to watch Gordan's reaction.

Gordan leaned forward and placed his elbows onto the table. His large hands came together under his chin, one hand over the other fist.

"I do like to ensure that a mission will be successful, waiting for the right moment to start. I also freely admit that, from the first time I saw you, I found you very physically attractive"

"Oh, really?" she asked sarcastically.

He ignored her. "But one can't allow beauty to override good sense; I had to try to find out why such a vivacious woman would have no attachments at such an advanced age."

She nearly choked on her BBQ chicken sandwich. "How old do you think I am?"

Again he ignored her. "I haven't found out anything so embarrassing that I needed to rule out a possible date in the future."

Now he sat back, waiting for a response.

Just then the door opened, and the overhead doorbell rang out when it did and as it closed as well. The sheriff, John Schmidt, strode in, looking as imposing a figure as John Wayne cut in any movie. Everyone called the 6'6", 270-lb. sheriff "Big John," and it suited him just fine.

The sheriff tiptoed past several people, saying, "Excuse me" and holding his service weapon with his right hand, not because he thought he would need it, but because it was the perfect height at his waist to smack people on the top of the head as he walked past.

He stopped in front of the table Valerie and Gordan were seated at.

"Hey, Sheriff," Gordan said, honestly happy to see the man.

Valerie nodded, "Afternoon, John." She looked up and smiled.

"Hey, Gordan. You ever think about carrying a phone? I don't know if the citizens of the county thought they were hiring me to be your answering service." He shifted his weight and placed his right hand on top of his .45 now.

"Sorry, Sheriff. Should we step outside or anything?"

"Nah — here's the guy's number." He handed Gordan a business card. "Said to tell you that Captain Schroeder called."

Gordan made a face like he'd smelled something bad. "Ah, shit."

"Not a friend?" the sheriff asked.

Valerie was paying close attention to both men.

"I don't know, I haven't seen him in a long time, but I'm not sure I want to walk down memory lane with the officer who tried to get me kicked out of the service."

Valerie wasn't the only one who had questions now. The sheriff asked his.

"What did you do?"

Gordan's brow furrowed. "Why is that…. Never mind. I was dealing with a guy more concerned with painting by the numbers than killing the enemy while protecting his own men." Gordan shook his head. "Thank you, John. I'm sorry, but I can't say it will never happen again, even if I get a phone."

"Maybe someday, over a beer, you can finish that story?" the sheriff asked.

"Can I buy you lunch for your troubles?" Gordan pointed over at the register.

"Maybe next time." The sheriff tipped his hat at Valerie and said goodbye to Teddy as he headed back out. Two dings from the bell.

The playful mood was gone; Gordan looked out the window, chewing slowly, his eyes focused on nothing.

Valerie interrupted whatever his thoughts were. "Maybe you should call, find out what the guy wants?"

Gordan turned back to face Valerie, and she made out the moment his eyes refocused. "Yeah — you're probably right." He began to roll his sandwich up into the foil that was flattened out under his sandwich.

"No, don't go. Here's my phone. Just step out, and then you can enjoy your meal." She smiled and nodded at her phone that she now offered him across the table.

"Really? Thank you. I'll just be a minute. I can't imagine what the guy wants." He reached out and took the phone, their fingers momentarily touching.

Gordan stepped out into the setting sunlight and walked around the parking lot end of the building so that he could speak without bothering people entering or exiting Teddy's — or allowing them to hear.

Gordan looked down at the number and dialed; the phone rang about four times before being picked up.

"This is Captain Schroeder"

Figures, Gordan thought, *the guy is out of the service but still goes by "Captain."*

"This is Gordan Hudde returning your call, Walter." Gordan used his first name to prevent Schroeder feeling like he still outranked him.

"Gordan, I'm glad I could find you."

Gordan interrupted. "Yeah. How did that happen?"

"You remember 'Bulldog.' Well his real name was Robert Mahoney, and he ended up working at the FBI on anti-terrorism; I bumped into him during a veterans event in Washington. I guess he has some contacts in CIA still, and I found the town. I'm not blowing your cover or anything, am I?"

"I retired years ago."

"Yeah. That's what he said."

"Is there a point, Walter?"

"Yeah. I'm sorry. There is, and it's a bit conspiratorial, if you have a few minutes."

"I really don't."

"Well I have some documents I can send you."

"Whatever it is Walter, I don't know why you believe I'm the guy that needs to see it or why I would even care."

"Because it's about fellow veterans, Gordan. I think someone is targeting veterans."

"So, go to the police."

"I've gone to the police; they think it's all about suicides. The FBI said the same thing, but now I feel like I'm being followed and maybe shouldn't even be talking on the phone."

"You're right — you sound like a nut. That's the same nut that tried to screw me over the last time I saw you."

"OK, I deserve that. But don't let your feelings for me allow you to let down your brothers; the war never ends for some of these guys."

Fuck — you're still a bastard. Gordan grabbed the beard on his chin and pulled down as he thought. "They say twenty two vets kill themselves every day. What makes you think a few are part of something bigger than that? You understand averages, right? If nobody kills themselves for a few days, and then a few guys you know do it at once, it's just part of the statistical anomalies."

"Gordan, I run a group, Vets for Veterans. We sponsor group meetings and offer advice on doctors, care, and getting through the red tape of the Veterans Administration. The guys I'm thinking of had never told anyone they were experiencing those types of thoughts. Hell, one of the guys was engaged to be married. He had a lot to look forward to."

"That's what successful suicides look like."

"Look, I can send you some police reports along with my thoughts and my group's files on these guys. I don't think I need to worry about privacy laws now. You don't even need to come up here."

"Go ahead and send it to the Sheriff's department. I can't promise you anything except that I'll look the stuff over."

"OK. Call me sometime late next week."

"Whatever." Gordan hung up.

The bell rang overhead two times as Gordan returned; he couldn't help but to smile at Valerie as she sat at the table, finished with her meal, waiting patiently.

"Sorry." Gordan handed back the phone. "If you go over on minutes or anything, I'll gladly pay."

"That's OK. I had Teddy wrap up your sandwich for you, and I've got a property to show. So I have to get going."

She stood up and waited for a moment, expecting something more.

Gordan noticed at the last second, just as she turned to leave. "Hey, Valerie?"

"Yes?" She turned back looking at him, raising her eyebrows a bit.

He stood up and walked with her to her truck. "Maybe someday I could grill you a steak, and we could share a beer on my patio. The view is spectacular."

She turned and thought about saying something a bit vicious but decided against it. "I think I would like that, Mr. Hudde. I'd tell you to call me, but..." She slid into the old pickup and started it up before she held her phone up for Gordan to see as she backed out and started driving out to the street, heading east through town.

Gordan couldn't help but feel sad. Talking about the situation regarding the veteran's administration and the suicides made him question his own sanity and place in the world. How had he come through everything without being killed? How had he mentally handled the horrors that he had seen?

4

THOMAS PARKER WALKED the wooden path out
to the beach on the coast of Delaware. His black trou-
sers and highly polished black shoes were out of place
on the beach pathway. It was very dark this night, and,
after just a few feet down the path, he disappeared,
due to his dark jacket. He didn't need to see, as he could
hear the waves crashing on the beach as a storm passed
someplace further out to sea, and he kept walking east.

He walked without turning his head and never var-
ied his speed. When he needed to, he stepped down into
the sand, not caring at all about sand in his shoes. He
walked near a dune with tall wispy grass growing like a
weak beard on a strong chin.

Thomas took out a pen and scrawled briefly onto
the first page of the yellow legal pad he was carrying.
He set the pad down and then began to strip from his

business attire. When he was naked, he set the pad on top of the small pile of clothing and then took off his prosthetic arm, placing that on top of the pad, holding it down from the winds.

Thomas turned and began to walk out into the waves; he swam past the surf and disappeared. A lone, dark figure turned from the ocean wind and walked the wooded walkway back to the pavement to his car, out of the wind. The man made one call. On the other end, someone said "Yes."

"Zero hesitation. The subject has disappeared." And the call was over.

Three days later, Thomas Parker's lifeless body was discovered in the sand nearly ten miles south at Ocean City, Maryland, by a five-year-old girl collecting shells in a small bright red bucket on a very pleasant fall morning. Her screams were almost not heard over the gulls that were angered at her interrupting their breakfast.

5

Nearly ten years ago, Bagram Airfield, Afghanistan
HUDDE WALKED UP the corrugated steel runway and climbed the ramp of the C-141 Starlifter. It appeared he would be the lone Army passenger as the plane was void of anyone other than the Air Force loadmaster and several stacks of pallets shrink-wrapped and now secured by heavy red-and-yellow nylon straps.

The loadmaster walked toward Hudde and motioned back over his shoulder toward the front of the aircraft.

"Nicer ride up front," he yelled to be heard over the roar of the jet engines.

Hudde just smiled back as he unsnapped a set of aluminum frames and nylon webbing that made up the plush seating arrangement. It was always odd to be on these military flights without being bogged down with several hundred pounds of equipment and, most importantly, a couple of parachutes.

The rear ramp began sliding skyward, and a man in a brown suit jacket and jeans jumped in and spoke to the crewmember.

His reddish-blond hair was a little long for him to be regular Army, and his uniform had Hudde thinking that maybe he was with a foreign country or maybe part of the special-operations guys; he was holding a large manila envelope as his only luggage. He turned and looked down, stepping carefully to miss the rail system and other rigging hardware that was everywhere on the floor of this freight flyer.

"I know you." He smiled warmly and extended a hand, seeming to look hard at the name plate on Hudde's dress greens to make sure.

"Gordan Hudde."

"Glen Turner."

"Pull up a seat, Mr. Turner." Gordan pointed at the uncomfortable sling seat.

"You going to a ball or something?" Turner referenced Hudde's dress greens, and he gave Hudde a Cheshire-cat grin.

"I'm heading to my Court Martial, so maybe you want some distance."

"No, like I said — I know who you are. My friend said you saved his life; matter of fact, he said you saved a bunch of lives."

"What are you doing Mr. Turner? Where is the envelope going?" Hudde turned the line of questions.

"Eyes only." Turner held the envelope to his chest as if he had to hold it tight.

"There you have it; I don't need to be sharing secrets on my way to the Court Martial. I don't want it ending in a hanging."

Turner shrugged his shoulders and cleared his throat. "Bulldog is my friend; I know all there is about that operation, so I really just would love to hear one thing: Why did you turn everyone back to the original ambush site?"

Hudde studied Turner for a moment. "Everywhere our men were going, there was an ambush waiting. The tangos obviously knew our plans and were just waiting for us, so I figured that we should do something even we didn't plan for. It's really that simple."

Turner shook his head. "No, Sergeant. It isn't that simple. No one else made that call. You had three other guys there that night who outranked you, and they not only didn't make the call, but now I hear they're remaining silent while you're getting screwed over for being right."

"Yeah. Politics." Gordan Hudde sighed and sat back against the frame of aircraft. He ran his hand over his clean-shaven chin while he thought. Finally, when he had decided to speak again, he sat up straight and looked Turner in the eyes.

"Captain Schroeder is a hard man and, I think, a pretty good Ranger. OK. But if you tell him he needs to take a route from point A to B, then he'll get every man killed doing it exactly as it was planned, himself included. I don't think he can adapt and change in the middle of an operation, and Top? I mean, the First Sergeant — he took a bullet in the ass during the first minute of fighting. The dude's ancient and shouldn't be out there; I mean he's probably 38 or 39 years old now!"

"Well, the Lieutenant...." Turner started but Hudde interrupted.

"That was the butter bar's first combat mission. Hell, he doesn't even have a nickname yet."

Turner smiled and nodded his head in understanding.

"Bulldog said you busted in that door and killed a half dozen *hajis* to save his ass. He said...let me get it straight... 'You looked like a lion in a room full of jackals.' I can tell you he's pretty pleased you were there."

"Well, if he writes a song about me, I may live forever." Hudde grinned. "Seriously, half of that was fear and adrenaline the other half dumb luck and an act of God." Hudde shrugged, "And, besides, one of the Delta guys killed the last two, I think."

"I like you, Staff Sergeant Hudde. I think you should come with me when we get to Germany. I'll make sure they pin some medals on you for your heroic actions. Then we'll retire you and you can come work for me. What do you say?"

"I'd say, 'You're fucking with me — right?'" Hudde sat up a little straighter.

"Here." Turner handed Hudde the envelope. "Go ahead It's for you." Then he sat back and waited.

Hudde grasped the aluminum key and pulled. It tore down the length of the envelope, allowing Hudde to see a document written on what looked like CIA letterhead.

"No shit."

"That's right — no shit. We'll send you stateside for training. Of course 'training' is a code word for 'Our turn to treat you like shit for a while, and then you come back here and continue to make good decisions.'"

6

GORDAN KEPT HIS head down while standing in line at the grocery store; he had come to realize and accept that he liked individuals but disliked people.

Leonard Kind, the storeowner, stood in the elevated office area that was common for small stores built in that area from seventy to eighty years ago. He could quickly scan the entire sales floor and see what almost all his employees were doing as well. He had added a few CCTV cameras in the cash cage and the back room, as it was a necessity for this day and age. Yet he hadn't really used it other than for finding out who didn't lock the back doors on a few occasions.

The small-boned blonde in front of Gordan had a pretty full shopping cart, and he closed his eyes to breath in slow and full, reminding himself that he damn well had no other place he had to be.

A kid screaming out brought Gordan from his trance.

"Ow! Ma — that hurts!"

The skinny blonde had the four-foot-tall boy by the ear, pulling him closer. Gordan noticed a bruise on the towhead's left cheek turning that dull grey after what was most likely a few days. He also noticed a bruise on the woman, up the back of her neck as her chest-length hair dropped over her shoulder; this one was a much-fresher dark purple. It disappeared under her light jacket when she stood back up after whispering sternly into the boy's ear. The baby in the carrier in the cart kicked and squirmed, "goo-gooing" and drooling happily down the front of his chin.

"Oh, hey, Mrs. Regis. How are you all doing this fine morning?" the cashier said.

Gordan guessed the cashier was trying to get her attention more than make small talk. As usual, Gordan felt he'd stepped into the exact busiest time to get his groceries.

"Oh, I'm sorry, Kathy." Mrs. Regis began unloading the groceries onto the rubber belt.

"What the fuck is taking so long!"

Everyone turned to look except Gordan; he kept his head down and looked up from under his black-and-silver hat with the jump wings emblazoned on the front instead of some football-team logo.

"Oh, Mr. Regis, it's all my fault, carrying on so with the missus!" Kathy the cashier nervously took responsibility for something that Gordan suspected had played out before.

Gordan guessed that Mr. Regis was about 6'1" and maybe 180 or 190 lbs. He also guessed he was in his late 30s or early 40s. His dress shirt was wrinkled, and there were growing sweat stains spreading from under his arms. The tie was askew and loose around his neck; his shoes were not shined and appeared well worn — a character straight from *Death of a Salesman*.

Mr. Kind appeared from nowhere, and Gordan thought he heard him ask Regis about smelling alcohol on his breath. Mr. Kind was maybe 140 lbs and about 5'7", a frail, grey Black man in his late 70s. He fell backwards easily when Regis pushed him away.

A teenaged bag boy yelled to Mr. Kind that he would call the sheriff and ran to the door that led to the upper office.

"What?" Regis yelled out with his hands held out shoulder high as he did a wobbly pirouette.

"None of you ever fell on hard times? None of you ever had a drink or two? Fucking hypocrites." Regis pulled a flask from his back pocket and took a swig.

Mr. Kind had climbed to his feet and began to bag the Regis groceries with thin and bony small hands. He looked over and complimented Mrs. Regis on her baby, trying to keep everyone calm until the sheriff arrived.

Mr. Kind's eyes met with Gordan for just a moment, and Gordan saw that the man was nervous and tired.

"Don't you worry, Mr. Kind. We all are all right, and I'll have you out of here in a jiffy." He turned to give a reassuring smile to Regis.

"Daddy, ma won't buy me a candy bar!" The towhead ran toward his father.

Mr. Regis spun and slapped the small boy, who fell to the floor.

"What the fuck is wrong with you? You know times are hard. If your momma told you 'No,' then that's it!"

Regis pushed the boy with his right foot just as the boy was getting to his feet, sending him stumbling and then crashing face first into the next register stand that was, at the time, unattended.

The boy rolled over, screaming, a trickle of blood coming from his nose. "Maaaaaa!"

Gordan started to slide past the two carts to make his way to the front of the store. Mr. Kind made eye contact and shook his head "No."

Regis turned toward Gordan and placed his hands on his hips. "What the hell do..."

Gordan cut off the rest of the sentence when his extra-large hand wrapped around the throat of Regis cutting off sound and breath. Gordan picked the man up like a dirty diaper, holding him up and out in front of him as he headed for the parking lot. Gordan used the body of Regis to open both sets doors to get outside.

Once outside, Gordan shoved Regis hard, sending him flying forward. Unable to catch his footing, Regis crashed into a car parked on the side of the store.

"We all fall on hard times, Regis. Doesn't give you the right to lay hands on the boy or your wife." Gordan was not sure what he was going to do next.

Regis pulled himself up the side of the car and turned to face Gordan. "I know who you are, soldier boy. What are you going to do? Huh? You going to stomp me now like you did the Tolbert brothers last year?"

Gordan looked around the small plaza and pulled on his beard as he thought. The bagger from the store ran back inside when Gordan saw him standing out front.

"I don't know you, Regis, but I do know you're making a big mistake."

Gordan's eyes lit up with an idea. Grabbing the back of Regis's neck, he began to push him across the parking lot toward the other side of the plaza.

Ten minutes later, Quincy Kind met sheriff's deputy Ralph "Bronson" Smith at the door of his small store and began to tell the story of how Steven Regis had once again caused a scene in his store and that he was about finished allowing them to shop there. His anger would subside later, after he helped the boy with an ice pack.

Bronson was typing into the computer in his squad car when Sheriff Schmidt walked up and leaned on the doorframe of the open squad-car door.

Bronson stopped and slid out. "Mr. Kind said it was Gordan Hudde that slapped Regis around a bit and took him outside. Nobody knows where they went."

"Oh, shit. Did you call for the ambulance?"

Bronson squinted up at the sheriff. "You don't think...?" Bronson allowed his words to tail off.

Big John shook his head and scanned the area; spotting Gordan's dark-blue Toyota Tundra parked out in the last spot, he started walking in that direction. "Yeah. I think you'd better," he said over his shoulder.

The sheriff touched the deep-blue hood of Hudde's Toyota; it was cool. He looked back at the front of the small store and the tree line behind it. He turned and looked around at the small plaza, a laundromat on the south end, an insurance agent's office, a cell-phone store, and the bar called "The Watering Hole" anchored the northern end.

The sheriff took off his Stetson and squinted up at the afternoon sun before it drifted behind a front that appeared to be moving in. A brisk and surprising cool breeze began to blow at the same time the sun disappeared behind the bank of dark clouds. The sheriff knew Gordan Hudde well enough to be shocked that he would do something so... *obvious....* Yeah — that was a good word.

"Bronson," the sheriff called out.

"Yeah?" Bronson listened past the wind.

"You better head into the tree line and check about. I would hate to miss something obvious."

"Sure, sheriff." Bronson bitched under his breath as he reached into his squad car to pull out a rain poncho.

He pulled the poncho up over his head, holding his Stetson with his right hand. He reached into his left pocket to pull out the plastic hat rain protector and began to stretch it out over the Stetson.

He put the hat back on just as the cold, late-September rain began to slap down onto the windshield of his cruiser. Bronson turned to yell out to the sheriff that he was heading out when he spotted two figures walking across the parking lot behind the sheriff.

"Well, it looks like we can call off the search." Bronson pointed back over the sheriff's shoulder.

About halfway across the parking lot, before getting to his own vehicle, Gordan Hudde stopped and allowed Regis to continue on his own. Regis walked with his head down, holding one hand above, as if he could slow the sopping he was getting.

The sheriff started walking out into the parking lot, meeting Regis nearly halfway out.

Regis stopped trying to shield his eyes from the pounding rain as he looked up at the bigger man.

"I'm guessing I'm under arrest?"

"You're guessing right, Steve. I've got half a dozen witnesses willing to have you hung for beating on your son." The sheriff paused, looking back at Hudde, standing still, halfway again out in the parking lot, a grey form in the pounding rain.

"Don't tell me he took you for a drink at the Watering Hole?" The sheriff saw a large manila envelope hiding under Regis's coat. "What have you got there?"

"Nah, sheriff — no drink. I'll let him tell you about this." He slid his coat up to cover the yellow envelope from the rain. "I'm supposed to ask you a hypothetical question."

"What?" The sheriff was in no mood for games.

"If you really wanted to kill somebody, if you needed to make someone go away... well, who would you call?"

The sheriff placed both hands on his hips and made an exasperated-sounding exhale; he shook his head; water splashed off from the plastic covering his Stetson. The big man turned to look back at Hudde, a dark-grey, ghostly visage standing like a statue in the momentary deluge. The sheriff turned back to lock eyes with Regis.

"Hell, I can't answer something like that, Regis."

"Never mind, sheriff. That's just what he said you'd do and say. He was right — you just did answer the question; I'll go get with Bronson, let him take me to your offices." He turned and splashed towards Bronson's car.

"Yeah, you do that, Regis." The sheriff was already walking towards Hudde.

Hudde saw the exchange stop and met the sheriff halfway again.

"You want to tell me what the fuck is going on here, Hudde?"

Hudde was shielding his own envelope under his denim jacket; he walked a bit further and threw it into the cab of his truck before turning around.

"Don't you want to go somewhere dry first?"

"I'm a little impatient here, son." The sheriff stood uneven on even ground, with one hip slightly higher than the other; his right hand rested on the big .45 grip that stuck out from under his wind jacket.

• • •

"Relax, John." Hudde spoke to him like a fellow soldier, not allowing the sheriff to pull rank. "Don't forget that I've been all over the world handling all kind of really, really bad situations." He paused and smiled a wry smile up at the sheriff. "Don't worry, John — not everything is a nail for me."

"OK, smart ass. You want to tell me about what happened and what's in the envelope both of you were carrying?"

"Sheriff, there is nothing I'd rather be doing. I observed Regis there" he nodded in the direction of Bronson's squad car "slap his son around in Kind's store and took him outside. I recognized a man with troubles, so I thought I would do the neighborly thing and buy the man some *peace of mind*. Well, that's what the brochures say, anyway." Hudde smiled up at the sheriff again before he turned and pointed back at the plaza, almost unrecognizable at the moment in the torrent.

"What? I'm failing to find the humor here, Gordan."

"I signed the man up for life insurance John, if anything happens to him, his family will be taken care of for a few years, give them time to get on their feet."

"Oh, come on, now. You didn't do him any favors—you threatened him; why else did he ask me that question?"

"Steve there is going to try harder for a while, and maybe it will give him time to find a new job. Who knows? He may even work some things out. If not, well, there's always option number two." Hudde began walking toward his truck.

Hudde stood up on the side rail of his truck and smiled over the roof at the sheriff.

The sheriff shifted on his feet. "You fool; you're the first person I'm coming to see if something happens to that man."

"I'll have some coffee on for you when you do, if you think you have to." Hudde turned to slide into the truck and then popped back up. "Hey, bring something to eat if you do need to have that conversation with me someday."

Hudde finished with a wave. "Have a great day sheriff!"

He climbed in and started the truck. Turning on the lights, he drove off.

The sheriff was still shaking his head when he arrived at Bronson's vehicle. It might work — who knows? Besides, locking Regis up every couple of months wasn't seeming to fix anything, anyhow. He didn't see Regis as a possible killer, he obviously was a mean drunk, and things sure weren't going his way right now, but, hell, you never know.

The sheriff walked over and slid into his own vehicle. He turned off the emergency lights and turned on the defroster, as the quickly cooling air that had come with the rain had created condensation inside.

He took off the Stetson and threw it on the passenger seat, running his hand back through his thinning hair. He thought about Gordan Hudde's involvement in last year's child abductions. A stalled investigation had kicked into high gear once Hudde started "helping," but the FBI took full credit once it was solved and a few of the children had been saved.

Hudde had never offered an explanation, nor had he ever filled him in on any of the details when he had disappeared near the end of the case. Schmidt asked Hudde once what Hudde's involvement was, but he had not received an answer — just a smile. But it was Hudde's eyes that he'll never forget; they said "Don't ask," and there was something a bit sinister that Schmidt felt at the time. As the local sheriff, it didn't seem right that he didn't know, and yet, even now, he felt a bit relieved that he was still in the dark about it all.

A shiver went up Schmidt's spine, and he turned on the heat as well. *Stop it*, he told himself. *If Hudde had been working within the FBI investigation, he must be on the up and up, or they would have taken him in back then...* Yeah, that sounded right; Hudde always seemed to be a law-and-order kind of guy. Who wouldn't want some more of that in a community?

7

IF ANY OF his fellow soldiers had looked up and observed Terrence Keels, they would have been shocked. All of them knew he'd been a hard-charging infantryman when he was active. They all knew he was one of the best to ever fire the M320-40mm grenade launcher. They all knew he would never quit and never surrender; it's just that they all knew he washed out of airborne school due to his fear of heights.

So looking up at a 30-story building to see Keels standing on the roof ledge looking down would have been a real shocker to his buddies and the cadre at Ft. Benning.

There were no screams to get noticed, there was no waiting to be saved by a brave police officer or talked down by a fire-department employee.

If anyone stopped to really take notice of everyone on the street, they would have noticed one man looking up and watching intently, a cell phone to his ear. He was nearly 6'1" and lean but not thin; when he spoke, there was a slight French accent.

"There seems to be a slight hesitation...looking... looking...left foot seems to be moving...gone! He has carried out his orders." The phone disconnected.

The man ignored the screams. He turned and left them behind. He ignored the tires squealing and the crowd that began to form and began walking down the street to his car, which had brought both Keels and himself to this area of town. Now he was riding back alone.

• • •

Gordan stopped and turned to look back at his wood-shed, now 3/4 filled. He turned to look at the small pile of wood he had left to split. The air definitely felt like fall was coming fast. The sun had convinced him that it was warmer than it was; the physical exertion still had caused him to build up a bit of a sweat, and he moved between the trees, looking for a sunny spot.

Sheriff Schmidt's squad car popped up over the ridge and rolled slowly in his direction.

The widow mechanism whined as Schmidt rolled down his window.

"Hey, sheriff." Gordan walked over closer.

Schmidt took in the area near the garage. "You know, they have a thing called 'a chainsaw' now; it might save you some time."

Gordan smiled as he turned and took in the saw, axe, and splitting maul strewn about his small yard near the shed. "Sure, maybe when I get to be your age, I'll be forced to look into that." His teeth flashed from under the dark beard.

The vehicle rocked as Schmidt opened and then exited his squad car.

"Wow — I kind of thought we were friends." The sheriff took a large manila envelope that he was holding in his hands and acted as if he would throw it back through his front window.

"Maybe I just won't deliver your mail."

"Sorry, sheriff. Look — I even bought a phone." Gordan pulled it from his front pocket and waved it in the air.

Schmidt turned and handed the envelope to Gordan. "Your former Captain?"

Gordan nodded his head. "Yeah. Looks like it — though I'm not sure where it's going." He waved the envelope before throwing it onto the pile of logs.

Schmidt turned and took in the area surrounding Gordan's place. "This has got to be one of the best spots to build in my county, Gordan; I'm more than a bit jealous."

Gordan joined him in looking around, and then he took a deep breath of the fresh mountain air — a mixture of pine, dirt, and hardwoods, with just a hint of the stream flowing at the bottom of the hill.

"Thanks, sheriff. That's right — this is your first time up here; would you like a grand tour?"

"Maybe some other time, but maybe you could tell me more about Regis the other day down at Kind's store."

"Nothing really to tell. He started slapping around the kid, and I just couldn't stand idle." Gordan walked back toward the maul while he spoke.

The sheriff followed. "So you didn't bounce him around a little before we got there?"

Gordan stopped and spun to look back at Schmidt. "Shit, is that what he's saying? There had to be half a dozen witnesses there to tell you different."

"No, I don't think they would tell me the truth if you did, but he didn't say anything. I was just wondering..."

Gordan walked directly up to the sheriff to look him in the eye. "I'm not interested in getting involved, John." Gordan wanted to make it personal. "I moved here for the peace and quiet, and I'm sure as hell not planning on running for local office either...if that's what you're starting to think."

"Oh, no! I really wasn't thinking...maybe just wondering why you didn't slap the guy around a bit, I guess; I mean, he certainly would have had it coming to him."

"John, you came to me before, and whatever happened, it turned out about the best it could under the circumstances. I was just trying to stop anything from getting out of hand, OK?" Gordan started to turn but then stopped. "I'd help anytime you ask, you know, without needing anything in return."

"I think I know that, Gordan, but what if something happens to old Regis? What happens when I have to ask you questions?"

"I don't want to be glib here, John, but how many times have you made contact with Regis?"

The sheriff shrugged. "I don't know — between eight and twelve times, all together, I'd guess."

"So you throwing the book at him the other day probably wasn't going to be the last time. Maybe if he believes it had better be his last time, maybe he'll try harder for a little while."

"I suppose..."

Gordan interrupted. "John, you always need to do your job. Never let our friendship or any help I may have rendered you get in the way of that."

Gordan followed Schmidt as he fit himself back into the car. "Thanks for my mail."

Big John nodded his head as he headed back down the switchback driveway off the wooded ridge line that held the concrete, steel, and wood home that Gordan had built special more than a year ago.

Gordan reached down with an oversized hand and let the maul's handle slide down between his fingers until the heavy head slapped his thumb and forefinger. He raised it with his other fist over his head. It was almost wrong that he felt so good today, so, with a primal scream, he attacked the remaining logs.

• • •

More than a thousand miles away in Wichita, Kansas, Michael "Jimmy" Legrand was looking at a greening bronze picture frame of a strapping young 17-year-old in

1944; at 6'1" and nearly 210 pounds, he felt, at the time, like he could help the nation win the war singlehandedly. He'd lied on his paperwork to get into the Marines before he graduated high school. His parents had been afraid for him but were proud when the letter that he dropped into the mailbox had arrived back home to let them know he was off to San Diego for Boot Camp.

Later, as Legrand sat on the deck of one of the five hundred-plus ships used to transport Marines to the island battles ahead, his fellow Marines laughed at his inability to stop his legs from moving rapidly, and, as "Jimmy Legs" was too much to say, "Jimmy" stuck.

Jimmy had observed the most incredible shelling from these same ships. He and his comrades knew that no one could withstand such destruction, and, as they were thrown violently side to side in the small landing craft in the early morning and sudden eerily silence of the big guns, they thought they would do nothing more than mop up a small and nearly destroyed enemy.

But Hell on Earth greeted them when machinegun fire and mortar rounds began to rain down on them once they were within sight of the destroyed and smoldering beaches.

Jimmy went from a wide-eyed Kansas farmboy to a killer with death eyes in a matter of weeks. He stood on beaches where the bodies of his fellow soldiers slid and rolled in what could only be described as a red tide. He watched in horror as burning men ran from holes in the ground. He was equally horrified at the satisfaction that he felt at the time. He had seen women jump from cliffs with children in their arms from the fear of what the Americans would do, and he had seen the emancipated deathly forms of the men captured by the Japanese and the rows and rows of unmarked graves of those who had paid the ultimate price.

Jimmy had experienced and survived all these things for the country he loved and returned to be somewhat of a successful businessman, husband, and father. But the country he loved had now abandoned Jimmy; he did not know that the Veterans Administration had dumped his paperwork into a file that would not be accessed until well after his death.

Jimmy, at ninety-one, looked as if he, too, had survived a Japanese POW camp. His parchment-like wrinkled and patchy skin was stretched across frail and thin arms and hands; he reached down and allowed a scoop of dry food to fall mostly into the cats' dish.

His once strong and forceful stride was now a short shuffle, his feet not really leaving the floor. He just pushed one a bit forward after the other; his slippers made the sound of paper shuffling with each step. His breathing was very shallow, and he stopped to lean against the railing of the stairs he no longer used, not to look at the family photos on the wall but to rest before making it to his favorite chair.

His grandson had been kind enough to take a day off from his job and drive him to St. Louis to visit the VA three months ago, but the doctor's appointment ultimately had been rescheduled, and he waited for the call to let him know when it would be.

His daughter lived more than two hours away, and yet she tried to visit twice a week, except in the worst winter weather; that weather would be here soon.

"Jimmy" turned and dropped into his favorite chair; the dust rose and danced in the sunbeam that snuck between the drapes behind him and made a direct line to the tassels of the throw rug his wife had bought just before her death late last year.

He coughed; it felt violent and burned, and the blood was bright red on the back of his hand; he reached out for the tissues his daughter had left on the TV stand next to the remote.

His thin, frail arm returned to the TV tray for the blue plastic cup which he always tried to keep full of water; he seemed so tired and parched.

His arm could barely lift the cup; the shaking hand and arm needed to rest, and he set the cup in his lap for a moment.

He began to cough again; the cup tipped, and water fell to the wooden floor pooling under his chair. The cat jumped off his windowsill perch to investigate the noise.

Jimmy Legrand's breathing became much faster and shallower. The cancer had spread to a point now that no amount of care would help. His chin fell to his chest, and, as he died, he gripped the arms of the chair as tightly as he could; he didn't want to be found cold and alone on the floor.

. . .

Janet Cummings looked at the computer screen and then closed her eyes and dropped her head into her hands. As the current Director of the VA in St. Louis, there was just no way she was going to earn maximum bonus for the year. She picked up the phone and called in her senior staff for an impromptu meeting; there was no way she would *not* meet her "numbers" because her spring vacation depended on the extra cash.

She directed the departments to purge whatever records they needed to, so that they had 100% successfully met all timelines and guidelines for the care of the veterans who had come through their doors. Anything that they could not delete they would say the veterans were offered outside care for from the dozens of other government-approved providers. Maybe they could blame and play off the poor record keeping of those entities. She promised them all the highest review of their own as the incentive they needed to falsify the records.

Satisfied that her vacation finances were secured, Cummings called her girlfriend so they could meet for lunch.

8

OUT OF HABIT, not necessity, Gordan turned on the turn signal as he neared his driveway on the winding Smith Creek road just northwest of the town of Otter, Georgia.

His dark-blue Toyota truck thumped over the culvert, and then he took a hard right as his driveway followed the road as it headed east along a heavy hedgerow, with quite a few trees separating the two. To his left, a meadow opened up which tilted to the west, toward the aforementioned Smith Creek. Gordan had built a large metal shed on the eastern edge, where the trees had thinned out and it was naturally a little flatter.

His driveway now turned back into the wood line, slowly heading up at first and then quickly to a switchback that then took him up to the front of his custom-built home. It sat on the south end of a ridgeline that ended here at his property, maybe seventy feet higher than the surrounding meadow and land.

The townspeople whispered about the mansion that was being built, but it was only about 1800 square feet. His architect had called it "...an above-ground bunker," and it was fitting; Gordan had from that point forward called it the "bunker." Three and a half feet of reinforced concrete made up the outside walls, and what few windows they installed were either bullet resistant or bullet proof. His safe room was literally a safe and was nearly the largest room in the bunker; the federal government would be concerned if they knew what he kept in there.

While Gordan felt comfortable that he could handle himself nearly anywhere, this was the only place that he could really feel... relaxed — a spot in the world where he could sleep without feeling that he needed to have one eye open.

This is where he had begun to review the information sent to him by his former Captain, Walter Schroeder.

It was a jumble of information. Gordan pulled out news clippings and placed them across his coffee table. There were a few pages of police documents regarding the deaths of two of the men.

Schroeder had gotten some of the medical history of all three men — not that odd, as most military men keep and maintain a file for the inevitable moment the government tells you all your files have gone missing.

Gordan could not find anything from the men's military experience that linked them together.

One of the men had never even fired a weapon in anger; he had been unfortunately hit by a roadside bomb before he had ever engaged the enemy in combat.

They were men, according to Schroeder, that seemed to have a life after a war. They all appeared to have plans, whether they were new jobs, marriage, or something else positive that should have anchored them into a better frame of mind. But Gordan knew that some things reached out from the darkness and took hold no matter how well adjusted the rest of your life was.

The only item Gordan found that linked these men is that they had come together at Schroeder's Veterans for Vets organization.

Gordan finished the beer he had opened when he'd started reviewing the documents and sat back, closing his eyes, hoping something would come to him.

He drifted off and fell into a recurring dream. It was restless sleep, and he was more tired when he awoke then when he had first laid back. He grabbed another beer and headed to the oversized shower.

He turned up the hot lever and stood in the now-steaming water. He took a sip from the beer and the placed the bottle carefully onto a shelf built into the stone tile. He stretched out his long arms, feeling the tension go as the hot water washed over the striations of muscle in his shoulders down the wide back. The scar in his scalp began to turn pink while the older ones from the two bullet holes in his side, which had been browned by the Georgian sun while he worked this summer on his property, turned an ash grey.

He took a moment to look at himself in the mirror. He had run his body hard for the last few years, but he felt like he was a few years short of his "prime." Maybe Valerie was right — his waist was short. He shrugged the massively muscled shoulders and wrapped a towel around his hips, taking a new beer out to his back patio looking down on the meadow and the part of Smith Creek he could see from his elevated perch.

His skin began to steam in the quickly cooling air as the sun set just off to his right.

He closed his eyes and tilted his head back, exhaling and then inhaling deeply.

When he opened his eyes, it seemed much darker than it had just moments before. The moon was a specter of half of itself.

He decided that he would go to see Schroeder in Virginia and see if he could help put the man at ease; he did, after all, feel an obligation to his fellow soldiers.

• • •

Fryderyk "Bull" Warczinski was once a big man, at 6' 4" and 250 lbs,, he was the guy everyone turned to in his 10th Mountain Division Infantry unit for heavy work.

He had carried the "pig" machinegun up and down the steep slopes without complaint and had been "a rock" within some of the battles his unit had been involved in.

He had served in Afghanistan until a rocket-propelled grenade had blown a hole in that broad Polish back.

Bull's life had been saved on the mountain by quick-acting medics and the helicopter unit brave enough to land in a hot LZ on uneven ground; he was forever thankful for them.

He had undergone surgery in Germany and then had been flown to the states, eventually discharged with severe kidney damage and back problems, limiting his ability to walk and move for the rest of his life. Follow-ups with the Veterans Administration led to the scheduling of additional surgery.

Bull was near thirty-two years old, but, as he lay shivering under a heavy blanket on this early fall day in Wisconsin, he felt closer to being seventy-two. Now closer to 165 lbs., Bull felt as weak as a kitten.

The VA had ordered him an antibiotic for a possible infection but had refused to see him on his last visit. He had scheduled another appointment, and they had called him, pushing the date back further.

Bull was well past caring about being a tough guy, but this fever was causing him to forget things. He got up and walked gingerly into the kitchen, but, when he arrived, he couldn't remember why he had come in there.

After a sip of water, Bull went back to under his blankets on the oversized sofa that he now nearly lived in.

His blood pressure was dropping nearly as rapidly as his breathing was increasing. The septic shock and fever was taking a final toll on Bull, and he convulsed as his organs failed. He remembered just as he died that he was looking for his phone to call 911.

9

GORDAN PICKED THROUGH the streets just southwest of Warrington, Virginia, looking for the home of Walter Schroeder. He found the small, red-brick single-floor home with a single-car garage with a small red car, maybe a Honda, parked off to the side; Gordan noticed the wheelchair ramp leading to the front door.

Gordan walked toward the door and turned to look out at the street and surrounding homes; it appeared to be a very nice neighborhood, although a little too tight for him, as he felt he could hit three homes with a grenade if given the opportunity. *The hell with good fences: Just have no neighbors within sight*, Gordan felt.

"Staff Sergeant!"

Gordan turned to see Walter Schroeder standing just inside the doorframe. His red, white, and blue lower-leg orthopedic device was, of course, the first thing Gordan observed. Otherwise, he looked exactly as Gordan remembered him, his hair in a high-and tight, fit-looking, and very straight-backed. Gordan guessed he still folded his socks and underwear in the military fashion; Mr. Dress right dress.

"If you got two of those, maybe you would have been able to max your PT training," Gordan said as he stepped past Schroeder into the home.

"This is my wife, Jill." Schroeder waved at his wife standing just inside the kitchen.

"Hello, Mrs. Captain Schroeder." Gordan was taken back by the attractive, thin blonde standing before him.

She held up a mug "Can I offer you some coffee, Mr. Hudde?"

"You can, and please call me 'Gordan' or 'Hudde' if you're yelling at me; it will remind me of the good ol' days." Gordan stepped in, and they shook hands.

She turned and retrieved a mug from a cupboard and then carefully poured into it, stopping at nearly full. "OK, then, please call me 'Jill.' Walter has been so excited that you would come and check out his information; he is so concerned, and I worry about him."

Gordan stole a glance back and forth between the two Schroeders.

"Is everything alright, Gordan?" Jill said as she handed him the steaming mug.

Gordan whispered as if Walter couldn't hear: "Does he have money or something? How did he catch you?"

"Are all you Army men the same?" She punched him in the shoulder, and Gordan checked to ensure he hadn't spilled the hot liquid.

"I have to go to work; you two play nice." Jill Schroeder pulled a coat out of a closet near the door and then kissed Walter on the cheek and waved goodbye to the both of them.

"Wow," Gordan exclaimed. "I never thought to ask you if you had gotten married, had kids, any of the normal things."

"I understood we aren't really friends; here, have a seat at the kitchen table." He gestured before sitting down himself.

Gordan pulled out the wooden simple chair and slid into it. He took a moment now to notice the decorations and personal things that the Schroeders had purchased to make their home; he suddenly thought of the barren walls of his bunker home.

"Nice place, Walter. So, tell me: How'd you trick the hot blonde into marrying you?"

Schroeder nodded several times and smiled. "I'll take both as a compliment but if you came here to prod me into an old argument, then you've wasted your time. I'm just not interested."

"If you want me to be honest, then I'd have to tell you that you did me a favor back then; I liked the Rangers, but I was not planning on staying there very long. I always wanted something more, and the agency was just the thing, so it all worked out for me." Gordan immediately felt odd about how he'd phrased it. "I'm sorry it took you losing your leg to get me there."

Schroeder nodded, "Me, too." He bent down and pulled up a pile of papers, spreading them across the table between their coffee mugs. "Where do you want to start?"

Gordan sat up straighter and took a sip from the rapidly cooling mug. "I've been reviewing some of the horror stories on line about the failures of the Veterans Administration, from Phoenix a few years ago, and then all across the country."

Gordan held up his hands and shrugged. "It seems criminal, so don't get me wrong — but where is this conspiracy above and beyond that which you are talking about?"

"Did you review the information about my guys that I sent you?" Schroeder leaned in closer. "Those guys were not contemplating suicide, Gordan — of this I guarantee you. They were three very well-rounded individuals, and I sat in with them during open group. In fact, I would ask these guys to show up and lead the group discussions just because they were so solid."

Schroeder looked intensely at Gordan. Looking for something and then not getting it, he continued. "The men had plans, Gordan. They were getting their lives in order. They weren't on drugs, prescribed or otherwise, and they had no problems at home. I'm just perplexed that they would do this."

Gordan ran his left hand over his Spartan-like beard for a moment. "Isn't that just it though, Walter? They were good soldiers and completed what they had planned — no crying for help, no dramatic displays of need. They just went out and did it. Isn't it always the people left behind who seem to be hurt the most, needing to move on without them?"

"And you think I can't move on?" Walter sat back and shook his head "No."

"Right." Gordan leaned in. "They were like family to you. You have taken them in like a big brother, and naturally, you're one of the hardest hit with their loss."

Schroeder put both elbows on the table and leaned forward, putting his head in his hands.

"I hope you didn't come here just to argue the same thing my wife has been saying."

Gordan allowed the silence to sink in for a few minutes continuing to stroke his beard.

"No, I want to see everything, because I want to find someone to complain to. After seeing what has been happening to my brothers, I have a desire to look someone in charge in the eye and get answers."

"Good — so where do I begin?"

"From your beginning. Why did you think it was necessary for you to start Veterans for Vets — and don't leave anything out."

Walter Schroeder then wove his tale for the next two hours, with Gordan occasionally stopping him to ask questions and other times writing things down on some scrap paper before him.

Walter Schroeder was possibly the poster boy for perseverance; while others may have gotten lost in the bureaucratic nightmare and maybe gotten poor care in the process, Schroeder had gotten through it with his health intact.

When he was sent from city to city to see other Veterans Administration doctors, Schroeder had been there with bells on.

When he was informed that his documentation had been lost, he had *hand-delivered* copies of what was lost to the departments that had demanded it.

All the while, Schroeder had been in good health, and nothing had become life threatening.

But Schroeder had observed the problems others had with the Veterans Administration, from the WWII vet to the returning injured soldier from the Middle Eastern conflicts. He had set that never-budging movie-star chin and then took that "dress right, dress" attitude and decided that he would hold the government personally responsible for the promises that had been made to all veterans. And he made it clear that they should deliver on those promises in more than a perfunctory manner. He wanted them to respond to the vets' request with the same rigor that they were making demands of the vets.

Gordan liked what he was hearing from Schroeder, his behavior, and his attitude; but he didn't want to compliment him yet. He wanted to visit his facility.

10

SOON IT WOULD be too cold for a leisurely stroll, but today it was just right for a cup of coffee and a light sweater. The Lincoln Memorial stood as a backdrop as Yvonne Lane looked back toward the Washington Monument down the mall.

She believed in form over fashion, so she always had sensible shoes for walking to meetings or grabbing a bite to eat. Meeting the Deputy Secretary of Defense here was not a big deal. As she sipped her coffee, closing her eyes, she listened to conversations as they came and went like a slow-motion version of the Doppler Effect.

Meredith Ryan strode into the mall from the opposite direction as Lane had come. He had wolfed down a sandwich, and, after wiping any possible crumbs from his suit jacket, he headed toward Lincoln.

He spotted the dark hair piled high — similar to a beehive from a '60s photo and started walking in her direction. The brisk air may have kept some of the foot traffic down, but now he wished he had grabbed his jacket before exiting his office at the Pentagon.

Before he announced his arrival, he couldn't help but notice the pert posterior of Lane. For a woman in her late fifties, she seemed to stay in good shape.

"Lane," he said as he stepped into her line of sight.

"What the fuck, Ryan — did you crawl here?" She pursed her lips and looked at him from over her sunglasses. Her arched eyebrows mocked him even more.

"I was hungry." He was immediately upset with himself for answering her.

"First, I've been told that the announcement will be made either the end of this week or the beginning of next week. If you haven't conducted your business by now, it may be too late."

He nodded. "I'm good."

"Please tell me you were smart about it and diversified and not all at once."

He exhaled loudly and looked up at the sky. "It's getting cold. Get on with it."

"The new facility was supposed to be completed by now; you need to push some buttons."

"I'll look into it and try to find out what is slowing it down. But isn't the General providing enough in both facilities and resources?"

He could feel her eyes boring into his skull, and he was glad that they were in public.

At this distance, he could see himself in the reflection of her oversized lenses. He wrapped his arms around his chest to warm up and do something besides stand there in silence.

"Ryan, quit being such a pussy."

"Oh, that's helpful," he quipped.

She slowed her speech down like a schoolmarm talking to young students.

"For the next stage of testing, he said he is going to need the entire facility. What do I know except that if the golden ring is attached to that element of the project, then we need to provide it." She studied him another silent moment. "You're all in already — just do whatever needs to be done."

She turned and walked away, taking long strides all the way back to her desk as Chief of Staff of Veterans Affairs. She had begun talking to herself more and more as this operation had come into being, and, while Ryan was vitally important, she would not allow his cold feet to, in any way, jeopardize what she had helped put together over the last two years.

For thirty years she had conducted herself with the highest standards. She had completed all tasks efficiently and effectively and better than the men who had slowly but surely all gotten past her in promotions, money, and power.

And then, one day, the stars all aligned themselves, and she had seen an opportunity. Even as it had seemed so multifaceted and so difficult, it had appeared to unfold before her eyes as if she was somehow so special to receive it. It had so much potential on so many fronts that all her years of unpolluted, uncorrupted service had evaporated. She had helped come up with the plan, she had found the people who needed to be involved, and she had found the leverage to get them here — to the edge of success.

This government was so large and unwieldy that it was easy, unbelievably easy, to manipulate and corrupt it. She just had to acknowledge that the good that was done by the bureaucracy was like the Washington Monument that she had just taken a left at. As huge and as impressive as it was, rising up to the sky, it got smaller the higher it went up. The real action was buried deep below, like the foundation of the exhibit; but the foundation of this operation would be seen as dark and evil. She had been afraid to admit that at one time. Now she felt comfortable — in fact, she now embraced it.

Fuck all of them. She would be the evil queen — the successful, rich evil queen.

• • •

Jeffery Boone still carried his full height of six foot three inches well into his seventies. Some men found their energy sapped and started to hunch and succumb to old age, but Boone would not be one of them.

He strode confidently through the white-glass and stainless-steel halls of his pharmaceutical company, Biophaze. People who recognized him scurried from his path, not wanting to be questioned by the CEO. He was used to it, and, although he did not want fear to be a motivating factor in an employee's work ethic, he didn't care at the moment *what* motivated someone, as long as it *did*.

He stopped at the double doors with the sign "Authorized Individuals Only." He swiped his magnetic card, waiting for the familiar *Swoosh!* sound that inevitably came after.

At the next door on his right, he again swiped his card, and a loud, metallic clicking noise followed when the lock released. Everyone inside the room stopped to look at the intruder as it seemed to be human nature to ignore an intrusion. Boone knew it; he nodded at the white-coated lab technicians and the scientists who stood over computer keyboards, tinkered with glass vials, and spun centrifuges.

There were three steps leading into a glass-enclosed office at the rear of this rectangular lab; Boone needed only one to go through the door at the top.

The small man seated at the computer did not rise; in fact, he did not look or concern himself as all the others in the building seemed to do.

"Come in, Jeffery. I think I have some good news for you today."

"Jeezus, Akihiko — you'd better, because we have bankrupted ourselves funding this chase down the rabbit hole."

Akihiko Watanabe was born in Japan from Japanese parents. They had migrated to London soon after his birth, where it was found that young Akihiko had a brilliant mind. He had disappointed his parents when he had graduated Cambridge University at 15, nearly a year older than the youngest to ever do so.

It threw some people when the five-foot-three-inch Japanese man spoke with a heavy English accent, but Boone was no longer one of them.

Watanabe stood and offered his chair to Boone. "Have a seat, mate. You look positively ill."

Boone was nearly the same height seated as Watanabe was standing. "Seriously, Akihiko, the company is leveraged way past where we should be, and our stock has dropped past its lowest recorded price since we went public. I'm afraid our future is looking very bleak."

Akihiko Watanabe grinned at Boone but said nothing. He was enjoying this.

Boone closed his eyes and took a deep breath. "Tell me you've made a breakthrough. Tell me something positive — I beg you."

Watanabe reached out and placed his hand on Boone's shoulder. "Old man, you run the company that created the cure for Alzheimer's."

Boone breathed very deeply, and now tears began to well up in his eyes. "You're serious — right?"

"I'm waiting on the paperwork from the FDA for the treatment IND (Investigational New Drug) on this latest serum at this very moment; it could come back any day now."

Boone jumped to his feet and looked down. "Why the hell are you this far along without me being informed of the progress?" His joy had momentarily been subsumed to the news that this had remained unknown to him until now.

"I just had to be sure, Jeffery; I was going to bring the documentation up later today, but I am positive about this."

Boone's mind began spinning. "Not a word to anyone. We need to make an announcement to best affect our stock price. Oh, Lord! We're saved!" He raised his hands skyward.

Boone walked in some tight circles, hands on top of his head. A thought came to him, and he stopped and pointed at Watanabe.

"Success rate?"

"Near 99 percent." Watanabe stood still, hands in his white-lab-coat pocket.

Boone began rolling his hand out in front of his chest as he searched for words. "Um...um..."

"Take a breath, Jeffery." Watanabe searched the desk for his pipe, a habit he'd picked up at school nearly twenty-two years ago.

"Side effects?" Boone finally blurted out, too loudly.

"In comparison, very mild." Watanabe smiled through clenched teeth as he placed the pipe there. He started to lead Boone back toward his door, pushing him by the elbows.

Boone shrugged him off and walked to the blinds, pulling down on the vinyl strip to look out into the daylight. "Delivery system, dosages — come on, man! Tell me!"

Watanabe pulled the pipe from his mouth. "All good news. It's not a cure, but a serum that may be able to reverse the symptoms — as long as the patients continue the treatment. I know we can use a liquid capsule and maybe a medicated patch as well." He waved at Boone with his pipe. "All good for you and your bottom line — isn't that correct?"

Boone turned and stepped in to slap the grinning Watanabe on the shoulder. "I'm afraid that, at any moment, I will awake and find myself still in bed."

"I'll be up shortly, Jeffery. In the meantime, have a drink, and enjoy the moment — I know I have."

"Yes, yes — I'm going to do that; oh, my Lord." Boone straightened up and went down the steps.

Watanabe tapped his pipe and then lit the bowl with a large "strike anywhere" match. He blew out the match and watched the smoke curl as it floated past his face slowly, like the uncoiling of a DNA molecule. He closed his eyes and took a deep breath; he liked the sulfur-dioxide smell.

Watanabe walked over and looked at the file that he had pulled up for Jeffery Boone on his computer screen; he had solved this puzzle nearly eighteen months ago, not long after he had made the deal with the US government.

11

Friday, 11 days ago
TRAVIS BALDWIN HAD helped win World War II, and yet he had never fired a weapon or marched onto foreign lands. As the Machinist's Mate First Class on the *USS San Diego* (CL-53), he had been deep inside the beast during every battle.

Now he seemed to battle for every breath.

After a long and difficult public-transportation trip into the Veterans Administration hospital in his city, he was told that the x-ray machine was out of order but that they would call him when it was back up and running.

They gave him a list of over-the-counter cold and flu medications and then had him wheeled him out to his wife, who had fallen asleep while waiting for her husband to be seen.

The aide needed to yell for her to hear the instructions. The two shuffled out and waited at the nearby bus stop for their journey home.

The undiagnosed pneumonia would take Travis long before anyone from the Veterans Administration would ever call their home; they had never even logged his visit.

• • •

Gordan took in the old business park on a dreary day in Virginia. Further back on the property, larger warehouses loomed in the early morning grey light. The office area up front was brick and cracked glass; in the distance, a diesel engine geared down to slow or stop. Cobwebs hung in the corners of the overhang, and pigeon nests stuck out from spaces above the visible beams.

"Nice place." Gordan's coffee steamed in the cool morning air.

"Well, it was the right price. Come on" Schroeder swiveled and headed up the concrete ramp to the double steel doors.

Gordan followed as the lights came on and he could make out some handmade signs. He studied the star-like graph that showed veterans all the different organizations that could possibly help them: The VA at the center, and all kinds of services shooting out from that organization.

"Let me get this straight." Gordan paused as he saw a pamphlet for a shrink who was doing work for the group; he picked it up and unfolded it.

"The VA is tasked with taking care of veterans and is given billions of tax dollars."

Schroeder was making coffee in a mineral-encrusted coffee maker. "Yeah."

"But they can't do everything, so the government adds to their budget to pay guys like you to do additional work?"

"Well, I'm given a grant to continue my work. It certainly doesn't pay for everything; we need donations of time and money to make this work."

Gordan pointed at the strange graph on the wall. "All these people do the same?"

"I'm sure they do." Schroeder opened a set of double wooden doors, which opened into another larger room with an assortment of chairs in a loose clam-shell formation; some folding tables ringed the room.

"I've got to get the donuts in your truck." Schroeder headed back outside.

He returned in a few moments with the two boxes of breakfast pastries they had picked up on the way in this morning.

"So I'm guessing you get visited several times a year by some bureaucrat to make sure you're spending the money wisely?"

Schroeder set the orange boxes down and slipped his finger under the masking tape that held the tops down.

"For what?"

"To make sure you're doing what you said you were doing with our tax dollars." Gordan looked at Schroeder, who had stopped to think about the implications. His mouth pursed and brows furrowed as the Boy Scout had never once thought about that before.

"Well, I've been doing this only a few years. Maybe sometime soon? I fill out a ton of paperwork every year to keep the funds coming — I can tell you that."

Gordan made a dismissive gesture with his hand. "Yeah, nobody would ever miss-represent their motives to make an extra buck."

"Where are you going with this, Gordan?"

Gordan shook his head. "Don't worry about it. I'm just throwing as much information into the hopper as I can and shaking it up to see what falls out."

"Well, there is nothing illegal or immoral going on here — I can tell you that."

Gordan ignored him and walked into the back of the room, looking back to the front office. "When is the first group expected in?"

"They all should be rolling in now. It's a group that either works nights or late mornings. This is a pretty well-adjusted group, and this is where the three suicides came from."

Schroeder turned as the sound of tires displacing gravel drifted into the building.

"Have you had others who committed suicide?"

"Yes — but not from this group. These guys have issues, but it just seems that they all had some positive things happening for them that keeps them grounded better than some of the others. This is my oldest group. I encourage all of them to come in when they can during other meetings to inspire others and give hope as well as act as a positive role model. Some of them even give out their number and 'sponsor' members — like AA or something."

"And this is once a week?"

Schroeder nodded in the affirmative.

"Very good." Gordan nodded at the door as some men began to trickle in, grabbing coffee and a snack.

There were earnest handshakes and slaps on the shoulder. The one thing they all had in common is that they all immediately identified the new guy. Unlike other groups, these guys came and confronted Gordan, asking questions and looking to offer help if needed: A band of brothers.

"You serve with the Captain?" one of the men asked.

"He barked some orders at me in the past." Gordan grinned. "Does he have you all fooled?"

"For an officer, he's OK" another man said.

Schroeder stood at the front of the room "Alright, alright. Settle in, and grab a seat."

The six men took seats; it was the first time that Gordan had payed attention to the service wounds that several of the men had.

Schroeder continued: "Anyone have something good they can share?"

"Sure. I got yelled at by my 'know nothing' boss, and, not only did I not quit — I didn't kick his scrawny ass."

The former Marine took a bite from a donut that he was holding in his prosthetic hand.

"Thanks for that bit of positive news, Corporal." Schroeder made a stink-face at the young Black man. "That man back there is a former comrade, SSG Gordan Hudde, a ranger like me; he's been in the shit and is firmly one of us."

The six men all turned in unison and nodded.

"I would love to have him come up here and tell you all what his life has been like; maybe he can tell you how he helped save my ass once."

Gordan was a bit taken back by the first admission Schroeder had ever made that his actions long ago were a positive thing. Gordan stood and walked to front of the room.

"Good morning, men." Gordan nodded, acknowledging them all. "Honestly, I'm not much for sharing, and I'm afraid that, if I told you my nightmares, you'd laugh."

There were some ruminations and quiet protestations from the men in the room.

Gordan held his hand out to stop them, and he continued. "But I would love to hear how this officer somehow did something positive and created this group." He grinned, knowing that all the men in front of him were enlisted.

There were some chuckles. Obviously, everyone understood military humor.

The Marine stood. "No offense sir, but everyone here shares something before we take them in."

Gordan shook his head in mock disbelief. "Always the jarhead who has to be difficult."

The young Marine sat back down, and one of the other men reached over and slapped the back of his head.

There was a chuckle that spread.

"Alright. I promise that one day, maybe some other time, I'll share," Gordan said.

"What are you — some kind of cop now?" somebody asked.

"I'm just a concerned former soldier that has questions is all. Now, if you don't mind, I'm going to hang around just to listen to your group. If there is anything you can tell me about some of your team members who are no longer here, anything..." he paused to make eye contact with each man "...even a rumor you heard, I'd like to know why they would take their own lives."

The meeting continued, and Gordan sat in the back silently, listening to an assortment of stories. Some of the men shared how frightened they now got when approaching anything near the side of the road that shouldn't be there.

Some of the men shared dreams that kept them awake.

The one thing in common is that they all shared positive stories about how their lives continued, despite the fears. Despite the difficulties of their injuries, they were young and determined to go on.

After the meeting, Gordan spoke with all six of the men. Nobody had any information that could have been a sign by three in question that suicide was an option that was being weighed.

"What did you think? Schroeder asked as the last man left.

"A good group. I didn't get the feeling that any of them were in danger of taking their own life."

"You would have thought the same of the others."

"Is this how they all go?"

Schroeder reached up and scratched his cheek. "Well, with this group, yeah. Some more difficult guys come in at night, it seems, battling with drugs and/or alcohol, maybe some other issues."

"One of the best things I ever did was to bring in some WWII and Korean War vets and let them tell some stories about how difficult it was to get back to normal life when they had come home. But all of them had led successful lives despite it all."

Gordan nodded. "Nice. I can see how effective that could be. Now about the drug and alcoholic types: How do you address those folks?"

"There are other groups — AA veteran groups and the like. We don't want them here high and causing problems for the guys trying hard to get past it all."

"Makes sense. Do you think your three went to see any other groups, maybe the same doctor or shrink?" Gordan shrugged his shoulders, "Anything?"

"I can't think of anything, Gordan."

"Maybe you can call the wives or girlfriends and see for sure?"

"Sure, Gordan. I'll try."

"Good. I'm going to see if I can find any other suicides that seem questionable and see if you and I can visit the survivors."

Schroeder slapped Gordan on the shoulder as he exited. "Thanks for this, Gordan. Whatever we find out, I feel like this will eventually help all of us."

Gordan yelled over his shoulder, "I hope so. Walter. I do hope so."

12

BRIGADIER GENERAL EMERSON Seibert always felt uneasy anywhere near the Pentagon. He didn't appreciate the invite when the Deputy Secretary of Defense called him to an office lunch.

Complete in his dress greens, Seibert's medals and uniform were perfect, but Seibert just never looked like an Army man. At the age of fifty-eight, he had long ago lost the urge to stand in a mirror and try to figure out why. His sloping shoulders and weak chin were an effect of genetics, and he'd long ago stopped worrying about that, for it was the same biology that was responsible for what lay between his ears, and that is how he had risen in rank.

Seibert was most comfortable where he was the highest-ranking person, and that was Fort Belvoir, where he was responsible for nearly sixty-five thousand.

He turned into the office and presented himself to the secretary; even she would not be impressed by his presence. In fact, she hardly noticed as she buzzed the office of Meredith Ryan.

"General Seibert, good of you to come." Meredith ushered the general into the plush office of high shag carpet and deep-red mahogany furniture.

"I ordered some sandwiches, chicken. I hope you don't mind; there is an assortment of condiments that they brought in." Ryan motioned to the table left of the oversized desk.

Once the door was secured and they were seated at the table, Seibert began to unwrap the foil-enclosed sandwich and look over the selection of sauces. He knew why he was here but was damn well sure he wouldn't offer any information unless it was solicited.

Ryan took a paper napkin and stuffed it into his neck; he looked over at the general and smiled. "I've done this before," and he shook some barbeque sauce under the bun.

Seibert just smiled and took small bites. When here, he often thought that he'd taken the wrong career path. This seemed so much more lucrative and, honestly, eas-ier, as there were no physical expectations placed on a desk job. He was always aware of the military-combat veterans and the disapproving glances his uniform and his presence invited.

Ryan swallowed, took a drink, and then cleared his throat. "Emerson, I hope you took my investment advice."

Seibert may not have had the attributes of many combat soldiers, but he had the poker face and nerves of a world-class poker player; his face did not show anything.

"Why, yes, sir. I did."

"Rich."

"Sir?"

"We are all going to be rich — rich, Seibert, beyond anything we ever thought." Ryan nodded; it was a subtle, almost unperceivable, movement of his head.

"I need to know where we are on the construction of the Fort Valley facility."

OK, Seibert thought, *there it is*. "We were a bit behind, but it is almost completely finished now. I was going to contact the doctor and have a walk-through to ensure he is satisfied with the end result."

"And the secrecy of it all — are you certain that it is still intact?"

Seibert sat up a bit straighter. "Civilian construction believes it is a secret military facility, and the military all believe it is something secret for the CIA, NSA..." he waved his hand in the air dismissively "...whatever top-secret group they want, it doesn't matter." He started to say something but stopped.

"Go on," Ryan encouraged.

"It really is quite impressive."

Ryan reached for a fry and then used it to point at Seibert. "That Lane loves to squeeze my nuts over this. I mean, without the two of us, she would never be able to pull this off, and then she struts around…as if she did any of the heavy lifting."

Seibert just nodded. He was thinking the same thing about Ryan right now.

Ryan took a swig of whatever it was he was drinking. "Yeah. I may check it out one day…"

Seibert made his eyebrow raise just the slightest, and Ryan saw it.

"…when it's all over, of course, after it is all OK." Ryan looked a bit embarrassed.

"Oh, of course." Seibert nodded but was praying the guy would just stay away and let him do his job. "Maybe for starters, the next time we meet, it can be at Belvoir. I'll be happy to pick up dinner at the O-club."

Ryan looked at Seibert and decided that it was a sincere invite. "Sure, General. I'd be happy to let you buy me dinner."

"Believe it or not, I've never had a better steak." Seibert began to rise. "I really should get back."

"OK, General. Maybe we should touch base in two weeks?"

"Sure. At Belvoir — correct?"

"OK, then. Call me with a time."

"18:30 hours every Friday. Don't be late." Seibert nodded and headed out on a good note; in two weeks, he wouldn't have to make this drive or walk through these halls.

• • •

"Holy shit!" Robert "Bulldog" Mahoney screamed out as he leapt from his office chair.

"Damn, old man. You got fat and slow on me. Is this what government employment does to you?" Hudde grinned.

"I ain't fat, brother. I'm just too short." The shorter man grabbed Hudde by the shoulder and pushed him over to a chair in his office.

Mahoney slapped Gordan hard on the shoulder. "You still look like a beast. You breaking down doors and kicking ass?"

"Good genetics. Naw — I'm retired and living the country life, but you know that already." Gordan smiled at Mahoney, knowing that he had given out the info that Schroeder had used to get in touch.

"What's this shit Schroeder says you're working on for the Famous But Incompetent?" Gordan made a surprised face.

"No, that's wrong; I'm the CIA attaché to Homeland Defense, my brother. I give out info... if they're nice to me." Mahoney grinned like the Cheshire cat.

"What do they pay you with, baked goods?" In a suit jacket and tie, the man was even more the fireplug than ever. Gordan felt he was more than capable of taking care of himself.

"Damn, Gordan. It's like you came here to hurt my feelings or something."

"If I were here to do that, I would suggest they burn the other side of your face off. Right now, I can't tell which side I like most." Gordan reached over and placed his oversized hand onto the burn scars on the left side of Mahoney's face. "Seriously, man. You look damn good, and I'm happy to see you."

Mahoney sat up so that he could look out his small office window. "What can I really do you for? Name it."

"It's Schroeder. Did he tell you what he is doing and why?" Gordan sat down and looked about at the maps and documents cluttered everywhere.

"Honestly, I didn't listen much. I've heard some rumors that you were doing your own thing, and I thought maybe you could help him."

Gordan's brows furrowed.

Mahoney's eyes rolled. "Don't worry. Nothing specific out there about you — just that you've been... active." He grinned broadly. "Yeah, that's a good word."

"Fuck." Hudde stood up and looked at the location of the pushpins on the American map. "So there is nothing out there, no matter how crazy it sounds at face value, about people taking out veterans?"

Mahoney threw both his hands out before him, palms up. "Seriously?" He waited for Gordan to say something; Gordan turned and looked at him, raising his eyebrows.

"No, Gordan. Nothing. But listen: I served with many good guys. I can't always do favors for anyone who knows where I work."

Gordan pointed a thumb at his own chest.

Mahoney shook his head. "No, man — you're different. Anything you ever want, if I can do it, I will."

"Simple as that?" Gordan asked.

"Well, let me think." He put his right hand out in a fist and then flipped out his thumb. "Let me count the guys who saved my ass; one..."

His hand hung out there for several moments while Mahoney appeared to think. "Oh, yeah — just one, you stupid motherfucker."

"Alright then, don't forget." Gordan started to walk out of the office but stopped and turned. "Hey, man. You should come visit sometime, have a beer and relax. Oh, and one of my new friends has the best barbeque anywhere." He nodded and smiled. "The best food, man."

"OK, Gordan. I may just take you up on that sometime." Mahoney gave a mock half salute as Gordan spun and walked out.

13

FORMER PRIVATE ROLAND Jones was led down the crisp, whitewalled hallways at the special medical facilities building on Ft. Belvoir.

Jones had signed up for testing of new painkillers, or so he thought. The two men in white lab coats unlocked a solid white door and opened it. Stepping aside, they asked him to have a seat inside.

"Are you guys sure this is for the pain-med study?" He looked at each man's face for acknowledgment.

"Absolutely, sir. Please make yourself comfortable."

Jones entered and listened as the lock turned behind him. It was another white room, small, maybe eight foot by ten, with a table and one chair. He sat and looked at the small wooden table before him with a metal drain grate directly below it; there was an assortment of three knives and a glass of what appeared to be water in it on the table.

There was a plastic knife to his left, in the center a silver steak knife, and on the right a fixed fighting knife with a black tonto-style blade. Jones admired it but did not touch anything. There were two grey blocks just at the edge of the table about a foot apart.

He glanced up and noticed that the high wall in front of him ended in what looked like a mirror that ran the length of the room and tilted into the room at about a forty-five degree angle. He realized that he was probably being observed.

In the observation and control room above, Akihiko Watanabe looked over the clipboard that contained the synopsis of Jones's overall health. Other than the obvious loss of his right foot, he was as healthy as any twenty-six-year-old male could be. He had absolutely no mental-health issues. This was why he had been selected for this test.

There were three vials with silver ends on them, making them look similar to heavy, oval-shaped light bulbs, lying on a tray on the control panel before him. Two of the vials were empty, and the third had a light-brown tint.

Watanabe needed to stand to see over the control panel and into the room below. The microphone that stood at the center of the console, with its heavy metal gooseneck, bent only so far, and he needed to stand, anyway.

There was some feedback to some hidden speakers above him, and Jones looked up.

A man with an accent asked him to place his hands palms down onto the grey squares on the table.

Jones reached under him to slide the chair closer and found that the table and chairs were bolted to the floor. This caused him to reach out a little more than he was comfortable with to place his hands onto the squares.

Watanabe looked down, satisfied. "Very good, young man. Now, please try to relax."

Who could relax under these circumstances? Jones thought. "Um ... mister? I'm here for the new pain medication?" He looked up, waiting.

Watanabe pushed the rectangular red button below the microphone. "Of course. Now, the one thing I need you to focus on is to not remove your hands from the grey squares from this point forward. Is that understood — no matter what I say — from this point forward?"

Jones shrugged his shoulders. "Sure."

Watanabe pushed a button, and strong exhaust fans kicked in; Jones heard a rumbling noise as it started and then a roar until they stopped.

Watanabe watched the clock that would be visible in the video if they watched it later. After three minutes, he pressed the red button again. "You may have a drink of water."

Jones started to lean forward, and his right hand started to rise because he was a bit thirsty, but then he remembered and stopped himself.

The voice, maybe British or Australian — Jones had never been good at telling them apart — said, "Very good."

"Great. You guys brought me here to play 'Simon says'?" Jones mumbled.

Watanabe screwed the first of the empty vials onto a silver-and-black female adapter at the right of the microphone. He set a timer and then stood, as this would now be automated.

There was a puff as the clean air from the vial was forced into the room from a vent above Jones. Watanabe continued to watch the clock, and, right on time, the exhaust fans kicked in.

Jones heard the rumble and then the air-conditioning or heat or whatever. Then there was silence. If he could see the clock behind him, it would have been exactly three minutes later that the voice returned.

"Pick up the plastic knife, and stick it in your eye."

"What kind of sick fuckers are up there? Of course, I won't do that!" Jones yelled up at the glass above his head.

"Of course not," Watanabe said out loud to himself, as he did not press the microphone button.

Watanabe unscrewed the first control vial and placed it into a foam-formed silver box similar to a briefcase. He then screwed the second into the same female adapter and set the timer.

For Watanabe, the seconds ticked off like minutes. He was getting so close to getting the Army what they wanted, and he wanted to be able to move into the new facility and get started with the mass testing right away.

For Jones, this was ridiculous. He was here to get some better medication — something to help with the pain and that was non-addictive. Why had they brought him in to play games?

The fans kicked on overhead.

Jones took a deep breath and allowed his head to hang, all the while keeping his hands firmly on the table. *What the fuck — if I end up getting the right stuff from the VA, then why complain?* He shook his head and said "SNAFU" under his breath.

That voice called out, "Pick up the silver knife, and stab it into your thigh."

Jones's head snapped up. "Come on — what is wrong with you people?"

Watanabe repeated removing the empty vials and then screwed in the slightly brown vial. He set the timer and then stood impatiently, watching the second hand creep.

Watanabe watched as this time the "puff" cleaned out the brown from the final vial. He stood and imagined that he could see the dust fall from above down onto the seated man below.

Jones began to feel odd. His head twitched; he suddenly had a feeling that he needed to scratch his cheek.

He was feeling warm — no, *hot*. His nose began to run, and his eyes were watering.

God called out to him, "Pick up the black knife, and cut your throat."

Watanabe leaned over the control panel. He saw the twitching start in the man's arms and become uncontrollable in waves. Jones watched as a black hand pushed out on its own — off the grey dot, snaking out toward the deadly looking knife.

His hand formed a fist around the handle, and then his wrist rolled and the blade of the knife slowly pointed at the ceiling. The convulsions were growing and racking his body in waves of uncontrollable shaking. His left hand grabbed his right wrist, and his body fought with itself.

Watanabe wanted to bang the glass and yell out, "*Do it!*" but he did nothing other than watch the clock and the man below fighting for his life.

Jones began to lower his head in the direction of the knife blade. His shaking now was as uncontrollable as a man getting electroshock therapy. Sweat poured from his hairline; his mouth was incredibly dry. The entire room was beginning to spin, and his face was getting closer to the point of the blade.

While he felt he had to stab himself with the blade, something deep within him was helping him to stop it.

Suddenly he lost all control of his bladder and bowels; he threw up all over the table before him as he threw the military style knife across the room. Exhausted, he fell off the chair, into his own filth.

Watanabe had both hands clenched into fists, watching so intently that, when the total physical failure of the man below happened, he, too, shook, in frustration.

"Shite!" he screamed and threw a fist at the ceiling. He stepped to the center of the room and closed his eyes; after taking a few deep breaths, he walked to the wall and lifted the clear plastic that was covering a horizontal valve. He reached in and turned until he could hear the water pouring into the observation room. After a minute, he turned it off and beckoned the response team.

His subject would be removed, cleaned up, and placed into observation. He made some notations into his log and then walked the metal case back to his office.

He felt like he was so close to finishing this project.

14

Sunday, 9 days ago

GORDAN PULLED UP in front of the small home in Leesburg, Virginia. Gordan thought that the yellow paint was ugly, but he wasn't here to critique the place for *Better Homes and Gardens*.

Gordan turned in his seat. "So you're sure that this guy had nothing to do with Vets for Veterans — right?"

Schroeder was reading the newspaper clippings that Gordan had placed into a cheap drugstore binder.

"Yeah. I don't recognize these names at all." Schroeder closed the binder and set it down on the truck floorboard. "How did you pick these three deaths?"

"I looked for close survivors making statements about being taken by surprise, and I looked for the reporter stating that there was no sign of mental illness or drug use. Otherwise, I couldn't see us reaching out to them."

"OK."

"So, you're the guy doing this counseling. I'd like you to talk to them."

"And ask them what, Gordan? 'Hey, do you think there was foul play in your son's death'?" Schroeder shook his head.

"You run a group to help veterans. Ask her about what she thought he needed — what *you* may need to reach out to these guys to help. Try to find out what VA facilities the son used or if he was in pain. Just let the conversation be natural; I'll step in when or if I feel I can help."

Gordan pulled the handle and exited his truck, stopping on the sidewalk; when he heard the opposite door slam, he pressed the key fob, and his horn honked once.

He hated doing what they were about to do. He just never felt like he had the right words. If you needed him to act, Gordan could do so without thinking. He could still run, jump, and shoot better than almost anyone he knew. But speaking with the surviving parents was something that made him uncomfortable; maybe it was survivor's guilt.

Gordan pulled on the screen door and allowed Schroeder to walk to the door in front of him. Gordan had to hold the screen door as he entered, as the spring was so tight that it would have trapped his foot in the door if he had released it too soon.

Schroeder rapped on the door.

They could see a smaller flat-screen television playing *The Price Is Right* through the window to the right of the door.

A woman in her late fifties opened the door.

"Are you the young men who called earlier?"

Gordan cleared his throat and lifted his right hand to shoulder height, "I am, ma'am."

"Come in, then. I put some extra coffee on after you called."

She led them past the TV; Gordan noticed that a pretty woman was standing in front of a new refrigerator on the show.

She showed them to a lightly stained wooden table with four chairs around it. She stopped and turned to them. "Did you know my son?"

Gordan held out his hand. "Ma'am, like I said on the phone: I'm Gordan Hudde, and this is my old Captain, Walter Schroeder."

She barely held his hand when they shook, and then she took Schroeder's hand.

"I'm sorry that I didn't know Martin, Mrs. Cook, but I'm hoping that, if I can talk to you about him, it may help me in my endeavors to help other returning veterans."

Schroeder pointed at a chair. "May we?"

Mrs. Cook was looking down at Schroeder's prosthetic leg "I'm sorry — did you do that over there?"

"Yes, ma'am." Schroeder pulled out a chair and took a seat. "Afghanistan — a rocket-propelled grenade."

She shrugged her shoulders. "I'm so sorry," she said as she put her hands to her chest. "It all seems so pointless."

There was a moment of silence; Mrs. Cook seemed lost.

She snapped out of it. "Coffee?" She looked at them expectantly.

"Please, black" Gordan said.

"No, thank you, Mrs. Cook," Schroeder said over his shoulder.

"Please — you boys can call me 'Carol.' I feel so old, and all that 'ma'am' stuff just makes it worse." She smiled rather weakly and then went into the next room.

She came back with two big, sturdy mugs; Gordan appreciated not having to grasp one of those dainty little teacups so many people break out for guests.

Schroeder started to describe his group and what they do to support returning veterans. He went over some of the difficulties he had navigating the Veterans Administration and deftly explained how his group, he hoped, would help others.

Carol listened with her hand held up around her throat. "I just don't know how your group could have helped by son. When the police called me that day...." She looked down into her mug; tears welled up in the corners of her eyes. "I was in shock. I mean, I know my son was unhappy with the way things had turned out for him, but I just didn't think that he would do that." She looked up at the ceiling, her eyes wide, and took a deep breath.

Walter reached across and took her hand; with her other, she dabbed her eyes with a napkin.

"Was there anything that, now," Schroeder paused, "months later, you realize that he was giving a sign that he was capable of taking his own life?"

She dropped her head and sighed, "His father."

Neither man dared say a word or make a noise as she gathered her thoughts.

"They were always going at each other. Sometimes, maybe, it sounded good natured, but it wasn't. He felt his dad's disappointment; it cut him so deeply. I look back now and I wonder if it wasn't *that* — more than the injury or the war — that made him do it."

She took another deep breath and then suddenly made a face as if she'd realized that she had just said something out loud that she had only dared think in her head before.

"Please — oh, please: Never repeat that."

Gordan shook his head and held his hand up.

Schroeder responded, "Of course not, Carol. Nothing you say will ever be repeated."

"Oh, thank you. We're having enough problems. I don't need David to hear that; that's for sure." Carol closed her eyes and shook her head slowly.

Fifteen minutes later, they were starting the truck and pulling out, heading in the direction of their next appointment.

Gordan looked at the map in his lap. "OK — what are your thoughts?"

Schroeder looked out the window. "We, I mean people, are so fucked up, aren't we?"

"Sometimes it seems like it." The rubber barked as Gordan hit the gas.

"I felt the pain in her voice, Gordan, when she made that statement about her husband; I just knew that this case wasn't anything like my boys."

"I agree. Now off to Frederick, Maryland."

• • •

About seventy-five miles to the southwest, near Fort Valley Virginia, the vehicle taking Akihiko Watanabe and Emerson Seibert had just turned east from the main road and was bumping along a dirt road that seemed to be disappearing into deep woods. After a few miles, they approached the gate to the property of the new top-secret facility.

The dirt road was actually fairly well kept, except for a few ruts that the heavy trucks had caused during the rain. Seibert tapped on the shoulder of the soldier driving, and asked him to stop just before they reached the gate.

Another dirt road led up and away to the north; Seibert dropped his window and pointed it out.

"This access road goes to a much-smaller steel maintenance shed that holds the equipment you will need to maintain the grounds and this road."

Watanabe didn't care, "Oh, very well," he acknowledged.

The window stayed down the final few yards as they approached the small guard shack at the gate.

The guard nodded at Seibert, and the gate rolled back; the passenger window rolled back up.

"Are all the guards armed?" Watanabe asked.

"Our soldiers can't seem to go anywhere without being armed." Seibert smiled and shrugged his shoulders.

"Is that prudent, General?"

The big GMC Yukon rolled forward through the gate and around a bend until a very large steel hangar came into view.

"Doctor, if a fully armed platoon came up here, I assure you they would get through the gate and into the hangar, but you would be safe and sound until help arrived. In fact, if World War Three begins, I may come here to join you."

Watanabe nodded. "All very encouraging, General. It has been so long since this was just a proposal that I made..."

"Well, it's done now, doctor," Seibert interrupted.

The giant garage door began to swing up and into the building, and the driver wasted no time in getting inside the moment that the bottom of the door had cleared the roof of the vehicle.

The facility was poorly lit, and the lights of the Yukon lit a path to the side of the building as the door dropped back down to block out the sunlight altogether.

The driver hopped out and walked forward, dropping a large switch; a double row of dim lights began flicking on, one after the other, from overhead at the door to the back of the hangar. They lit the interior like a full moon on a clear night — nothing that anyone could work under but enough light that you wouldn't trip over something left out on the ground.

Now visible was something like a concrete four-walled closet with a single steel door, freestanding, as if it had been pushed up from the dirt below and then asphalt had been laid around it directly in the southwest corner of the hangar.

In the very center was something a bit larger, with big steel double doors at the center, maybe something the size of a double-car garage.

All the way to the rear, almost impossible to see from a distance and in the near-dark conditions was another closet-sized concrete building with the same single steel door.

Watanabe looked about, taking in the nearly empty vast space. "I imagine this exactly when I discuss it with the people from the Pentagon."

"Would you follow me to the elevator, doctor?" Seibert began walking forward.

There was a card reader at the side of what appeared to be steel sliding doors. Seibert pulled a card from his front left pocket and held it out for Watanabe.

"This is your card, doctor; please notify us if you lose it, for it will open everything here that locks."

Watanabe looked at both sides of the white plastic. It was void of any picture or indication of what it would be used for.

"It can't be traced to here by any means and has no identifying marks in the case it is lost and then found by anyone other than you."

"Of course." Watanabe nodded. He reached over to the card reader and then looked back at Seibert.

"Any way you hold it up there, it will get read."

Watanabe flicked it past the reader, and the two large steel doors separated. They stepped inside, where the lighting was much better. An elevator that typically would be used for heavy freight stood before them.

Seibert nodded at a card reader off to the side, and Watanabe waved the card in front of it. A loud metallic *Click!* was heard, and then Siebert grasped the handle and threw it up and over to the right; the doors separated easily as they could hear the bearings rolling on well-greased wheels. A safety screen separated horizontally in front of them; half disappeared into the floor, and half went up into the ceiling.

The two men stepped inside, leaving the asphalt behind in the soft glow of the man-made moonlight.

"You got this so far, doctor?" Siebert asked.

"My bodyguard will do it anyway, but, yes, General. It is similar to any heavy lift we have over in London."

He pulled down on the strap hanging off the safety screen, and the top and bottom met in the middle again; the main doors slid closed automatically after.

Seibert turned to Watanabe. "Would you like a cup of coffee or something to eat first?"

"No, thank you."

"OK, then. The office and labs first — or your specialty training facilities?"

"The office and labs."

"That is second floor; the first is the barracks for the staff and the kitchen, and the fifth is the testing floor. You have the ability to set the security parameters for everyone within the facility." Seibert pointed at the card reader in the elevator control panel.

Watanabe pressed the second-floor button before swiping his card. There was an audible buzz to notify the person that this was not an option. He then swiped his card and pressed the button for the second floor. The elevator began its decent into the ground.

When the elevator stopped, the outer doors opened, and Seibert pushed the screen to get it out of the way.

They could have been standing in the facility at Belvoir — everything was white with grey steel doors, and the only thing missing was all the glass that the Belvoir offices had.

There was a bit of an odor present. "I wouldn't lean up against anything," Seibert said. "I'm guessing we have some wet paint around." He led Watanabe to the lab door.

Watanabe waved his card, and the door released; Watanabe walked in and began to inspect the equipment.

Along one wall was an extremely powerful electron microscope and a wall-mounted monitor for easier viewing; it looked a bit like a submarine periscope.

Watanabe was saying, "Yes, yes" after looking at each table or piece of equipment.

"And, like Belvoir, your office is slightly higher, overlooking your staff."

Watanabe stepped up into his office area. A large locking cooler was near the door, followed by a long prep-table with a sink and gas nozzles. A large desk with a computer monitor at the far end faced so that it was looking back into the room. A chalkboard took up a large area on the back wall, with a dry-erase board and a cork board flanking both sides.

"Fabulous, General." Watanabe looked pleased.

"OK, then — continuing," Seibert walked out and turned deeper into the floor, "this door is to the cooler." He stepped back and watched Watanabe swipe his card; as soon as the door opened, bright lights came on, lighting up the stainless steel tables and refrigerator with six small square doors in rows of two.

"You can see that you can keep six bodies — or a couple more, if you take up the tables."

Watanabe allowed the door to close. "Very acceptable," he said, and they continued down the hall.

"Medical facility," Seibert said as he pointed at the next door on the right.

Watanabe patted the door and continued down the hall.

"This last door on the right is X-ray." Seibert stopped, but Watanabe continued to the only door on the left, the last on the floor except for the one at the end of the hall.

Watanabe passed his badge over the reader, and the now-familiar noise notified them that the door was open.

Watanabe pushed through first and found the light switch. The first one lit red lights, such as the military uses for night operation. He turned them off and found the second, which lit the fluorescent lights. They snapped on, one after the other, lighting what appeared at first to be a long, narrow hallway.

But about six feet to their left was a window similar to the one over Watanabe's control panel back at Belvoir. It was designed to be the perfect height for the shorter man, and when Watanabe pressed his face up to it, Seibert had to bend to do the same. It, too, canted outward at the top at a forty-five degree angle.

"Lights?"

Seibert pointed further down the long, slim space. "All at the control panel."

They continued inwards; Seibert counted the lights overhead. When he got to sixty, he stopped as Watanabe stepped forward and began to look at the control panel before him.

Watanabe began flipping some switches, and the window began to glow, with light coming from the other side.

Seibert again stooped and looked at the room on the other side. It was a cavernous room with thirty-foot-high ceilings and longer than a football field.

The opposite wall had door after door the entire length of the vast room. Approximately six feet apart, each door was painted grey with a large white number from one to fifty.

Seibert pointed at the control panel, and Watanabe began flicking them on. A bank of monitors began coming on over their heads.

"Each room is covered by CCTV," Seibert pointed out.

Watanabe shook his fists in front of his face. Seibert was concerned.

"What's wrong, doctor? Did we screw something up? I'm sure it can be fixed."

"On the other hand, good man, I'm a Jammy bastard, I am." Watanabe grinned.

Seibert looked confused.

"It means 'I'm lucky,' old man — I mean, across the pond it does; anyway, it used to."

"So you're satisfied so far?" Seibert knew his fortunes were very much tied to this man, and he was going to make sure this little Jap-Brit-hybrid bastard was pleased.

"Absolutely, my good General — absolutely." He placed his hand up on the soft, sloping shoulder of Seibert. "Can we go below now?"

Seibert began walking out of the long hallway. "Sure, doctor — by all means."

"With these facilities, General, I'm willing to bet I give your Army what it has ordered in six months or less."

Seibert spoke back over his shoulder, "If that positively affects my bank account, doctor, then I'm pleased as hell to hear it, and so will the folks I work for — believe me. Let's take the stairs and check to make sure your card works here as well. These will release in the event the sprinklers are set off." Seibert turned to the steel door at the very end of the hallway and waited for Watanabe to swipe his card once again.

The stairwell was battleship grey, and their steps boomed like a kid banging a hammer on the outside of a steel drum. Seibert decided not to speak over his shoulder as he led the scientist down into the belly of the beast.

It took Seibert three tries to push the exit-door handle and get the door to open into the bottom-floor hallway. They first came upon a set of steel double doors, and they entered into what Seibert would describe as a dreary high school gymnasium.

Thirty feet above them, they could see the two-way glass near the ceiling running the full length of the room. Three large, square, steel-shuttered vents broke up the ceiling, but even in the poor lighting, Seibert could make out the CCTV mini-domes and the odd silver track that hung a foot below the ceiling and disappeared into the walls at either end of the room.

Watanabe walked to the first of the fifty doors dotting the east wall. He ran his hand over the foot-high white "number one" painted on the grey door. He swiped his card and then pushed the door to the left into a hidden recess in the wall. This room was no more than five feet by nine feet with a small cot, a toilet, and a stainless-steel sink. He looked up and observed the dark, small dome above for the camera system.

"Does that meet your expectations?" Seibert stood with his hands folded before him.

Watanabe nodded. "Beyond my expectations, actually, General. I don't imagine a long stay for most of the subjects brought here."

"I think the Army is expecting to use the facility for detaining some undesirables in the future — but you never heard me say anything." Seibert winked as if he was sharing something special, but Watanabe didn't care.

Watanabe was going to ignore the General completely, but then he couldn't help himself. "General, I do not care about anything but the science. If my studies can continue, then I will be happy to allow your Army to do whatever they wish with some of the accidental opportunities."

"Accidental? Doctor, what are you talking about?" Seibert almost reached out to grab the man by the shoulder as he walked further into the vast, dull-grey room, but he felt that he'd better not.

Watanabe saved Seibert by stopping and turning to address him.

"The mind — all the neuro-sciences, from psychology to physiology — is relatively new. My study will advance all the studies by leaps and bounds."

Seibert looked as confused as he was. "But what about our...um...the serums you're producing for us?"

"Ah, all by-products of what I would really like to be attempting. You know the story of the little blue pill?"

"Why would I?"

"No offense, old chap. I'm just referencing the attempt to lower blood pressure that created a pill which resulted in erections for every male test subject."

"Oh, yeah. I think I heard that." Seibert hadn't.

"These things I am producing for your government are just by-products of my real work. Imagine that every undesirable human behavior could be adjusted with a daily pill?"

"Every?"

"Murderous desires, smoking, drinking, right down to biting your nails." Watanabe was happy with the earnest wonder in the face of the general.

"And who is going to sell these products?" Seibert's wheels where spinning.

"I imagine Biophaze will, eventually, although I may have some difficulty writing any peer-reviewed papers." Watanabe made a joke — something he seldom did — but it was lost on Seibert, who was recalculating how much more Biophaze stock he was going to purchase.

"Nice, doctor. I wish you the best of luck." Seibert didn't ask; he just began walking back out to the elevator.

"I hope that we can begin moving in immediately." Watanabe was as excited as he ever got.

"Right away; we have been hiring staff, all foreigners with no American family or ties, for security reasons, and we're prepared for today, as a matter of fact." Seibert did not mention that this highly secret and criminal operation could then be moved from his post and thereby limit his exposure.

"Well, then, I have been identifying good subjects for additional tests, and your people could begin soliciting them for their involvement."

"You're ready for that level of testing already?"

"Why, yes — your facilities on the base limited the scope of our testing so far, but we have been conducting smaller ones regularly."

Seibert shook his head. "OK, doctor. We will begin filling the basement for you. Hey, can I ask you a question?"

"Yes."

"Why do you need all veterans? Why can't we fill this place with people off the street?"

"We need to ensure that our test subjects have similar training and the will of the enemy forces that you would be using the weapon on."

"Oh, I see; that does make sense."

15

Monday, 8 days ago

WALTER SCHROEDER WALKED over to the plush chair in Gordan's suite and fell back into it. Nearing the end of a second day of finding and trying to speak with the survivors of veteran suicides was punishing mentally.

Schroeder sighed and allowed his head to fall back so that he was staring up at a stained ceiling. When he raised his head, he took in the decorations of the room.

"Man, do you think they use these outlandish colors to keep people from stealing the stuff?"

Gordan called out from the bathroom, "I notice the stuff when I open the door for the first time, and then, after that, it becomes background." Gordan came out drying his hands on a towel that he threw on the bed.

He went to the fridge and pulled out a green bottle. "Beer?"

"No, I'll have to drive back home."

Gordan popped the top and leaned against the small counter.

"Is all this getting us somewhere? I'm exhausted of talking around the death. I mean — have you learned anything at all, Gordan?"

"Well, from your three guys, we have the common thread of the VA and your not-for-profit group. I don't know anything else about them or relationships from out-side. With the people we have spoken to over the last two days, none have used your group, so the only common thing is the VA, other than the very vague fact that they all served; but what else could these men have in common?"

Schroeder sat up. "Where does that take us?"

"Honestly?"

Schroeder nodded.

"Nowhere; I mean this could be anything." Gordan shrugged his shoulders. "I'd love to say we could figure something out beyond that some guys just couldn't take it anymore, Walter, but I can't. We all would like to know how to fix people who get that low or desperate but, as far as I know, there is nothing out there. Ultimately, I think it has to come from inside the person."

"There has to be something. I just can't reconcile in my head that the men I knew would take their own lives."

Gordan took a sip of his beer and looked at the floor.

"Gordan, do me a favor and stick around a few more days, OK?"

"Maybe we stumble across something that starts a new thread to pull, but you have to be realistic, and, in a few days, we call it done."

"Absolutely, Gordan. When you say that's it, well, then, we did all we could — right?"

"OK, Walter. Deal." Gordan showed him to the door.

"I've got some friends pulling strings trying to get me into see someone at the top at the VA. Maybe you could come with me and see what kind of excuses they give me for the all the shit they pull that my guys constantly complain about."

"They might kill some vets through incompetence, but I don't think you want to go in there making accusations about them doing it on purpose. If they aren't killing vets now, then I know who they will start with." Gordan gave him a sheepish smile.

Schroeder looked up at the darkening sky. "Maybe I just want to get a pound of flesh out of them for everything I've heard."

"Let's talk tomorrow."

• • •

"There he is." Hans pointed to the man exiting the Veterans' Hospital and heading toward the bus stop: dark hoodie pulled up, not seeming to notice the starting of rain. "Joseph Copeland, formerly of the 101st, bad knees."

The man limped from the knee-replacement surgery that he had undergone from falling down a mountainside in northern Afghanistan several years ago. His life had continued to fall apart after being medically discharged. Now, after a nasty divorce, he lived alone in some low-rent apartments.

Hans nudged the white-coated man next to him. "You're up."

Allen Graham nodded. "Right. Just keep close this time."

"Don't worry about me. I'll be there."

Graham slid out of the white Mercedes van and walked quickly up to the wet Copeland.

"Joseph Copeland!" Graham called out.

Copeland stopped and turned; he saw the man in the white lab coat coming in his direction and assumed it was someone from the VA.

"Yeah, that's me." Copeland took a second to glance up at the sky to see if it would let up soon.

"I'm sorry. I need to get a couple of signatures." Graham tried his best to smile and be unassuming.

Copeland glanced back at the bus stop half a block down but then shrugged his shoulders, knowing there would be another bus soon.

"What do you have for me to sign?"

Graham reached out and shook Copeland's right hand and handed him the clipboard before reaching behind him. "You're saving my life for stopping."

Copeland felt a bite on the back of his shoulder. "What the fuck?"

"Oh, sorry." Graham walked around, dropping the small needle on the ground and kicking it into the street. "Nighty-night, soldier boy."

The van was right there, and Hans helped Graham lower Copeland into the back without incident. Graham stayed in the back momentarily to zip-cuff Copeland and then closed the door behind him. Copeland was already asleep in the soundproof and padded cell-on-wheels.

Graham walked around and jumped into the front passenger seat only a little wetter for the experience. "Only forty-nine more to go, my Hun friend."

"What do you think? About two weeks to finish?" Hans asked.

"Maybe longer." Graham winked at the bigger German man. "Maybe we get a couple of dates this way before we quit?" He moved his eyebrows up and down a couple of times.

"You're a sick fuck, Graham. Are all you Frenchies too perverted to actually get a girl on your own?"

"Hey, be nice — or I'll send my *le copain* to pay you a visit."

Hans looked over briefly as he drove. "You've got no friends. Don't try to bullshit me."

"Ah, so you do not know. When they were looking for some more muscle, I put a call in to my buddy. He's doing personal security for the mad doc himself."

"You talk too much."

"He was French kickboxing champion two years in a row." Graham studied the German's face. "Seriously — he's a very bad man, maybe a bit crazy."

Hans fake-spat at his feet. "Isn't everybody nowadays?"

• • •

Emerson Seibert looked across at the computer screen. He was being asked if he was sure about making the stock purchase. He was positive, and he pressed the button. Sitting back afterwards, he felt like he needed to smoke. Every extra penny he owned had just gone into Biophaze stock. This was the biggest gamble he had ever taken in his life (as far as he was concerned), even more so than participating in the scheme he was presently neck deep into. Nobody was going to question anything he did on his own post.

Seibert kept doing the math on the computer screen. He had purchased all the stock at or near the lowest point in Biophaze stock history: six dollars and seventy-five cents per share. That meant he now owned more than thirty thousand shares of their stock.

His hands were sweaty.

He reached over toward. the heavy tumbler. The scotch had nearly melted the two cubes, but there was enough left for them to make some noise as he raised it to his lips.

Seibert may not have known combat strategies; he may never have earned the respect of many of the men who had to salute him now. But his nose for political schemes and maneuvering was one of the best he had ever seen. This was going to be his big farewell to all things US-government-related, and it was going to be big…so big.

Someday it may come to light what he helped accomplish here, and then there would be some hand wringing and some careers destroyed, but his would not be one of them.

Uncle Sam would conceal the truth to the best of his ability to save face, even if only to use the drugs being created by the doctor. Maybe history would judge General Seibert long after the positive results had been observed on the battlefield. This was something that he was very sure of: Emerson Seibert knew the dark history of Uncle Sam.

The computer screen went dark from lack of activity, and Seibert nodded his head at his own reflection.

Seibert pushed back, and the wheels on the chair fought the carpet before beginning to roll backwards. He rose and padded down the hall to the bedroom.

His wife was on her side, facing away from him and deep under the covers. She whispered to him, for no reason, as they had been empty-nesters for many years now.

"Everything alright, dear?"

"Yes, honey. Everything is going to be fine. You just go to sleep."

He sat down on his side of the bed; swinging his feet up into the bed, he patted the shape under the covers.

"Just fine," he whispered.

He reached up and behind him and clicked on the small reading lamp. Reaching over to the nightstand, he slid off the top magazine, which was a listing of homes for sale in the Florida Keys. The cover had a beautiful, bikini-clad woman lazing on a boat skimming across shimmering blue water, her blond hair dancing behind her like a flag in the breeze.

16

Tuesday, 7 days ago

CELIA CLARK SHUFFLED out from her kitchen; three tiny china cups rattled on the ornate tin serving tray that she carried them and the teapot out on.

Gordan stood and asked again if they could help.

She set the tray down and then raised her long, thin black arm into the air and fanned her hand at Gordan and Walter as they sat in her sitting room.

"Nonsense, young man. Any friends of my grandson Tyson is going to get some tea and cookies, and they won't need to help none, thank you." She smiled at Gordan as Walter explained again that they didn't know her Tyson.

She pointed at the prosthetic leg. "You fought in the war with my boy and lost your leg, but he lost something too." As she took a seat, she nodded at the black-and-red plaid box of butter cookies on the tray.

"My one vice — them damn foreign butter cookies."

Gordan watched the woman, who had to be in her nineties. Her stark white hair was a contrast to her dark black skin. Her small, round eyes were made somehow smaller by the large thick lenses of the glasses she wore. When she turned her head, he could make out the cataract in her left eye. Gordan liked the spirit, the energy that she gave off. She may have been old and seeing the world with one good eye through several inches of glass, but Gordan had the feeling that she didn't miss a thing.

Gordan said, "Thank you" and reached over to grab the thick cookie that Mrs. Clark pointed at.

Gordan bit off a piece. "Hey, that is good. Thank you, ma'am!"

Gordan glanced over at Walter with a quizzical look and then turned back to Mrs. Clark with a smile.

"I expected it to be dry and sandy, but it's good!" He held what was left of it up into the air briefly before stuffing it into his mouth."

"Well, you learned something new today." Mrs. Clark smiled and passed a small cup of tea over to Gordan.

Gordan laughed at the cup. His enormous hands made it look like a small girl's set for a Barbie doll.

Walter took a sip of tea and cleared his throat. "So this was the address we found for Tyson, and we were hoping to talk to his mom or dad as well."

"Oh, he never knew his pappy, and that mixed-up and flawed daughter of mine left him here with me one night nearly twenty-eight years ago now." She shook her head sadly. "Mind you, she came around once. May God have mercy on my soul — I could not forgive her, and I sent her on her way!"

"The very last thing the Lord would do is to send us here to judge." Gordan nodded at the woman as she began to push off the floor and rock at the memories.

"You military boys are so respectful, and you believe in the good Lord. Please call me 'Cecil'; I don't get many visitors anymore."

Walter leaned forward and placed his cup on the tin at the center of the table.

"Cecil, did Tyson have any problems that you knew about before his death. Did he talk to you about his problems?"

She closed her eyes and continued to rock. Her hands held the teacup steady at her breastbone as her thin chest continued to rise and fall slowly in rhythm with the chair moving back and forth.

Gordan thought she may have fallen asleep, and he began to study the pattern of the white doily that covered the center of the table, when she began to speak.

"He was always a good boy. He was well mannered and respected his elders. I had to whoop him some when he was little, but that boy was going to make something of himself!"

She set the small cup down and then challenged both men with a steely look from her good eye. When neither offered anything, she took a deep breath and spoke very softly and steady.

"My boy Tyson did not kill himself. Tyson was starting to get his life in order after the Army; had himself enrolled in school and was excited as I ever saw him."

"Did he have a girlfriend?"

"No, sir!" she snapped at Walter for asking. "My Tyson said he could not get mixed up with that until he had a good job after school."

Again she shared a tough glance with both men.

Then, with a slight movement of her lips and a half-smile that slowly spread into a big grin, she said, "But the women came around. They knew a good man when they saw one — but he wasn't having anything to do with it."

"A man with a plan," Gordan said and nodded in agreement with Cecil.

"God's plan," she said as she looked down into her lap.

"Don't you believe that God has a plan for you...if you listen, that is?" She glanced at both of them.

"Is there anything else you can think of? Was his injury doing OK?" Walter leaned forward.

"Why, yes. He was going to get a new painkiller. I guess it was one of them that didn't get a man hooked, and therefore Tyson said he would try it. You know that shoulder would ache him something fierce when the weather turned cold, like it is now."

"Do you know what kind of drug that was, Cecil?"

She looked off into the window.

"Could he have a bottle in his room we could look at, maybe?" Gordan asked.

"No. I don't think they ever gave it to him. I think he was going to test them out or something, but I don't think that he ever got them."

"Cecil," Gordan got her attention, "I don't mean to bring up bad things from the past, but did the police test Tyson's blood after his death?"

"Yes — they showed me. They said he may have taken some pain pills but nothing for a while."

Now Gordan sat up further. "Did they use the word 'trace'?"

"Yes — yes, that's exactly what they told me."

"So that means maybe he took some only when the pain was real bad."

"No. I'll tell you the same thing I told them: My Tyson had me telling him for over twenty years about what happened to his momma, and that boy never had no narcotic, even one from the government, in him." She stopped rocking to make her point.

She wagged a bony and bent finger in their direction. "Don't you never let them tell you my boy took any drugs. He was willing to try something new for them but nothing illegal."

"Never a doubt, Cecil." Gordan raised his right hand like a Boy Scout pledge.

"Thank you, ma'am, for your hospitality and for telling us about your grandson. It was an honor." Walter shook her hand.

"You have a good heart, young man; God is using you at this very moment."

Walter stopped moving. "Do you think so?"

She stepped up into his personal space and looked up at him. "God's plan may have been for my boy to get your attention. The things you do from here may all be a part of his plan. Who are we to question his designs?"

"Thanks for the cookie, Cecil," Gordan winked, smiled, and waved goodbye.

Faster than he thought possible, she was at his side, hand on his shoulder and whispering into his ear.

"God gives us all gifts, child. My gift is to really see people for who they are." She pointed at her one good eye. "When you are called upon, don't fight it but rejoice in your ability to participate, your time to act." She stepped back and nodded at Gordan.

Gordan tried to maintain a smile. "What?"

She pointed that old, weathered finger at him. "Remember Romans 13:4, and just rejoice!"

"I'll try to, ma'am." Gordan nodded and turned, heading to the truck.

Once she'd closed the door, Walter asked Gordan, "Well, what did you think of that conversation?"

"I think I would have liked to have known her about sixty years ago," Gordan said as they walked down the wooden steps out to the pickup truck on the side of the road.

"Get your mind out of the gutter, and tell me what you think for real"

"Well I do believe in God, but that entire "I may be a prophet" thing kind of gives me the creeps."

"Yeah. OK — not that, either. I'm talking about the drug angle."

"Well if the Army prescribes you a narcotic, it's not illegal, and the police wouldn't make anything of it, especially in trace quantities."

"So we have another mystery — right? Another soldier who committed suicide, even with a bunch of positive things going on in his life. It makes no sense to me."

"Walter — still. Where does that leave us? A young soldier who didn't go to your group, and the only two things in common with the others, as far as we know now, is military service and trips to the VA." Gordan shook his head sadly as they walked down the broken sidewalk to the truck.

Gordan walked around to get into the driver's seat. "And just because the VA gave him some kind of new painkiller doesn't mean that that isn't a possibility, either. Maybe you can check into that sometime."

Walter snapped his seatbelt on. "What are you talking about?"

"Those drug commercials I see on TV, where they say thoughts of suicide are a side effect."

"Oh, yeah. I've seen those. You know, I've got some people looking to help me get an audience with someone at VA headquarters in Washington, as close to the top as I can get. Maybe now is the time I push hard on that."

Gordan dropped the truck into drive. "I wouldn't push too hard, Walter. You still need funds from them, right? And we sure as hell don't have anything solid to accuse them of."

"What? Other than gross incompetence that is getting our people killed?" Schroeder leaned back against the door and shared an astonished face.

Gordan raised one eyebrow. "I know, but I'm thinking of your operation there. You look like you're doing some good. I'd hate to see some bureaucrat pull your funding or tax status or whatever you need to keep doing what you're doing."

"If it lights a fire, I don't care."

"Seriously?"

Schroeder nodded.

"OK. Let me drop you off at home, and I'll see if I can get you some tinder." Gordan smiled. "I've been thinking."

"Sounds like a plan, Sergeant — but one thing?"

"Yeah?"

"What's Romans 13:4?" He pointed his finger at him and bent it to mimic the old woman, squinting with one eye and the other wide open.

"Walter, the next time your ass is in a sling, I'm going to leave you hanging. That's just mean — she was a beautiful woman."

• • •

Gordan parked outside the CIA headquarters building in Virginia. He had been here more times as a civilian than he had ever been while working at the agency. The shiny glass and concrete gave off an aura of quiet professionalism that he was proud to have participated in at one time. Once inside the main building, he walked across the checkered grey-and-white tiles and the emblem on the floor. He stole a glance at the stars on the wall and said a silent prayer.

He showed his guest badge to the uniformed guard, who scanned it and handed it and Gordan's identification back to him.

Gordan passed through the scanner, which screamed out a warning to the surrounding guards.

"Hey, Jim. How they treating you?" Gordan called out to one of the men he recognized.

"Man, they still let anyone in here." The guard walked over to say hello, but it was really to check the badge at close range.

"They still calling you a 'Special Guest.' I'm surprised."

Gordan took his hand back from the shake, "As long as Stevens is in charge, I'm guessing that will be the case."

"You heading upstairs, then?"

"No. No need to bother the man behind the curtain; I'm heading to the dungeon."

Jim waved over another man in uniform. "You know you need a babysitter to get down there." He nodded at the man in uniform even though he was talking to Hudde: "Don't forget to check out."

They walked to the elevator, and the uniformed guard put in a pass card to take them to the lowest level. When they arrived on that floor, the guard scanned his card again to get Gordan into the only door on the floor.

The only light inside at first was the light coming through the bulletproof glass square in the center of the door behind him.

Gordan waited for his eyes to adjust and then could make out the man in the computer chair across the room from him. Only one small screen was on, while an array of screens surrounded him.

The shaggy blond head turned with the chair as Gordan approached. "Hey, Mykhaylychenko. Why you sitting here in the dark?"

"What do you want, Gordan?" The Russian spoke with just a hint of an accent.

"Oh, come on, kid. Don't be that way."

"Gordan, you may not realize this, but you're a civilian, and every time you come here, I have to sit through months of questioning."

"Stevens covers you, doesn't he?"

"Yes, but..."

"But what?" Gordan furrowed his brows. "You and I did a lot of good for some kids that last time."

"Gordan, I don't do well under pressure. That's where you perform. I like the relative quiet of my computers running."

Mykhaylychenko cleared his throat. "Which sends me back to the original question: What do you want, Gordan?"

"Listen, kid. I've got a friend who thinks something strange is going on with some of his veteran friends. I don't think right now there is much to his thoughts, but he's going to get an audience with somebody over at the VA soon, and I'd like to liven up the conversation a little."

"Gordan?"

"Hold on before you start talking about 'security clearances' and all that. I know you follow what's been going on with the news. Somebody needs to be yanking a chain, don't you think?"

Ivan "The Kid" Mykhaylychenko took his glasses off and set them off to his right. "Gordan, I've seen the news. The Veterans Administration seems to have had many setbacks with staffing, computer-system failures, and human weakness."

"Bingo! You said it, kid — 'computer-systems failures.' You pulling up the un-redacted versions of the Inspector General's reports would certainly highlight their issues over there."

"Come on, Gordan. Everyone will know who got it for you."

"Who is 'everyone'?" Gordan began to pull down on his Spartan beard.

"CIA, NSA, DIA, the Russians, the Chinese — *everybody*. No, Gordan. I can't do it. Go get one of them to do it for you."

"Hell, Kid. Even if I knew all that, I still would come to you first."

There was silence as both men thought about the next step. Gordan broke first.

"Listen — just pull it up, and we'll see together if anything in there is important."

"No. First break into their system, and find the encrypted file. Steal that, break the encryption, and then read it." Mykhaylychenko raised his hands together. "No, thanks."

"I know you care about what happens to our people when they come home. My buddy thinks they are feeding our boys an experimental drug that has dangerous side effects."

"Seriously?"

"Yeah. He believes it is causing the unprecedented number of suicides that have been going on lately. Well, that's just one theory right now."

"Does the Director know you're here?" The kid bit his lip and looked up at Gordan standing over him.

"No, Kid. But if that's important to you, I'll head up there next and show him."

The Kid closed his eyes and took several deep breaths; Gordan did not move. Mykhaylychenko shook his head and said, "It couldn't hurt that much to just take a look."

The kid reached over and fired up all the computer screens surrounding him; soon the glow of them lit up the area. Gordan walked behind the chair and just listened to the keys being punched at a speed that was unfathomable to his own, nearly one-finger typing skills.

"Oh, *Christ!*"

Gordan opened his eyes. "What is it?"

"The Inspector General has accused the VA of a litany of crimes against veterans and their families. He then accuses them of a cover-up by transferring employees or allowing them to retire with full benefits. Whistleblowers have accused them of retaliation, and that, too, is being investigated."

"You got all that already?"

"Yes, and what is worse is that this was presented to VA upper echelon more than six months ago, and I can't find a single document or news story that covers their utter failure to address this."

"What about congress?" Gordan looked at the screen and pulled down through his beard in thought.

"I'm sorry, Gordan. Once the news stopped covering it, they appeared to move on to something else. I can see that they began to argue about the budget instead."

"And the senators would have read the same documents?"

"Well, they would have received redacted copies, but I'm guessing it would have conveyed the same message."

"I need a copy of that IG report — no redactions, Kid."

17

JOSEPH COPELAND AWOKE from his drug-induced sleep; he sat up and reached up to rub his head, which felt about two sizes larger than normal. A wave of nausea washed over him; his eyes adjusted just in time to see a toilet a few feet away.

After wheezing and spitting the last of his intestines' contents into the john, Joseph reached up, grasped the stainless-steel sink, and pulled himself up enough to run cold water over his scalp. Finally, he took a few sips to ease the twisted pit he felt in his stomach.

He was a prisoner — that much was clear. His cell was dark and cool; he still had his own clothing but no longer had anything in his pockets. There was no window in either of the doors, one on each end of the room. The only thing unique about this cell to Joseph was that the ceiling was probably three times higher than the cell was long.

A good fifteen feet above the floor, a small monitor screen flickered to life. A soccer game was being piped in. It put a crook in his neck to try to watch it, but he found it was comfortable enough when he lay down.

There was a noise toward the door at the opposite side of his head, and Joseph looked up to see a silver tray of something being slid through a slot near the bottom of the door.

Joseph attempted to spring to his feet but stumbled from the residue of the drug still working through his system. When he arrived at the door, he banged and yelled to whoever had delivered the tray.

"Hey — why am I here? I want a lawyer or my phone call!"

There was no response.

Joseph gingerly squatted to retrieve the food; a five-by-nine card was underneath the tray. Joseph turned and sat on the end of his bunk. He sniffed the meal. It was some kind of macaroni and beef with some buttered bread and a side of peas; it smelled pretty good.

Joseph took one small bite and was surprised at how tasty it seemed as he rolled it around in his mouth. He waited to take another bite after this one had hit bottom; he didn't want to throw it up.

He turned his attention to the small card; words had been printed on it by a printer. "Thank you for being part of our experiment; you should rest comfortably knowing that your participation will ensure our country's safety for many years to come."

What? That's delusional; I've been kidnapped and brought here! Joseph's mind screamed.

He banged at the door until his knuckles bled to alert someone of his special status, but no one ever responded.

• • •

The Deputy Secretary of Defense was not a title that Meredith Ryan ever thought that he was going to want. It was a prize that was uncovered, a treasure of untapped potential that came to Ryan like a vision from the Old Testament.

After years of kissing asses and fighting to get to the top of the investment world, he had finally greased the right wheel and bet on the correct horse. He had bundled an ungodly amount of cash for the last presidential run, and when his horse came in, he knew exactly what he wanted and why. He was just unsure, at that moment, of how he would fleece the United States Treasury; he just knew somehow that he would.

Ryan strode confidently into his office; his secretary rose from her chair and followed behind him.

"Sir, I've got Walter Schroeder on the line waiting for you."

"Thank you, Elain."

Ryan dropped into the oversized leather chair. "Captain Schroeder?"

"Sir, yes Sir!" Schroeder couldn't help the years of training.

"Captain, General Hoskins has called on your behalf. Honestly — it seems you have been burning up the phones both at the VA and here. So I thought I would reach out personally and see what I could do for you."

This respectful banter made Ryan furious that he felt it necessary and that he was speaking this way to a *subordinate* on top of it all.

Schroeder tried to keep the gleefulness out of his voice. "Sir, I appreciate the time you have taken to reach out to me and my group. I would just appreciate a small bit of time with the director at the VA to bring my concerns to light."

"Captain, as a civilian, let me say that I have also developed a lifelong respect for all things military and especially those returning from combat."

"Thank you, Sir."

"Well let me finish, because there is a "but" coming. But, we can't allow every returning serviceman or founder of a veterans' group get face time with the director of the Veterans Administration. I know that you, a believer in chain of command, would respect that."

"Yes, Sir — I do. But I have some personal friends who committed suicide, and I just know…I mean to say that, in my heart, I know that there is something wrong that needs to be brought to light...veterans need to be warned, investigations need to be redirected or something."

"Captain, you should take your conspiracy theories to the police. You really shouldn't be wasting the time...I mean, I'm surprised the General put in a good word for you."

"Don't take it out on the General, Sir. I didn't think it wise I tell him everything that I have been thinking."

"What are you leaving out?" There was a lump in Ryan's throat that seemed like a small dry spot. He reached out for a glass of water that always was close by.

"It involves drugs that may be being prescribed by the VA itself. Now I know it sounds crazy, but we're working on getting more evidence, Sir — and, just maybe, those at the top don't know it is happening."

Ryan choked and nearly spat water onto the papers strewn about his desk.

"What? What the hell are you talking about, Captain?" It was impossible that anyone could have stumbled onto his operation.

"Sir, I can't explain, but, maybe, if I can work with someone at the VA, I can figure out if this is as crazy as it sounds or if there is something there."

"Who is 'we' Captain? You said 'we'?" Ryan took another swig of water to wet the growing dry spot in his throat.

Ryan had worked harder than ever to build this structure that was going to make him wealthy beyond anything he'd ever imagined — and nothing or no one was going to stop them now. He had long ago begun to think Yvonne Lane was growing more difficult. Maybe this was a moment he could test her with a malcontent who was closer to the truth than he knew.

"Captain, I'm going to help you get past whatever it is you have festering in your mind that seems to be keeping you awake at night. You understand, I'm going to help you just because of the great service and sacrifice to this country you have already made."

"OK, Sir. I understand."

"I'm going to make a few calls and get someone to reach out to you, but you need to make sure you are not spreading any rumors out there that make it harder for everyone to help returning servicemen. Can you do that?" Ryan felt like he was scolding a child.

"Yes, Sir. That's not a problem. I haven't even told my wife about all of it."

"Good — that's real good, Captain. Now let me get your phone number so that I can reach out to the right people." Ryan smiled at how easy this was. Even if this guy was on to something, he'd just walked into the lion's den — or, he should say, the lioness's den.

• • •

Hans took a large mouthful of pancake with a chunk of sausage; he looked like he hadn't slept in three days — because he hadn't. His coworker, Allen, took a sip of his coffee and stared out the diner window.

Allen spread some apple jelly onto his toast and used it as a pointer before taking a bite. "What I don't understand is why they can't give us the entire list. That way we could collect a few of these guys at the same time; right? I mean, we could cut our driving and their wait time in half — easy."

Hans's black, bushy eyebrows rose slightly. "I think I could begin to digest this food better if you could remain quiet for a minimum of five minutes."

Allen continued to point with his remaining toast. "You telling me that you wouldn't rather double-up or triple-up on these trips?"

"Are you getting paid a bonus for finishing this quicker? They'll just give us a different task. Why rush? We'll just end up pulling perimeter security or something else equally boring." The bigger man checked his bushy black beard for crumbs and then rose from his chair.

"I'm going to go get some shut-eye, and, when they forward our next task, I'll call you. Knock on my door before that, and I'll be working alone." He threw a twenty on the table and started to walk away. He stopped and turned back. "And leave a decent tip for the pretty lass, you fucking cheap bastard." He turned and winked at the young waitress before heading out into the darkness.

18

Thursday, 5 days ago

MEREDITH RYAN ROCKED back and forth in his seat as his SUV bounced down the dirt road near Fort Valley, toward the facility that his misappropriated funds had built.

He hated the woods; he thought back to a time that his political appetite had caused him to go on a "hunting" trip in Alaska with some right-wing senator who, at the time, he needed for a temporary alignment in an attempt to get votes. He'd had some assistant help him to purchase all the correct equipment from clothing to the proper weapon.

The gun was locked in a cabinet and had never been fired, and the clothing had given all to charity. He had never been able to get the stench of burning wood out of it.

He had to admit that he was interested in the facility, but this was more to keep the good doctor interested and to continue the partnership with him and him alone. He could never allow the doctor to understand that the full government was not behind his secret work. Based on what the doctor's work consisted of, Ryan didn't believe the doctor was all that concerned about dotting "i's" or crossing "t's" on paperwork; but he may see a way to renegotiate for more money. Watanabe didn't seem to care about that, either, but better to be safe than sorry.

He was nearly positive that, by the time anyone may have understood what he had done, what they'd accomplished, the United States government would be neck deep in it. They'd be unable to acknowledge how the entire operation had begun and unwilling to give up the new serums the good doctor was creating.

They may ostracize him and ban him from any further or future government activities, but by then he would be richer than anyone he knew, and he wouldn't care. Of course, they would pretend to be aghast at how he came to his fortune, but they really would be envious that they didn't think of it first or find the disaffected doctor before he had.

Mr. Smith may have at one time gone to Washington, but Mr. Hyde is all that was left. Ryan smiled at his own machinations; he had thought of every move in this deadly and expensive chess game, and now they were nearly finished.

Ryan peeked around the driver as they stopped at the main gate; a guard waved, and the gate rolled away, allowing them inside.

Ryan felt a bit awed when the woods slowly parted to give way to the giant hangar surrounded by dense woods and a twelve-foot-high hurricane fence with triple rows of razor concertina wire keeping anyone with sense from trying to climb over.

The steel was battleship grey, and a giant dark-green door began to rise into the ceiling as they approached.

His driver switched on his lights as the SUV bumped up onto the concrete floor. The ride was smooth now, and they parked against the far side of the wall.

Ryan heard gears clanging, and the vast door began its descent, slowly shutting out what sun remained in the sky.

Ryan pivoted and swung his legs to the ground. The nearly two-hour trip had left his legs a bit stiff, and the blood began to flow as he stepped around to greet Doctor Watanabe, standing nearby.

"Welcome." The doctor reached out to shake hands.

"Doctor, I do believe we really ensured our secrecy with this location." He waved his arm and then added, "I hate the outdoors."

"Well let's go below, where you will not be reminded how remote we are." The doctor stepped back and pointed at the elevator.

Below ground, in the comfort of Watanabe's office, under the harsh glare of what could only have been government-approved fluorescent bulbs, the Deputy Secretary of Defense sipped a cup of coffee and relaxed.

"Sometimes I forget how good it is to get away from the hustle and chaos of day-to-day activities at the Pentagon. I could get used to this."

"Are you aware that we are now fully staffed and that our test subjects are quickly nearing one hundred percent as well? Soon we may begin my final tests. Of course, the Air Force will need to also finish on their delivery system."

Ryan shook his head. "You would never know it — it's so quiet."

"Secretary, I know there was a reason for this visit. You may be direct."

Ryan smiled a polite smile. "Of course. Thank you, Doctor. Even with all the time I have had to contemplate what I feel I need to say, it still is a bit delicate."

Watanabe remained silent but maintained eye contact.

Ryan continued, "While you have had a good working relationship with the Veterans Administration, I think it necessary for you to deal directly with General Seibert or myself and no longer with the Chief of Staff over at Veterans Affairs. It's not that we are no longer working to the same ends, but I'm afraid some of the inter-agency politics may interfere with positive results."

"Oh, I am sorry to hear that. I have enjoyed my occasional conversations and time spent with Ms. Lane."

"Soon, I will need to reveal our interest and investments to your employer ...Mr. um..."

"Boone," Watanabe helped.

"Yes, Mr. Boone. I would like that to be a meeting that we have without allowing United States governmental-policy bickering to be any part of it... I feel Ms. Lane has begun to have extracurricular desires that are not exactly within the scope that was once entirely agreed upon."

Akihiko Watanabe sat up straighter in his chair. "Mr. Secretary, the last thing I want to do is get involved in any government bickering. If I may continue my experiments, continue to advance the science of the brain — that is the only reason that I am here, the only reason that I agreed to work for your government. I am fiercely devoted to this work, and I will not be tolerant of anyone who interferes with it."

Watanabe realized that his blood pressure was elevated; he attempted to sound calm. "Please, the less involved I am with anything else, the more positive work I will be able to accomplish."

"Good. Then we are agreed. The General or myself and you are left to do what you do." Ryan stood and clapped once before holding his hand out.

"I look forward to your continued success."

Watanabe stood and shook. "You do not want to continue a tour?"

Ryan smiled. "What would I know? If you are satisfied with the facility, then I am happy and encouraged that your efforts will be successful for each and every one of the tasks you have been asked to assist with."

"I wouldn't be surprised if the current list of wishes is completed within the next six months."

"You don't say; that is very encouraging to hear. Now, if I can be shown back to my car?"

Back into the relative comfort of the back seat, Ryan closed his eyes and let the uneven road rock him to near sleep. He was satisfied that he could freeze out Yvonne Lane without alerting the good doctor that there could be any cracks in the partnership.

• • •

Valerie Baker closed her eyes and set her home-listing paperwork onto her chest before she reached across her coffee table and picked up the cell phone. She didn't recognize the number but answered anyway — a habit from years of experience as a real estate agent.

"Ms. Baker."

"Speaking."

"It's Gordan."

"Who?" she smiled to herself.

"Gordan Hudde!"

"I'm struggling to remember the name. Should I know you?"

"Ouch — that kind of hurt!" Gordan exclaimed.

"Just where are you, Mr. Hudde?"

"I'm still up in Virginia, Valerie; that's why I'm calling. I didn't want you to forget that you promised me a date."

"Oh, I remember you promising me a steak — nothing about a date." She sat up and pulled back on her long, dark ponytail, feeling it fall back behind her after lying on her couch.

"I guess you left the impression that we would at least eat our meal together up at my place."

"Did I?" Valerie paused, allowing another smile to grow across her face. "OK, Mr. Hudde. I guess I may have."

"You had me worried there for a moment." Gordan cleared his throat. "I guess it was a good thing I called to remind you."

Now she laughed out loud.

Gordan tried to remember why a man put himself through moments like this.

"Well, when are you coming home to feed me? I may waste away to nothing waiting for you."

"It's a favor. I feel bad running out on this guy, but I'm getting close — maybe another day or two. I'm guessing maybe next weekend I could make it up to you."

"If you didn't like him in the first place, don't you think you've done enough already?" She was sincere.

"I guess I've seen how passionate the guy is about what appears to be good work that he is doing here; Schroeder, my former company commander, has found his calling — I think."

"Speaking of passion, Gordan Hudde, I'll fight off all my suitors for another few days, but you'd better hurry. A better meal may come along soon."

"Damn, lady — that's just mean."

"Oh, that's nothing, Gordan. Call later, and maybe I'll tell you about my bubble bath and glass of wine; goodbye." She hung up before he had a chance to say anything.

Gordan held the phone in his hand and stared at it. *That was punishment I didn't deserve. The guys at SERE school could learn from that woman*, Gordan thought, and then he grinned.

19

Friday, 4 days ago

GORDAN KEPT HIS eyes on the traffic as he and Schroeder made their way over to the Veterans for Vets facility.

"I have been burning up the phones about this meeting they keep promising me. Thank God I can write off my mobile bill." Schroeder looked at the bright screen.

"And is it getting you somewhere?" Gordan knew what the answer would be.

"How about a line on a possible experimental painkiller?"

Schroeder put the phone back in his pocket. "I was hoping today we could ask everyone who comes through our doors — see if they've heard anything or been offered anything. That's a lot of VA experience when you see the number of veterans who are showing up nowadays."

Gordan noticed the oncoming traffic coming at them and said, "Hold on."

The truck tires barked and squealed, the bed of the truck sliding out for a moment before Hudde straightened it out. They rocketed across the lanes of oncoming traffic, with only the sound of one unsatisfied commuter's horn to let them know anyone had noticed.

"That guy had to stop at the red light two hundred yards up the street, and they're pissed that I may have slowed them down a moment. What a douche." Gordan looked out at the traffic stopped at the light down the street, trying to discern who owned the offending horn.

"Not much for the morning commute, are you, Gordan?" Schroeder blew the steam off his morning coffee and headed to unlock the double steel doors of his facility.

"Kill myself if I ever had to be a lemming," Gordan muttered.

"Yeah, well — do it without me in the truck."

"Didn't you hear? The psychiatrist you made me go to announced that I was homicidal, not suicidal."

Schroeder stopped in his tracks and looked back at Gordan, studying him for a moment.

"I don't find comfort in that."

Gordan grinned.

"Before you go on your next spree, do you think you could make coffee? I feel bad enough I didn't bring in any pastries."

"Just don't ask me to go back out into that traffic, or I know where my next spree starts."

Schroeder just shook his head.

Thirty minutes later, they sat waiting for the final member of the group to show up.

Walter Schroeder stood up and began the meeting with a prayer. After, he asked the members about experimental drugs while being treated at the VA.

Gordan could see how tight the group was, as one by one, each member seemed to glance back, expecting the final guy to walk through the doors.

After a half-dozen negative answers, Gordan stood. "You guys are missing the smart-assed Marine, right?"

Half a dozen affirmatives.

"Figures the jarhead forgot how to get here." There were some good-natured chuckles. "Any of you guys have his number to reach out?"

Each man took out a phone.

Nearly an hour later, after the meeting had broken up and all the men of the group had exited, Schroeder approached Gordan, placing a hand on his shoulder.

"I don't think Andrew James has missed a meeting since he found our group. These guys have become pretty tight; they all were concerned, especially when he didn't return a single call."

"You have an address, a work number; we can start checking it out. Leave your second to handle the facility here."

"Sure, Gordan. I'll be right back."

• • •

Meredith Ryan set the phone down on its cradle, closed his eyes, and took a deep breath.

He couldn't wait for the day that he could tell some senator to "fuck off" and threaten them with financial support for a rival, have them eating from his hands.

He rubbed his temples and pictured the look on the face of any one of those self-righteous bastards after he would tell them. *They release the most benign letters to the press that they have sent me asking for information, and then they call me to make polite threats or outright demand my job. Fuck them.*

He slowly allowed his eyelids to rise, permitting the light to incrementally get brighter, until his eyes were once again wide and he was back at his work desk.

He was looking at a wall-mounted monitor that had been forever set to CNN; they still laughingly referred to it as the "Clinton News Network" around here, even though most of the younger interns would have to Google the name.

He jerked to an alert, upright position, both his feet firmly planted onto the floor. He rifled the papers, frantically searching for the remote.

He stood, stepping around to the front of his desk and pointed the remote like a gun; the volume went from silent to too loud in seconds.

The perky blonde was happily speaking about some business news... "And some possible good news on the horizon if you have a loved one experiencing the symptoms of Alzheimer's or Dementia: The CEO of the pharmaceutical company Biophaze has announced breakthroughs in treatment, and this network has confirmed that the FDA is in the approval process..."

He changed the channel looking for the business one.

His mouth dropped open, and he stared.

The stock had nearly doubled in just the last few hours. Oh, Lord — it was starting! He took a step back, toward his desk, thinking about picking up the phone to call general Seibert but thought better of that as well; he took a deep breath.

He would see him for dinner a week from today anyway. It could wait — and who knows when or where the stock would top out at.

Ryan found himself pacing the floor, where he once was the most patient thoughtful one of this business alliance. Once he saw the news, he could think of nothing else.

His secretary notified him that a retired General was on line one.

"Who?" he asked him. He pressed the call button. "I don't recognize the name."

The secretary said, "He says he's calling on behalf of a group — 'Vets for Veterans' or something like that."

"How many friends can that guy have? Just tell him his Captain friend will get a meeting next week, and make him go away; tell him to take up a useful pastime."

"Sir?"

"No — just the first part. Thank you."

Ryan fell back into his thick-leather heavy chair.

• • •

Andrew James's eyes opened, and he was unsure for a moment why he was frightened.

He remembered the evening before exiting the grocery store with several bags and then talking to a couple of guys near his car.

They were foreign. *That* he remembered. British or French accent.

Then nothing.

He looked down at his transradial prosthesis. No — it was still there. He had heard horror stories of people having them stolen.

James sat up; he took a very deep breath to fight off the nausea and looked around at his bleak circumstances.

Everything was jet black except for the stainless-steel commode and sink. He felt like he could be back on a ship, but he felt no motion of a ship at sea.

The door on the one side of the thin room was like something from a ship or sub. It appeared water tight, but it was larger than anything he had seen in the military.

The door on the other side was heavy-duty steel but otherwise appeared normal; the hinges were either hidden or on the other side of the wall.

He tested the water from the sink; it was cool and eased the burn he felt at the back of his throat. A grey jumpsuit was hanging on a hook. He held it up and noticed that the number "45" was stitched onto the back, like something a guy on a pit crew would wear. He hung it back up.

Looking up gave him no hope. It was too high a ceiling, and the vents were way too small for a human being. He spied the camera in a smoked dome and used his good hand to throw up a bird. There was no doubting it: He was a prisoner of some kind.

"That's right; fuck you, whoever you are!"

He sat on the bunk and tried to think.

• • •

Gordan rolled once around a small park, looking for the closest parking spot to the apartment complex that Andrew James lived in. A cold wind thrashed the treetops, urging the leaves to get off. Gordan didn't want to make Schroeder walk farther than he had to. He didn't want to walk in the cold, and he was concerned that they were the only two white men he had seen in a few blocks; it appeared James lived in a tough neighborhood.

He found a spot, and they made their way to the courtyard between four-to-five-story tall identical apartment buildings.

Four young men got up from the steps leading up to the doors and began sauntering over.

"My, my, my. What have we here? Farmer John and Soldier Boy done went and got themselves lost."

Gordan pulled up on his denim jacket to give himself some added room to move. He guessed he was the "farmer," as he'd layered the denim over a dark-blue hoodie sweatshirt and a flannel shirt under that. His outfit was more than enough for the current weather, and an added benefit was that the denim was tough to cut.

Schroeder's light jacket was emblazoned with all kinds of military patches, probably given to him by all the men and women who had used his services. He stopped the men approaching with a raised hand.

"We were looking for our friend Andrew James?"

One of the smallest of the men surrounding them began mimicking Schroeder's speech pattern and mannerisms.

"Good day, sir. Have you seen Mr. James?" he mimicked Schroeder's speech pattern.

There was some hooting and laughter.

Gordan knew what this was; it was a shakedown, and potentially very dangerous. These men had probably done this many times whenever they came across people who looked out of place.

"I'm afraid you haven't paid the fee to conduct a search on our property. Once you do that, we can talk, my man." He grinned wide and looked about to make sure his friends were all in agreement; there had to be a price.

Schroeder stepped forward. "Look — we just want to make sure our friend is OK. We don't want any problems."

Gordan glanced about and observed that nearly every window he could see in the courtyard had a face or two in it.

The little man pulled up on the waistband of his own hoodie and showed the grip of a small framed pistol. "You don't seem to get it. Throw your wallets on the ground, there." He pointed at Gordan, "Hey, Farmer John: That ride looks pretty new. Why don't you toss me the keys?"

Gordan Hudde had grown up on the streets; from a young boy getting beaten pretty badly to an adult, he had been in every form of combat imaginable, except professionally, in a cage, where there were rules. He understood that fighting overwhelming odds meant taking a chance. It was a dance, a deadly ballet where a single misstep could lead to serious injury or possibly death, but Gordan did not fear it.

He had been underestimated often, usually due to him being relatively short. At just a hair under six feet tall, he seldom was seen as heavy, unless you took the time to look at the thick neck and shoulders or his big hands.

These guys were on their own turf; they were brimming with confidence and didn't appear to believe that either Hudde or Schroeder would say "No." Two of the men had cold hands deep in their pockets. Pulling a gun or knife from them would take precious time even if a hammer spur or large knife didn't get caught up on the way out.

The mouthy little one had just pushed his coat back down below his knees and the forth guy was looking back at the opposite complex.

Gordan shook his head and stepped forward. "Why is it always the littlest guy with the biggest mouth?"

With his right hand in a single-knuckle-strike position, he hit the largest man, closest to him, in the throat. That man staggered backwards, grabbing his neck and coughing. Gordan continued with his momentum and kicked out the knee of the next man with his right foot, spinning further to strike the little mouthy man in the face with his left foot. It was all about maintaining your weight's driving force and keeping his two hundred and thirty-five pounds moving forward through the targets.

The final thug stood still looking to his right as Gordan stopped his spin by placing the muzzle of his forty-five into the man's ear.

Schroeder bent to pick up the weapons scattered about the ground, but Gordan warned him to put on his gloves first. The mouthy one was out, one lay on the ground holding a possible dislocated knee, while one was kneeling, still coughing for breath through his damaged larynx.

"Maybe you could help us find our Marine friend," Gordan whispered to the man.

The last of the thugs was standing as still as a statue, his eyes locked Hudde's.

Gordan whispered, "You are about two ounces of trigger pull from getting a .45 caliber lead Q-tip. We're looking for a friend. We didn't ask for any trouble."

"I only know he lives over there." His eyes briefly left Hudde to look over at the building.

Gordan stepped in close. "I will kill anyone who fucks with us from this point forward; if my truck is fucked with, I will return with more of my friends, and I have to tell you that I'm the nice guy in my gang."

The affirmative nod was nearly imperceptible.

"Now collect your buddies, and go indoors. I do not want to see any of you again."

Gordan and Schroeder began backing toward the correct building; a young boy met them on the steps.

"I know where he lives." He nodded in the direction of the stairwell.

"Thanks, kid. Should we expect more trouble?"

"Nah — those are the worst that live here. I don't think your truck will be safe for very long."

"Let's hurry, then. You lead." Gordan pointed at the stairwell door with his free hand.

The kid's eyes lit up. "Sure!" They headed up to the third floor.

Schroeder knocked several times. Nothing happened.

A door opened from down the hall, and an older woman waved Gordan down.

"Yes, ma'am?"

"Good for you. Those young men had it coming to them."

"It's a sad circumstance," Gordan replied.

"They should all be in jail, they frighten so many people."

Gordan nodded in agreement. "Do you know the young former Marine who lives next door?"

"He's a good, polite young man. I do see him fairly often but not in the last few days."

Gordan turned back toward Schroeder. "Hey, Walter. Give your card to this woman in case she sees him sometime soon."

Schroeder pulled a card from his jacket and smiled at the older woman as he passed it to her.

"Thank you, ma'am." Schroeder handed the card over and tipped his head. "We are a close knit group of men, and we worry if we don't where our members are."

"Oh, that's so nice. I'll let him know."

"Thanks again."

Gordan turned to Schroeder and whispered, "Let's get moving."

Gordan slipped the kid a twenty and said, "Thanks, kid. Stay safe."

"Whoa," the kid said.

Gordan turned. "What — I underpaid?"

"I was hoping for a new video game, man!"

Gordan pulled out his wallet and looked at a hundred-dollar bill; he shrugged his shoulders and handed it down to the kid as they went back to the first floor.

They made it back to the truck without incident. Schroeder turned to Hudde. "I haven't had that much adrenaline flowing since Afghanistan. I always knew in the Army that you were into fighting, but I didn't know you were that good."

"Yeah — that was fucked up. It could have gone bad pretty fast." Gordan ignored the compliment.

"'Could have gone bad'?" Schroeder gave him a quizzical look.

Gordan looked back with a touch of a grin. "Well... ended in death, police called, you or I wounded...that kind of bad, I guess."

"Holy shit — I don't need that kind of trouble. Now what, though? Do you think we should call the police?"

Gordan shook his head. "For what? Those guys?"

"No — I'm not that naïve. For my guy, James."

"Do you have next-of-kin cards on file for your people?"

Schroeder shook his head "No." "Starting today, I guess we will."

Schroeder's phone began ringing, and he dug it out from his coat pocket.

Gordan could hear only enough to know it was a male voice on the other end; he hoped it was the young Marine they were looking for.

Schroeder never seemed to get a word in — just a few "Yes, Sir's" and affirmative grunts. He said "Thanks" and jammed the phone back into his coat.

Schroeder turned and patted Gordan on the shoulder. "Who has some pull around here, huh?"

"What?"

"I've got an appointment tomorrow morning with the Chief of Staff at Veterans Affairs!" Schroeder was grinning like the Cheshire cat.

"Yeah — so?"

"What the hell do you mean 'So?' This is important, very big news. I can ask about the screw-ups my people complain about all the time and maybe find out if these veterans' deaths are on their radar."

Gordan made a turn and then made some eye contact. "First, do you think if this person even had any info, they would share it with you? And second, what would that sound like? And finally, third, why would they invite you on a Saturday?"

Schroeder looked disappointed. "It's a start. Not every non-profit group gets some face time with somebody that high up in the VA."

Gordan cleared his throat. "Oh — absolutely go. By all means, go — and good job getting in. Maybe I can go along or feed you a bit of information from some documents I'm not supposed to have."

"What are you holding out on me?"

"Don't get your panties in a bunch I have the VA's Inspector General's report from last year; it's pretty revealing."

The truck bumped up and over the parking at Vets for Veterans, and Gordan slid to a stop on the side of the building. He turned in his seat as much as his shoulders would allow, and he stared back at Walter Schroeder. Gordan began running his hand down the black Spartan-like beard as he always did while deep in thought.

Schroeder stared back from the passenger seat as long as he could. "What?"

"Walter, you cannot say where you got or even heard this, but the Inspector General knows and seems to have conducted a pretty detailed investigation into misap-propriated funds, theft, and fraud going on in the upper and middle VA management."

Schroeder made a dismissive face. "Everyone who ever reads a paper knows this." He turned and pulled on the door handle, starting to get out.

Gordan reached out, stopping him. "No, Walter. They have names and everything. Don't you see? It's been in the hands of upper management, and nothing has been done about it. Senators and Congressmen must know, too, but I haven't heard or seen any big reports, have you?"

Schroeder relaxed back into the big bucket seat. "No, I haven't."

Gordan stroked his chin. "This had to have been reported to the Department of Justice."

"*Had* to be?"

"Crimes are, at a minimum, suggested in here that should lead to possible charges at the DOJ. I wonder: If someone looked at this, then who was that person, and where are the charges?"

They sat in silence for several minutes before Schroeder asked, "What do you think we should do?"

"Well, I would love to know why there isn't a federal trial going on right now."

"Damn, Gordan — why?"

"Why indeed."

20

Saturday 3 days ago

WALTER SCHROEDER STUMBLED from the bedroom and lazily leaned over the toilet, placing his right hand on the wall as he evacuated his bladder. His wife Jill, dressed for work, stopped momentarily at the open bathroom door.

"I better not have to clean up after you," she warned.

"Sometimes I can't believe I don't wet the bed," he said, impressed with his stream.

"Well, try not to wet the floor, for starters."

He washed his hands and then followed her out to the kitchen. Retrieving a mug, he poured himself a cup of steaming coffee.

Jill buttoned up her coat and reached for her purse on the edge of the counter as she headed for the front door. She grasped the keys hanging on a decorative hook near the door jamb.

Opening the door, she turned back to say goodbye, but her peripheral vision caused her to let out a scream. Gordan Hudde was sitting on the front step with a Styrofoam cup.

"I'm not quite used to getting that response from women in the morning," Hudde quipped.

"Fuck you, Gordan! I nearly had a heart attack!"

She made a fist of both hands and stomped a foot.

Walter was at the door. "Why not just knock?"

"I was enjoying the sunrise. I heard someone in the shower, and I thought I would just wait to see who came out all warm and smelling good." Gordan grinned at both. "That's obviously not you, Walter."

"Yeah — fuck you, Gordan," Walter said. "I won't be heading out for a while. Why are you here so early?"

"I just wanted to talk you into taking me to your big meeting today."

"No, I haven't changed my mind about that, but you can come in."

"Sorry, Jill. I didn't think you would open the door before looking out."

She pulled back her hair and stepped in close to Hudde. "You think I smell good?"

"Ma'am, yes ma'am."

She turned back to Walter as she stepped out the front door. "Walter, you haven't said that in some time. You'd best start paying attention." And then she *clickity-clacked* on her heels down the short sidewalk to the small car parked there.

"Yeah — you better pay attention, Walter." Gordan shook a finger at him as he closed the door behind him.

"Gordan, has anyone told you today to fuck off yet?"

Gordan grabbed his beard, thinking. "It does sound familiar." But he shook his head in the negative.

"Listen, Gordan — the meeting was set up for me. I know how these people work, and the simplest little slight could put the entire meeting in jeopardy of not happening, so dragging along a "plus one" isn't going to help."

He smiled and patted Gordan's shoulder as he walked, mug in hand, toward the back of the house.

"Lock the door behind you; I'll call you when I'm back." He waved over his shoulder.

• • •

Joseph Copeland banged on the black steel walls and screamed out; this time it was just frustration. He heard a dull bang in return, but he had no idea if it meant anything.

He stopped trying to figure out why he was being held in this cell only when he fell asleep; otherwise, the questions just kept coming and then repeating, and he never got an answer.

He felt like he had been here nearly three days. It was hard to tell, as there were no windows; his phone and watch had been confiscated, and the lights stayed on all the time.

No one had spoken to him. Hell, he hadn't seen another human being except on the monitor above him. He had no idea where he was or what reason anyone would have to hold him.

He realized that there were three soccer matches that were being played on a loop on that monitor high above him, and now boredom was also creeping into the situation.

He had been getting three square meals every day, so that was a positive thing. He wondered if he should try to save the meal tray to make a shiv or something, but they would be looking for the empty, and that would be easy to detect. So he held that thought only as a last choice or chance.

He wet his hands at the sink and slid them over his head, slicking his hair back. He held his hands at the back of his neck and slid down against the wall until he was seated on the floor. *Why?*

• • •

Walter Schroeder made sure his handicapped sign was hanging properly before he checked himself out in his rearview mirror, cinching his tie just a bit tighter now that he had arrived at the VA in Washington, DC.

After riding around with Hudde for the last few days, he had begun dreaming of owning a pickup truck. He knew his wife was comfortable with the Honda, but he was second-guessing the small Ford he was extracting himself from now.

The horn sounded once as the doors secured; he stepped up onto the sidewalk and headed toward the bright-blue canopy that protected the two guards who stood on either side of the double glass doors.

Walter acknowledged both men with a nod and then headed in to the front desk.

Walter made it to the correct office and took a seat once he signed in with the young man at the desk.

An hour and a half later, a loud voice could be heard from the hallway, and then Yvonne Lane entered the office with a cell phone plastered to her ear, a light jacket over her arm.

Walter couldn't help but to notice an hourglass figure on the woman, but something about her demeanor had him believing that she was all business. Maybe it was the stern look on her face, combined with the way her hair was pulled back so tight. Maybe it was the tone of her voice as she complained about the timing of some event with whomever she was on the phone with.

He stood and waited politely, but she never acknowledged him. She just waved at her assistant and then entered the inner office.

"It won't be long now, Captain Schroeder," the assistant said but then looked down immediately when Walter thought he would inquire how far behind schedule she was.

OK — I can do this, Schroeder said to himself. The Army prepared everyone the same for "Hurry Up and Wait." He sat back down and closed his eyes; he heard everything but reacted to nothing.

Two hours late.

Three hours late, and the door opened; when Walter opened his eyes, the light coming from behind Lane almost hurt. It did highlight what an attractive-looking woman she was.

"Mr. Schroeder, I can see you now."

He stood and nodded at the secretary. From what he had seen and heard so far, he didn't plan on getting an apology.

She pointed at a chair out in front of her simple desk and then walked behind the desk and sat.

"Mr. Schroeder, I've been told you have been making many inquiries about my department, and you seem to have quite a few friends with enough rank that people from above me to the Department of Defense are begging me to get the harassment to end."

Schroeder was taken back; he'd waited here for three hours to be berated by this bureaucrat? He could feel his ears burning. When he looked at the clock, he thought the second hand had stopped moving. This was not what he had envisioned.

"Excuse me, ma'am. I've got some questions regarding concerned veterans — you know: the people you serve. They want me to get answers."

"Captain, please. I have no way of keeping track of what is happening day to day to any individual or the services that they may have a complaint about. You are wasting your own time as much as mine. I have taken the time to review your own medical file and the report regarding the group...um..." she flipped open a manila file... "Vets for Veterans?"

"So?" Schroeder was on his heels.

Lane continued, "So I was thinking maybe you could actually follow the proper chain of command before any of your paperwork gets lost, and your own personal claim needs to be resubmitted, or maybe the IRS re-examines the documentation for your little non-profit?"

"Why are you so hostile?" Schroeder blurted out.

"I'm sorry. I'm short staffed and days behind on work that needs my attention, and you want to jump past all the options available to you to speak to someone at the top? You appear to have received all the care you needed, and now you are living off the government through a non-profit — isn't that correct?"

"Well... kind of...yes, but..."

"But nothing, Captain; America thanks you for your service, but now you need to move on and allow us to do our jobs without your interference. Just how many calls have you made over the last six months?"

Lane stood and walked to the door, not waiting for Schroeder to get up.

Schroeder saw himself ten minutes in the future, sitting shell shocked behind the wheel of his tiny car.

He set his chin and fought with his own desires to totally respect the chain of command. "I need to know what happened to the Veterans Administration employees who have been identified by the inspector general's audits."

She opened the door and turned toward him; he could feel the heat from her eyes.

"What? I'm guessing you saw the congressional hearings, and that's all you need to know. Good day, Captain."

Gordan had warned him against this, but he could feel the burn from his ears. It spread to his cheeks from the total ease with which she now dismissed him.

Schroeder had one page that Gordan had given him from the inspector general's investigation; he pulled it out from his inner pocket and unraveled it.

He turned directly toward her and began reading out loud; he got to a list of names and continued reading.

Lane slammed the door. She was suddenly flush herself. "What are you reading?"

"It's a page from the IG's report; it seems to have names and everything."

"Where did you get that? You should have no access unless it has been released by my department — which it hasn't — and totally redacted!"

Schroeder waved the single page in the air. "This was on the floor in the elevator."

"It's a crime to possess that," she sneered.

Schroeder was feeling the blood come back to his leg. "I'm turning it in. As I said, I found it. I was wondering where the investigation is within the Department of Justice on the possible crimes of your employees."

She walked back and sat back down at her desk. "Just what is it that you want, Captain?"

"I want to know why strong young men are committing suicide." He paused and thought, *What the hell?* and went for it "I want to know what kind of drug you have been giving veterans and if it has side effects — like causing suicides."

He remembered what Gordan had told him. He leaned forward and tried to watch closely. He saw the color leave her cheeks; he watched as she took a short breath, like she was experiencing a heart attack, and then she gulped a large breath. He watched as her eyes went up and to the right just before she spoke.

"So you're one of those conspiracy wackos; I understand now." She rose and walked to the door. Opening it up, she waited for him to exit.

He took his time and then stopped right in front of Lane at the door. "If you think I was a pain in the ass before, just wait." He smiled for the first time in nearly four hours.

Lane closed the door and walked back to her chair. Her legs were shaking as if she had just finished a ski run at Telluride in Colorado.

She dug through her Louis Vuitton briefcase; finding her phone, she dialed the doctor.

"Dr. Watanabe, this is Yvonne Lane." She nodded, although no one could see her. "Yes, I know what Ryan wants, but I need your people to add a name to your list."

She picked up the other file she had on her desk. "Captain Walter Schroeder, a former Army Ranger. Yes, I have an address and phone number. Hold on a second."

• • •

Jill Schroeder walked across her living room to hand Gordan a mug of fresh coffee. "Honestly, Gordan, what do you think about Walter's conspiracy theory? You should know that I encouraged him to call in help, but I thought it would help him discover that it was all nonsense. I never thought that there would be anything to it."

Hands on her hips, she stood over Gordan, studying him; he didn't want to step into some domestic quarrel.

"Listen, Jill. I'm not sure that I believe anything nefarious is going on here, other than general incompetence added into the bloated bureaucratic nightmare that the government is." He smiled up at her while taking a swig of the good black brew.

She turned and stepped over to the sofa. Gordan waited until she was seated and looking back at him before he continued.

"Walter believes it, and now having a missing friend isn't going to help dissuade him of it. If we don't find something concrete by the middle of next week, I'm going to be heading home, and Walter should probably give up on this — unless he's going to write a good thriller."

She closed her eyes and tapped the end of her nose with the tip of a finger, deep in thought.

Gordan admired her for supporting her husband the way she was. She was a strong woman and, from what he'd heard, a good nurse. He hoped that Walter would quit tilting at this windmill when he left next week; it looked like it may cause some arguments if he didn't.

Gordan heard the small four-cylinder engine idling in the driveway, and he understood that Walter was home.

Jill opened her eyes and locked them on Gordan's. "And before you go, you will do everything you can to make him see it your way?"

"Sure, Jill."

"Good."

The door opened, and a chill wind followed Walter Schroeder, who didn't close the door or acknowledge either Gordan or Jill.

"Jesus Christ, Gordan! You should have seen her. It was just like you said, man — and everything you said!"

Jill walked over and slammed the door closed. "Walter!"

"Oh — sorry, honey." Walter walked over and got himself some coffee.

Jill came into the kitchen and placed a hand on his shoulder. "You think you need that?"

He grabbed the cup of coffee and grabbed her hand, pulling her along to the sofa.

"So this bitch...um, Lane, ah...Yvonne Lane keeps me waiting for nearly three hours and then comes at me with all this attitude, man — you should have seen it."

Gordan interrupted, "What kind of attitude?"

"Man, she starts asking me if I understood anything about the chain of command, and then she said something about not caring who I know or can convince to call on my behalf. I mean I was almost catatonic because I don't even remember an introduction or some polite banter before she was kicking me in the balls!"

"So, why are you grinning?" Gordan asked.

"Well, I was on my heels there for a second, and she was showing me out the door. Then I hit her with the deaths and suicides, and that slowed her down a second, so I hit her with names from that report you gave me."

Gordan's brows went up. "You *what*? I told you not to go there."

"Man, it shut her down! She closed the door and sat back down at her desk — started threatening me with arrest for having that page."

"Walter — you showed her the page!?"

Jill was watching like she was at a tennis match.

"Don't worry. I told her I found it in the elevator. But, hold on — that's not the best part...I asked her about experimental drugs being given to veterans..."

"And?" Jill now asked.

Walter turned to his wife; he put both hands up in the air, doing small karate chops at thin air.

"Gordan told me everything to look for, and when I said that...bam! Everything Gordan told me happened! She stopped breathing for a second..." he turned back to Gordan, "her eyes, Gordan; just like you said: 'Up and to the right,' man — up and to the right." He shook his head and tried to calm his breathing.

"Then what?" Gordan began to run his hand down his beard.

"She kicked me out — well, not before threating to get my funding taken away."

"What? Can she do that?" Jill placed a hand on Walter's thigh.

"I'm sure she can, but that's interesting, Walter." Gordan stood up and walked to the window. "You say you saw her react to the drug thing?"

"Oh, man — did she! It was as if I had reached across the table and slapped her."

Jill grabbed her own coffee mug and walked back toward the open kitchen area. "So you insulted her — what did you expect? This doesn't prove anything, does it?" She asked the question, and Gordan could hear the hope in her voice.

"No Jill, it doesn't prove anything, but it is suspicious. Let me ask you, Jill: How would you react if some citizen came into the hospital and accused you of giving patients cancer?"

Jill was taken aback. "I'd explain how ridiculous that was and hope they would understand that I would never condone or allow that under my watch."

Gordan walked past her and held up the coffee pot, looking at her; she shook her head "No," and Gordan refilled his own.

"Exactly the correct response, if you were to ask me. Walter what do you think?"

Walter was nodding his head "Yes." "Yes — exactly yes! I wouldn't threaten and then throw the person out."

Gordan walked back to the chair nearest the TV. "So we all agree that her behavior was odd. It may not prove anything, but it was...off?"

Walter said, "Yes."

They both turned to Jill and waited. her eyes briefly flashed back and forth between the two men. "Yes," she said, somewhat defeated.

Gordan went back to stroking his beard. He spoke aloud, but it was not directed at anyone. "So what does it mean?"

They sat in silence for several minutes, each of them deep into their own thoughts.

Jill got up and went deeper into the house without saying anything to either man.

Walter watched her go and then turned back to Gordan. "She's not going to be happy."

"Sure, Walter, but she reached the same conclusion herself. See if that sinks in; maybe it will help."

"I don't think so; she hasn't really been all that excited about this from the start."

"Hey, Walter?"

"Yeah?"

"Neither was I, but this last bit has me a little more curious. If the VA is doing a test with an experimental painkiller, it wouldn't be nationwide. It would be just one or two facilities — right?"

"I guess..."

"Do you think the VA's Chief of Staff would be involved in that?"

"Well, maybe..."

"Even if she was aware, would that cause the reaction you got? I mean, they are trying to help people with pain. Why be upset if that got out?"

"I don't think so." Walter scratched his head.

Gordan put his hands up in "full stop" sign. "Wouldn't you suggest that you couldn't talk about it but that you are trying to help veterans, so please go back and just do your thing — please stop harassing our people. Wouldn't that have been a reasonable response?"

Walter was nodding. "Unless you were accidently killing people."

Gordan jumped to his feet. "We don't know anything, but we are more suspicious. Sleep on it, let it stew. Maybe tomorrow we recalculate. Nice work today, Walter."

"Thanks, Gordan. I appreciate it. Your paperwork and interrogation tips really helped."

Gordan slapped him on the shoulder before turning out the door.

21

GORDAN LOOKED DOWN at the two fast-food bags on the floor of the passenger side — one bag full of burgers and the other French fries. The least he could do is not eat the Schroeders out of house and home while he was there.

He imagined that Jill Schroeder was probably not all that happy about last night's conversation. He couldn't blame her: Maybe the darkness and the desire to find intrigue led him to fall into Walter's conspiracy. A good sleep and a hot shower made Gordan feel less sure that Walter had found out anything important yesterday, and he had ended up doing exactly what Jill had asked him not to do —encourage Walter's theory.

Maybe the folks at the VA had been having some bad days, and their Chief of Staff had been getting her ass handed to her over the blunders. Maybe she just needed to get it out, and Walter was the guy that she had no allegiances to that she could whack without getting into trouble.

He pulled into the driveway and allowed the current song to finish playing on the sound system before turning off the engine.

Gordan slid out and walked around the truck to retrieve the bags of food. Jill met him at the door in a robe, her blond hair pinned high up on her head.

"I'm getting ready for work Gordan. Go ahead and watch TV or whatever until Walter gets back." She turned and headed back into the home.

Gordan shrugged his shoulders and set the bags down on the kitchen counter before pulling out a sandwich and heading back to the living room. He examined the remotes until he found the correct combination to get the cable up and running.

The early NFL games had started, and Gordan settled in on a game being televised from Florida. He based the decision solely on the uniforms of the cheerleaders; he didn't care about the games.

Jill came out in her blue scrubs, blond hair in a ponytail, white shoes that ultimately were good walking sneakers with a nonslip sole.

"Grab a burger, Jill," Gordan called out.

She came in sliding into a coat. "I don't eat that crap, but thanks anyway."

"More for me."

"Good — eat them all, and don't give any to my husband, either."

"Where is he?"

"I don't know; he got a call when I was heading into the shower. He said to have you wait here; he seemed pretty excited."

"Roger that." Gordan slid back in the recliner and hoped somebody would score soon.

"Gordan?" Jill stood at the door with a concerned look on her face.

"Please don't let your imaginations run away with you today."

Gordan held up his hand. "I swear."

"Thank you." She turned and closed the door behind her. He imagined the disapproving look she would give his truck and the two tires deep into the yard.

Gordan stood and grabbed another burger. Stopping, he turned and stuck his head into the fridge; he found a beer in the back before he returned to the chair.

He dropped the wadded-up wrapper next to the first on the coffee table and then tilted back the nasty light beer, finishing that as well. Lunch was over — now, where was Walter?

Gordan pulled up on the lever on the side of the chair and allowed it to rock all the way back. *Oh, well — it could be worse.* He closed his eyes and drifted off to sleep.

Gordan had that moment when he awoke where you wonder just where the hell you are; it's a common feeling for military personnel. He snapped the chair back to upright and looked around.

Some fat guy in a bowtie on TV was going to teach him how to make a fortune in real estate; Gordan needed merely to order a small fortune in reading materials and attend some seminar.

He reached out for a napkin to wipe the saliva from his chin. He stood and stretched. After a few more minutes, he realized that this was not a commercial on TV but an entire show.

He grabbed the remote and kept flipping until he came across another game.

He gargled with some tap water and then grabbed his phone from the outside pocket of his jean jacket.

His call to Walter went straight to voicemail. "Dude, I'm at your house. Give me a call and let me know if you're going to be back anytime soon." He glanced at his watch. "It's fifteen thirty hours."

This was the most sleep and lack of movement Gordan had had in years; he needed to move. He locked up the Schroeder home and headed to his truck. He drove over to the Vets for Veterans location.

When he pulled into the parking lot, he noticed that the little car was not parked there.

Gordan stopped and walked into the facility.

Gordan didn't want to admit that he couldn't remember the young former Air Force First Lieutenant's name; "Sir" always worked.

"No, he hasn't been here at all today, Mr. Hudde."

"Fuck. If you see him, make sure he knows I'm looking for him."

The young man looked up from the table. "Yes, Sir."

Gordan backed his truck into the empty parking lot next door, another abandoned business. He sat back in the seat and rubbed his temples for a moment, taking a few deep breaths, trying to center.

Veteran suicides were happening all over the country — maybe an anomaly, nothing obviously standing out from what Gordan had observed. He still felt that soldiers may look for help less and then follow through more often — a tragic thought but logical.

Schroeder's charity and outreach center was looking to help, and that took veterans who were looking for help and were able to accept that help. Gordan didn't feel that the two were mutually exclusive; in fact, it was statistically more likely.

One person you knows goes missing — poof, just disappears — is out of the ordinary. If Schroeder didn't turn up later, if he wasn't in an accident or something, Gordan couldn't accept all the above as coincidence; especially after he had been burning up phone lines and pissing off people all over Washington, DC.

He opened his eyes and ran his hand down over his beard. That's it, then! A missing Schroeder meant that all of Gordan's doubts and ribbing Schroeder about the ramblings of a madman had to go away. He had been wrong.

And then what?

He nodded to himself: Exactly, then what? Who would be killing veterans? The VA? Seemed somewhat dubious as that's their constituents, the buyers to what they are selling.

A foreign entity? So they take out the guys who are already out of the fight? That didn't add up for Gordan.

How about a terrorist organization that was trying to demoralize troops. Maybe. He certainly couldn't rule that one out, but it, too, seemed a reach.

Gordan pulled out his phone and dialed Robert Mahoney.

"Mahoney."

"Hey, Bulldog — it's Hudde."

"What's up brother? Still in town?"

"Yeah. I'm wrapping up my stay, I think. I was wondering if you could get some info out of the Famous But Incompetent?"

"I'll try. What do you need?"

"Look, man. I'm just kicking some stuff around, but I was wondering if there are an inordinate number of missing former military men around the Virginia, DC, and Maryland areas."

"That's not a vague question you ask at the water-cooler, Gordan. Jesus!"

"I know I know it's an odd thing, but if you can do it..." Gordan just let it hang out there.

"You know I will. This number OK?"

"Yeah, and you still haven't heard any tango plans for the east coast."

"Brother, you're scaring me. I hate being the mushroom."

"No, just asking. I don't have anything I would dare share even with an old buddie."

"Alright, I'll see what I can do. Meanwhile, something hardens up with whatever you're dancing with, you call me first."

"Of course." Gordan hung up.

Gordan knew this could end with some embarrassment if all this was nothing, but there was no harm as long as he wasn't running around like Chicken Little.

• • •

"What do you mean, you haven't seen him all day?" Jill Schroeder screamed at Hudde.

"I'm sorry, Jill. You know he left without me this morning, and I never touched base with him. None of my calls have been answered."

"And you didn't think to call me at the hospital?"

"If he came in after doing something out on his own, I didn't want to worry you. I'm sorry."

She put both hands into the hair at the top of her head and tilted it back, letting out a silent scream into the ceiling. She picked up her phone and started pounding out a call.

Gordan was afraid to ask; she looked up at him and spoke to him as if he were a child. "Checking the hospitals to see if he's been brought in."

She paced, and she spoke. Gordan could see the frustration build; before she could make a third call, Gordan interrupted.

"Jill, is there anything you can tell me about that call this morning?"

She gave him a death stare for a moment, and then her eyes lit up. "The call was on our old phone, and Walter picked it up after the machine had picked it up. I heard a voice as I walked through the bedroom."

"Great. Maybe he didn't erase it."

Gordan followed her back into the bedroom. There was a standard king-sized bed with small, light wood nightstands. The door to the bathroom was ajar; Gordan could see the shower curtain with little cartoon fish on it from where he was standing.

She bent over the nightstand with the wireless phone standing on a small platform that Gordan recognized as the answering machine. There was no flashing light, and, after she fumbled with the buttons, she shoved it all off the table.

"Damn it! He must have erased it." She placed her hand to her throat. "I'm sorry."

Gordan felt a bit uneasy standing in the bedroom with the wife of one of his platoon mates, without him present It wasn't like he couldn't control himself or that there was any chemistry between him and Jill. But this was a place where the two of them were intimate, and he didn't want to intrude. He began walking back to the front of the house.

"Jill, you said you heard a voice. Is there anything you remember?"

They stopped in the kitchen. She stood with her eyes closed as she tried to go back.

"I think I heard a name, but right now I can't remember...it was male... He said "Good morning. This is..." I just don't remember, Gordan."

"Tone — was he rushed?"

"No, no he was...maybe an accent, like he was from Australia or England or something." She looked at Gordan for approval.

"That could help — male foreigner. OK — you stay here and let me know if you hear anything. I'll be back in the morning unless I hear from you before that. OK?"

"OK. Yes, Gordan. I have one more hospital to call."

Gordan nodded and headed to the door.

"Gordan?" Gordan paused and turned. "It's probably nothing. I mean, maybe some former soldier called, and he felt like he had to go help — he's like that." And then she added, "It has happened before." She tried to muster a smile.

"This late, and without a call to you?"

"Well...no," she shook her head, "...never exactly like this before." She went back to making the phone call.

Gordan closed the door behind him; he stood on the front step and took a deep breath of the cold, dark-night air.

He spun to find that he'd locked the door handle on the way out; he banged several times before Jill, looking a bit flustered and still holding her phone to her ear, opened it up for him.

"OK. Thank you so much for checking. You have my number if by chance..." she was saying into the phone.

The person on the other end must have finished the sentence for her.

Jill turned to Gordan. "What now?"

"I'm sorry. I just started thinking seriously about this and remembered that Walter had one of those electronic map things stuck to his dash."

"Yes." Her face lit up for a moment, and then her forehead wrinkled as she frowned.

"I don't have any information on it."

"I'm willing to bet he kept the box somewhere."

She shrugged her shoulders. "If he did, it would be in his office, I guess." Jill turned and walked into what could have been a spare bedroom, but it had several steel file cabinets, a desk with a small table near it for a big computer set-up, with speakers and printer nearby.

Gordan sat down and pressed the space bar. After a few moments, the screen was fully refreshed, and Gordan pressed the Internet access. When he reached the GPS unit's home page, the sign-on and password auto-entered.

"Thank goodness Walter used that password saver."

When the unit number was requested, it took a moment, and a symbol spun while they waited. Finally, it came up on a map of Richmond, Virginia. Gordan zoomed in to a few-block radius; a five-and-dime, a couple of bars, a grocery store, the mandatory McDonald's — and, two blocks away, a veterans hospital.

"I'll go look for Walter's car." Gordan headed back to the front door.

Jill reached into the front closet and pulled out her coat.

"I think you should stay here, Jill. Who knows? Maybe that old piece of junk he drives died, and he lost his phone. Maybe he shows up without his keys. I think you should lock up tight and be careful when opening the door, but I do think you should stay here."

"Why should I be careful? Do you really think something awful is going on?"

"No, probably not. It's just a bunch of coincidences falling together to look like a conspiracy. I'm not sure I ever really bought into Walter's theories. I just wanted to help in any way I could." He smiled and turned away, knowing that, more and more, he was beginning to believe.

"OK, Gordan. Please call me."

Gordan didn't need to check and re-check his .45. It was always locked and loaded, secured in a holster behind his back. He reached into the duffle bag behind the passenger seat and removed two extra fully loaded magazines. If there was something nefarious going on, he was not going to be caught without enough rounds to get the job done.

When he arrived in the area, he took his truck around the four-block area and then decreased the size of his search area until he was on the block where Walter's car sat, idle.

The little Toyota was not alone on a street; it was in the parking lot with hundreds of others near the end of the plaza near the Mickey-D's, a short walk to the veterans hospital.

Gordan used the drive-through to get a large coffee and then parked another hundred yards away, positioned so that he could keep his eyes easily on the Schroeder mobile.

Gordan dialed the home number for Jill.

"Hello?" She sounded exhausted; he knew that an incident like this could cause an incredible emotional drain on a person.

"Jill, I have found Walter's car, and I thought I would check around and then check inside the hospital. If I find anything, I'll call you. Otherwise, try to get some rest, and I'll check with you tomorrow."

"Is the car alright? Does it look like he was in an accident or a carjacking or something?"

"Good question. But, no — everything appears to be fine."

"Thank you, Gordan."

She hung up just as a little golf cart with a flashing yellow light drove slowly past Gordan's truck.

Gordan had learned never to drink scalding hot coffee, so it sat to his right, steaming. The thick steam moved eerily around in the center of his windshield, ebbing and flowing with Gordan's own breathing.

A cold sprinkle of a rain began falling, causing additional difficulty viewing the outside world. Gordan gave in and restarted the vehicle so that he could put on the interior defrost and allow the windshield wipers to work intermittently.

Gordan liked to work on cases through a visual presentation, much like detectives do with a corkboard full of pictures and maps, allowing him to better understand how everything fit together. In the service, they used to build dirt relief maps to plan.

The CIA often had 3D images or built entire villages to assist in planning and training. Without any of these tools, he tried to build it in his head, laying out what little facts they had uncovered and holding them up to the suspicions and conspiracy theories that he and Walter had discussed.

Walter's disappearance had to be the final fact that solidified their suspicions of a bigger conspiracy. But what was it, who was running it, and to what ends?

Gordan began keeping time by the flashing yellow light of the parking-lot monitor. Five trips around, ten trips, twenty; then the cart stopped. An elderly gentleman in a polyester uniform pushed the plastic rain guard to the side and walked around to Gordan's side of the Truck, shining a flashlight into the back of the bed and then finally into the truck's cab.

There was an electronic whine as the side window went down. This wasn't a police officer. He had no weapon on his belt, but Gordan gave the man the courtesy to have his right hand on the steering wheel as he acknowledged the guard's presence with a wave of his coffee cup with his left.

The man, easily in his mid-seventies, cleared his throat before speaking.

"Everything OK in there, young man?"

"Sure." Gordan tried to smile to put the man at ease. "It's a crappy night for an open ride." Gordan nodded over at the golf cart.

"Yeah. We used to have a small pickup, and we did a lot of jump starts, but I guess management doesn't want us to do that anymore."

"Well, you can sit in my passenger seat and get some heat if you want."

"No, I couldn't do that, but I appreciate the offer. I'm told I'm supposed to run off any youngsters before there are any problems. You've been here a while now."

It was more of a question. Gordan understood it completely.

"Listen, um..."

"Gerry"

"Gerry, my name is Gordan. See that little Toyota over there with the one door a different color than the rest of the car?"

"Yes. I noticed it because it's been there my entire shift."

"Very good. That car belongs to a friend of mine, named Walter; he had a bit of a tiff with his wife, and she asked me to look for him. Now he's a veteran, so he could be across the street. He wears one of those modern flashy red, white, and blue things for a missing leg, but I was afraid to head over there just to have him walk up from somewhere else and drive off."

"Well, all these shops," Gerry waved his arm in a sweeping gesture covering the entire plaza, " are currently closing up, so I doubt he's in any of them. But, I'm a veteran, and I use the facility across the street myself."

He smiled at Gordan proudly. "3rd Infantry during Korea." He winked at Gordan. "I'd be glad to help you out."

"Thank you for your service, sir." Gordan pointed at himself. "I'm a former Ranger."

They shook hands through the window.

"Maybe you could do me a favor, Gerry. If I head over to the hospital and my friend Walter comes back to his car, maybe you could tell him to wait and have him call me."

"I can do that, Gordan."

Gordan got out of his truck and locked it up "Good. Thank you, and nice meeting you, Gerry."

Gordan walked off with his coffee in hand, heading across the street to the hospital through the now-freezing mist.

22

Monday — yesterday

GORDAN PACED THE hospital grounds, listening in on every conversation, waiting to hear a foreign accent and asking everyone if they knew of the British or Australian doctor. He mostly was dismissed outright, or people looked at him like he had missed a dose of medication.

He was getting tired and irritated — well, more irritated than normal.

He dialed the Schroeder home.

A weary-sounding Jill picked up. "Yeah, Gordan."

"I'm sorry, Jill. I haven't figured out anything yet. I thought I would stay on this until after lunch, and maybe by then, I'd have something else." He knew not to ask if she'd heard anything. "Did you manage to get any sleep?"

"I nodded off a couple of times on the couch, but I woke to every sound. Maybe I'll try to get some now. I'm not heading into work."

"OK, then. I'll call if anything comes up. You do the same."

"Gordan, shouldn't I call the police?"

"Sure, Jill. They would take some kind of report and probably not do much unless we find a crime scene."

She hesitated. "But what about the things Walter has been saying? Don't you think it may have something to do with it?"

"If Walter is correct, the police won't solve anything, and we'll further tip off the people involved that we are on to them. If he's wrong, police will want you to have a health-and-welfare check — lock you up for observation."

"Gordan, we can't do nothing but wait."

"We're not, Jill, and I can do a lot more looking on my own than by involving the police — until that may be necessary, that is." Gordan was crossing the street back to the Mickey-D's. Walter's car was still sitting alone, out farther than anyone else would want to walk this morning. At least now the temperature was climbing above freezing.

"Get some rest. I'll call closer to 1400 hrs."

• • •

Akihiko Watanabe waited for Louis Monreau to open the door to the big silver Mercedes. Watanabe never wanted a "bodyguard," but a gopher/driver was very nice to have, especially because he hated reading maps or using those GPS devices.

Monreau was tall and lean; he maintained the same weight as when he'd fought professionally as a kickboxer in Europe. He had actually held the title at 175 lbs. for nearly two years.

His suit was fitted; with a thin, black tie, he looked every bit a world-class athlete. He moved lightly on his feet, never getting off balance, never overextending himself. He never carried a gun — only a pair of brass knuckles.

He would never admit to his coworkers, but he really appreciated this work. He had never been in any real trouble, and, with months of pay coming in steadily, it was better than another man trying to kick off his head.

Maybe a socio-linguistics student would understand that he was speaking Levantine French; his darker skin and black hair would make Homeland Security suspect of his nationality.

Today was a happy day for Monreau, as he and the good doctor were going to be done with the Veterans Administration for good. Once they had taken care of some paperwork that the doc had left behind, they would never return.

Monreau was so sick of some arrogant American hearing him speak French and then mocking the WWII

French position, or the knuckle dragger would point to a "These Colors Don't Run" tattoo on a flabby biceps.

Forget the fact that they were so rude; they knew nothing of history. After all, didn't the French help these ungrateful bastards during their own revolution?

Watanabe always sat directly behind the driver; Monreau stepped back and then reached down after opening the door.

"This is it, then?" Monreau asked.

"Yes, I do believe today is it. Soon, all the hard work will prove my work is accurate." Watanabe took a deep breath and looked past the veteran hospital toward the west. "I believe it will be a beautiful day to travel out to the country."

Watanabe started heading up the sidewalk while Monreau closed the door and pressed the "lock" button on the fob in his pocket; the horn acknowledged.

He turned and strolled leisurely toward the side entrance, following his current paycheck.

• • •

Gordan looked across the street from his vantage point standing alongside the Schroeder mobile.

He had been up many hours; maybe he would pull his truck right over to the tiny car and catch a few Zs before heading back in to canvas everyone closer to lunch.

He ran his oversized mitt over the top of his head and then down through his beard. Maybe he would walk the hospital until this cup ran out.

First he opened the back driver's-side door of his truck and pulled off his denim jacket. It was heavy; the deep inside pockets were full of a variety of small things he thought he could one day find handy.

He pulled off the dark-blue hoodie sweatshirt and put the denim back on. Honestly, the denim was a bit of a security blanket, and he'd had it for years. The additional weight on him was comforting after years and years of carrying hundreds of pounds of extra equipment; it also covered the protruding grip of his handgun whenever his shirt may have ridden up.

He topped it off with a weathered Army black-and-gold baseball cap and headed back across the street.

He wandered the parking lot and found himself trying to imagine the drivers of the different vehicles parked in the lot.

Just when he thought he had it figured out, an elderly gentleman drove up in a 1950s Chevy pickup truck. It was dark metallic green, looking like it was brand new.

The driver looked to be in his seventies, and Gordan waited patiently while the man climbed down out of the cab and hobbled, with the use of a wooden cane, to the sidewalk that Gordan stood on.

"Very impressive truck you have there, sir." Gordan pointed. "That color is beautiful, especially in this morning light."

With some effort, the man stopped and looked back at the vehicle. "My old man bought this truck brand new in nineteen and fifty four." He smiled at the truck as if it brought back pleasant memories.

"Does it run well?" Gordan walked over and looked in the driver's-side window.

The man chuckled. "See, what I had done was to drag this old truck out of the barn, and I paid, probably too much, to get her all fixed up. The guys put all modern engine, exhaust, and suspension, but none of all that electronics crap. I can move my own seat and roll up my own damn windows. I can tell you this: I don't need a computer telling me which way to go."

It was Gordan's turn to chuckle; he held out his hand for the gentleman to shake. "Sir, I couldn't agree more; it's perfect."

The old man shook Gordan's hand vigorously. "I hope my grandson appreciates it as much after I go."

"A shame if he doesn't understand it," Gordan agreed. "You just make sure it's a while from now."

"Thank you; I'm doing my best, son."

Gordan moved off, happy that he was able to meet that gentleman today, a positive moment he would remember for a long time.

Around the opposite side of the hospital, Gordan found an entirely different parking lot, one that had many newer, nicer vehicles — the employee parking lot. Gordan noticed that the further away from the building he walked, the older and in worse shape these vehicles were, and they began looking a lot like the other parking lot.

Gordan walked back into the facility. The same staff was at the front desk, and he took a seat after throwing out his now-empty cup. His eyes grew even heavier as the minuets ticked off the clock. At one point, he realized that he'd been sleeping; nearly twenty minutes had elapsed.

Frustrated and a bit angry with himself, he began walking the halls, popping into any rooms with an open door, lingering outside some, trying to eavesdrop, waiting to hear a British- or Australian-sounding accent.

He was told to leave or asked his business several times but did not hear what he wanted. On the third floor, he walked into an open door.

"Finally, *Je me casse!*" Louis Monreau jumped up from a chair in the small room and pointed at a flat cart with several boxes stacked on it. "This goes into your incinerator. Do you understand? This all goes up in flames."

Gordan scanned the room. There was a little man in the corner who began to stand. He appeared to be of Japanese heritage; he had some kind of satchel between his feet.

Taller than Gordan, Monreau bent to look into Gordan's eyes. "*Allô!*" Monreau clapped his hands before Gordan's face.

Gordan nodded. "French, huh?"

"Oh, *putain*! Yes, yes, I am French. Now would you get rid of this, and make sure it is incinerated?"

"Yeah, sure. Top-secret stuff, huh?"

"No, it's just records, personal records. Nothing more important than that."

Gordan took possession of the cart and began to push it out of the office and then down the hall. A man in a green jumpsuit was walking briskly in his direction.

"Is this the paperwork for the incinerator?"

Gordan nodded.

"Thanks. I got it from here."

Gordan started to head to the stairwell and up to the fourth floor when he thought he heard, "Right, then. We're off."

It was British. The tall guy and the little Japanese guy were now standing at the elevator with five other people; only two of those looked like potential doctors. Gordan started to head in that direction but realized that, unless he full-out sprinted, he wouldn't make it.

He turned and ran down the stairs, making his way to the elevator doors on the first floor; the doors slid open moments after. Gordan made it a point to rudely bump into those he had not heard speak before, as he forced his way into the elevator before allowing them to exit.

"Sorry." Gordan didn't mean it.

He got a "What the fuck?" and a "Jesus!" out of the two he suspected; neither had an accent.

The Frenchie stepped into Gordan's space. "You got that paperwork taken care of already?"

"Sure, pal. I just deliver it. I don't load it into the incinerator. This is a union gig, mate." Gordan pushed back onto the main floor.

The little Japanese man stood at the rear entrance and called back, "Louie, may we?"

Gordan, shocked, pointed at the little man. "Australian, right? I think I'm good at hearing accents!"

The man shook his head. "You yanks. No, my good man. I was born in Japan."

He turned to walk out the door, Frenchie now in tow.

Gordan followed and, once on the sidewalk, yelled out as the man named Louie opened the rear driver's-side door of a big silver Mercedes for the little Japanese man.

"Hey — what about the accent?"

The little man stopped and stepped back to speak across the trunk.

"British, my good man. British." He shook his head at the Yank's error and then jumped into the back seat, allowing Louie to close the door and get into the driver's seat to speed away.

Gordan ran around the building and sprinted across traffic to get to his truck. He looked back to see the big Mercedes pulling out and heading north. Gordan fired up his truck and headed in the same direction. If he took the street, he would miss the light and maybe lose the vehicle.

He took a straight line. Jumping the curb, he barely missed a bus stop, and then he stomped on the gas to get through the light half a block behind the Mercedes. He said a thankful prayer for getting his truck outfitted for off-roading. He glanced into his rearview mirror also thankful when no lights came screaming after him.

Keeping an eye on traffic, Gordan called "The Kid," Mykhaylychenko, at CIA headquarters. He got a message and then left one. "Kid, this may be very important and I need your help. Call me back, and pull me up on satellite when you can, please."

He drove on, following as he had done many times in his career. The car ahead seemed not to notice as they performed no maneuvers to lose a tail.

• • •

"So this Army guy was here waiting for you when you got home yesterday, but your husband was not?" The police officer was standing in the Schroeder living room, looking down on Jill Schroeder, who was holding her head in her hands.

"Yes, but he is not an issue right now, officer."

"How can you not be sure these army pals aren't out sleeping off an all-nighter?"

The officer looked over at his partner, who was looking at pictures on an end table; she shrugged her shoulders and began walking to the door.

"Your husband's injuries intrude on any daily activities?" she asked.

Jill lifted her head and looked at the officer at the door. "No, not really at all—unless he attempts to be on his feet for too long."

The male officer interrupted anything the female was about to say. "And there was no fight — you guys are getting along fine?"

"That's right."

"I'm willing to bet they're both back before tonight. I'm willing to bet that his buddy," he looked down at his notes, "he probably knew all along where your husband's car was." He nodded in confidence at his partner. "Give us another call if he doesn't come back by tomorrow morning."

Jill Schroeder's headache was getting worse; now, she just wanted to try to get alone so that she could close her eyes. She walked to the door past the female officer and opened the door.

"Thank you for coming out. Maybe you could give me a report number or something?"

"Right now, that would just be a "contact" number; tomorrow, we would write a report," the male officer informed her.

"Thank you again." Jill closed the door and locked it. Leaning against the door frame, she pushed back a feeling of nausea but then lost the fight and ran to the bathroom.

• • •

Gordan's bladder was about to burst. The amount of coffee he had drunk over the last thirty-six hours was causing him to feel jittery and was no longer keeping him awake. Being in motion was helping him stay awake, but this meandering drive while he followed the silver Mercedes was bringing him to the brink of sleeping at the wheel.

Where is The Kid? If he could follow them via a satellite feed back at CIA headquarters, I could grab an hour of sleep without feeling I was missing something important.

His phone rang. It was Jill.

"Gordan, I called the police. They think you and Walter are out on a bender or something. They expect you both home soon. They told me to call tonight if you both don't show up."

"Jill, I'm doing everything I can. I will call you if something significant happens. Get some more rest, and keep praying for the best."

"Gordan..." her voice quavered with emotion.

"I'm here."

"He's given so much for this country. He's a very good man, and he doesn't deserve anything else to happen to him in this life. My heart will break." He could hear her tears.

"I've tried and lost before, but I've never given up, Jill. Walter didn't just disappear. A robbery or car-jacking would have been different — we would have found him. I promise that it will not matter who did this. I'll find them and Walter."

"And then what? What if it's something crazy, something involving important people?"

"That stopped being an issue for me years ago."

"I'm so tired. What does that mean?"

"It means that I don't care who 'they' are. I used to care, but back then I was a different person; that's not me anymore."

"He trusts you. I'm begging you."

"Eat, get cleaned up, and then rest, I'll talk to you soon."

Another person putting all their trust into him. Another desperate soul pushing all their money into the center of the table and betting it all on one Gordan Hudde. It had happened too often before, and he could only sure of only one thing: Death was the consistent winner.

He was suddenly wide awake, making sure he didn't lose the vehicle up ahead.

• • •

Walter Schroeder's eyes fluttered awake. He was face down, lying on cold, hard concrete, a pool of saliva under his cheek.

His head was pounding, and he struggled to a seated position against the black concrete block wall, trying to remember where he was and what he was doing here.

He slowly turned his head, taking in the odd room he found himself in. No — it was a cell. Narrow, but high.

He checked himself for injury, and only his head and stomach reported back with issues.

The low-slung bunk, the stainless-steel toilet, and sink all screamed *cell*. He couldn't remember what he had done to get here. A cell should have bars and only one door. This one had doors at both end and no bars whatsoever.

A green set of coveralls was hanging on a hook; he could make out some markings folded into the back. He stood slowly and pulled out the shoulders on the empty outfit to see what it was.

"Forty-eight," he said out loud. The nine-inch high numbers on the back were the only markings.

He caught some movement above and noticed, for the first time, the small TV high above him; was that on before?

He splashed water on his face and then drank from his cupped hand.

He sat on the bunk and closed his eyes; he was still very tired. He could hear some banging and something that sounded almost like music somewhere off in the distance; he fell asleep to an uneven beat.

• • •

"It doesn't matter where I've been, Gordan; I'm not sup-posed to work for you. Matter of fact, I'm supposed to report every contact I have with you to the man upstairs." The Kid obviously didn't like being asked where the hell he'd been. He almost lived in this place the way it was.

"Who is demanding updates?"

"You know who."

"Listen, Kid, you know I couldn't live without you; have you got me on screen?"

Mykhaylychenko shook his head; he knew he was wasting his energy. "Yes."

"About half a mile ahead — only two cars in between us — there's a big silver Mercedes. Do you have it?"

"Yes."

"Please let me know where it goes."

"Why are you way out there, and where are you going?" The Kid asked the obvious.

"Brother, if I knew that…." Gordan shook his head.

"That's some heavy woods, and only like an hour away!"

"More like two hours the way this guy has been driv-ing," Gordan quipped.

"The next task I need for your genius to work on is to find me a Japanese-looking doctor who works for the Veterans Administration. I'm sorry, but I don't have a name. Just a little, polite Japanese guy who is kinda freaky when he speaks in a British accent."

"The VA here?"

"I saw him this morning at the VA in Virginia. They were cleaning out an office."

"Hey, Gordan. Your target turned and is now heading east about three quarters of a mile ahead of you. It looks like a dirt road. OK — you're almost on it. And now you just went by."

Gordan went another mile down the Wilderness Road and turned off.

"Are they still going deeper into the woods?"

"Yes, about a mile in now. Hey, Gordan?"

"Yeah, Kid?"

"They're gone."

"What do you mean? Like the woods are too heavy, or they went underground? What?"

"Hold on. I think someone has blocked out this area using a mirror program. Gordan, you'd better be careful. Somebody important has messed with this bird."

Gordan spun the wheels as he left the dirt to get back onto pavement. He slowed at the mouth of the small dirt road.

"OK, Kid. I'm heading in. Can you call if you see the same vehicle heading out?"

"Sure."

"Hey, Kid? If you can't get ahold of me after a few hours, maybe you should call Bulldog Mahoney."

"OK. I'll do that."

The Kid continued to monitor Gordan until he watched as the dark truck disappeared off of his screen.

• • •

Monreau nodded and waved at the dark guy standing guard at the gate. He knew he spoke French, but Monreau also knew the guy was Muslim. He'd been recruited in Europe and had no love for America — well, for anyone, for that matter. Momentarily he thought he was happy that they had yet to move in here. He wondered if this guy was on the American "no fly" list; he should be.

He turned the slow corner of the dirt road, careful not to spin the tires and unnecessarily dirty the car. The large, framed steel building loomed out of the surrounding forest.

Monreau pushed a garage door remote hanging from the driver's sun visor. The giant door began to rise, and, when it was high enough, he drove under. His lights came on automatically, filling the vast, nearly empty chamber with temporary extra light. There were a half-dozen cars parked along the opposite wall; the place was quickly becoming totally operational.

He parked near the elevator and then jumped out to open the door for the doctor.

"So once you are done here today, you only have to clean out your office at the military base, and then we live here for the foreseeable future?"

"Yes. It's incredibly satisfying to see the progress."

"Will you be heading back later today?"

"Right now, I'm prepared to stay until tomorrow if we have to, but I would rather get back to the brownstone tonight if possible."

"That's the plan, then."

• • •

Gordan eased to the small fork in the road. He couldn't ask The Kid, as there were no eyes on target right now. He placed the truck in park and hopped out. Walking ten steps out in front of his truck, he closed his eyes and listened; nothing but the wind through the trees came back to him.

He could clearly see fresh tracks in the soft earth heading forward and not taking the turn to the northeast. He continued on foot until he came to the next slight bend to the south.

Gordan immediately jumped into the tree line. Ahead was a metal fence and gate, with a guardhouse. One man was standing inside the small enclosed shack. The afternoon sun was shining through the glass. Gordan figured the man would have difficulty seeing him through the glare.

Gordan slowly made his way back to his truck; he took the turn in the road at nearly walking speed. He stopped when he could make out what looked like a corrugated steel shed. Again he got out, now walking; it was a little bigger than a two-car garage. Out in front of the shed was a pickup, equipped with a plow and an old army deuce-and-a-half truck painted a solid green; everything stood silent.

Gordan figured he could fit his pickup behind the structure and it would not be seen by anyone parking out front.

After backing his truck between the trees and overgrowth, he stood quiet and just listened; ten, fifteen minutes went by, and he did not move.

He could not hear any human activity inside or out. He picked the lock of the man door and went in. Amazingly, there appeared to be electricity; he flipped a switch, and some long fluorescent lights flickered on.

It was every guy's dream maintenance shed: Two four-runners, every tool imaginable for jobs in the woods — kind of like Gordan's own shed down below his home in the mountains in Georgia.

He turned off the light and headed back outdoors. He realized that the wind was turning even colder.

He went back to his truck and returned with the dark hoodie under his denim. Then he slowly disappeared into the trees, looking for that silver Mercedes.

What he eventually found was more of that twelve-foot-high fence, complete with the three rows of razor wire, which just made Gordan that much more suspicious.

What the fuck have I and Walter fallen into?

It appeared that the land behind the fence was opening up a little further, so Gordan followed the open area
around his side of the fence until he saw the giant steel
structure up ahead.

Gordan squatted in the tree line. *What the fuck is
that monstrosity? You could park a couple of C17 cargo
planes in there.* He glanced at his watch; it was just after
1400 hrs. He waited and watched nearly a full hour;
patience was something he'd learned long ago. He saw
the path being worn into the ground near the interior
of the fence and suspected a guard. His patience paid
off when he observed two men walking side by side; he
could make out rifles slung over their shoulders. As they
came near, he could hear what sounded like idle chatter
but couldn't quite pick it up. They may even have been
speaking a foreign language.

He waited until they had passed and thought, *I should
wait to see how long it takes them to come back around.*
But he waited until they were near the back side of the
hangar, and then he followed on his side of the fence.

The building had a giant overhead door that Gordan
guessed would rise slowly up into the structure. He could
not see any other door in the front or on the east side as
he silently approached the rear from the wood line.

When he'd cleared the back of the structure, there
was enough space to build several football fields side
by side. One lone cement-block structure stood alone
almost directly in the middle of that space. Gordan could

make out what appeared to be brown shutters all around that small single-floor building. From the beaten-down knee-high weeds, Gordan guessed that the guards would walk directly along the back of the large steel structure and didn't bother to follow the fence several hundred yards farther out. One lone man-sized door was situated on the southeast back corner of the steel hangar.

Gordan followed the fence until the small concrete building was between him and the hangar. The next time he observed the guards walking across the back of the hangar, he cut the bottom of the fence from a steel post nearby and wormed his way under.

He ran hunched over, feeling the weeds drag under his knuckles as his arms swung low to help with balance, like the gait of an ape — something he had been called before.

He silently fell to the ground near the cold cement of the twelve-foot-by-twelve-foot small building. He guessed it may be a generator room, but there was no familiar diesel noise emanating at the moment.

He felt the brown shutters and found them to be steel, which made even more sense for some kind of hazardous material storage or an electrical room.

He peeked around the corner; nothing. He crawled to the opposite side and peeked around — a lone steel door.

He found it odd, but there was no CCTV cameras mounted anywhere, no ground-motion sensors—nothing but two roaming men and a man at the gate. He shrugged his shoulders and reached into the outside pocket of his denim; he took out his small lock-picking tools.

He crawled to the door and picked the door's lock; it was a standard lock — nothing fancy. Gordan now wondered if this could be in any way important. When he entered, he pulled out his small pocket flashlight and turned it on, flashing it across the dark interior.

The small beam was just enough to cut completely across this distance.

Gordan frowned; he had never seen anything like it on dry land. Coming out of the concrete floor was a dark-green, round, steel ductwork. There was a vented steel rectangular hood of some sort on the top, resembling a strange kind of viper rising up from under the building.

Next to that, a three-step platform had been built with what appeared to be a submarine's conning-tower door screwed into the concrete, with six giant bolts buried deeply into it. No way in hell he was getting into there, but now he realized that down there was more important than the large steel hangar out there.

Before he left, he felt a need to look down into the vent. He was hoping that it was large enough to force his wide shoulders down into it, maybe a legitimate way inside. He studied the top and found that a dozen small screws were holding down the top, with a layer of green paint added to make life more difficult.

• • •

Dr. Watanabe met with the engineers installing the latest equipment deep underground.

Deep-blue coveralls identified the workers who were up on a pair of electric lifts, ensuring that the disc was properly attached to the track that ran directly overhead, straight down the middle of the cavernous room.

Watanabe was out of his element, but he understood what the man was trying to convey.

"Given your matrix and types and consistency of liquids you have suggested would be dispensed, we have determined that this here piece of equipment should emulate the exact — er, ah, well, in scale of course — results of the live fire tests we've completed in Arizona." He smiled and waited for some kind of acknowledgment from Watanabe; he got none. "We should be able to test in just a few moments now."

Finally, Watanabe spoke. "Fascinating!"

"Shall we head up to control?" The engineer turned and headed out of the testing facility, turning to his right, toward the elevator.

By the time the two men were standing in front of the monitors and controls on the third floor, the men with the lifts were driving the lift units into the storage room, plugging them in, and exiting the room to head to the surface, where they would wait for their leader.

The engineer with Watanabe continued, "For the first test run, we will use a heavy yellow smoke; it's a non-contaminate so that we can also gauge the exhaust system. For the second test, we have a special liquid illuminate that, when shown under a black light, glows like crazy." He was grinning, very happy with this. "I'm telling you, Doc; we're going to impress you with the pattern you are going to get with the droplets."

"Sir, your tech is as foreign to me as I would guess my biology may be to you, but I find what you boys have done here incredibly ingenious. I am amazed by what I do not know."

"Thank you, sir." He cleared his throat. "The tubes have been pre-loaded and can be handled from here. Are you ready?"

• • •

Gordan Hudde put away his multi-tool and cussed. One of the screws would not break free. *When all else fails, try brute strength.* Gordan pulled on his mechanic's gloves, ensuring they were fitted properly, and climbed up on top of the concrete slab. He reached down and got the best grip he could on the vented slats along the sides of the hood.

He tested it first, leaning back a bit and pulling at about what he thought was about half strength. The hood held steady; he tried again, putting more into the lift. His legs and lower back began to strain, and he felt the slats begin to give. Just as he was about to give up, something gave a fraction of an inch.

He shined his light and found that he had managed to break the hood free from the paint, but there was still one small screw.

He pushed down on the top of the hood, and it settled down a bit. Then he steadied himself and heaved upward with all his might.

The hood moved but held; he gritted his teeth and used every bit of muscle from his legs up through his back. He let out a deep breath with a final push of everything he had; he wished he could scream like he and his men would when squatting heavy weights in the gym.

And then it gave. He went stumbling backwards, tripping on the sub-door, landing on his back with a twenty-five pound steel hood on his chest.

Even in the cool air, he was sweating and now breathing heavily. He allowed the hood to roll off his chest, and he fought to regain normal breathing. Instead of jumping up, he lay there an extra moment, waiting for someone to burst through the outside door or out the big, round steel door in the floor; they did not come.

Gordan walked over and looked down into the darkness. He pulled out his small flashlight, but it could not penetrate the darkness that extended past the army green that it highlighted within the first ten feet.

He took off his gloves and began searching the pockets of his denim; finally, he found what he was looking for — a small package about the size of a marker. He opened it and snapped the plastic contents in half; the room filled up with a green glow from the light stick.

Gordan stuck his head into the open end of the vent and allowed the light stick to drop. It fell for quite some time before he thought it stopped. Maybe it was stuck? Maybe it fell into an alternate shaft? Whatever had happened, that faint green light reflecting from the green painted steel deep in the earth made Gordan feel as if he were looking into a bottomless emerald abyss. He could not make out a bottom, even though he stared until his eyes watered.

He stood still in the dark, contemplating his next move. *Will my shoulders fit into the vent? Then where the hell would that go?* He leaned forward, allowing his shoulders to roll inward, testing how tight a fit it would be.

Suddenly a small yellow light overhead, covered in thick glass and enveloped in steel mesh, began turning like a bubble on an old police cruiser.

Gordan froze, thinking it was some kind of intruder alert. Then the steel louvers on the wall began slowly opening.

Gordan felt it first in his feet: A vibration, and then his ears popped, as if he were in a plane that was climbing.

With the realization of what was happening, Gordan fell to the corner of the room and placed his jacket over his nose and mouth.

Gas! Yellow smoke began to blast out of the pipe with tremendous force, and then it swirled around the room and Gordan, making even his short hair move in the wind. The blast of air continued until the air was clear again; then the roar stopped, and the louvers began to fall.

Gordan waited for whatever toxic concoction that was to affect him, and he nearly jumped out of his boots when his phone began to vibrate.

He seated the earpiece and heard The Kid's voice.

"Gordan — are you there?"

"Yeah, I'm still here." His breathing was louder than his whisper was.

"Are you sure you're OK?"

"For the moment. What do you have, Kid?"

"I just sent you a picture. Do you recognize that individual?"

"Nice work — you've identified my Oriental Englishman."

Gordan peeked out the door, "I'm on the move, Kid. If I lose you, make sure you call back."

"Gordan, you bumped into former child genius and bio-chemist Akihiko Watanabe, from the company called Biophaze."

"Should that impress me for some reason, Kid?" Gordan whispered as he ran in a crouch.

"Last week, they announced that they had a remedy for Alzheimer's! I wish I owned some of their stock. It was almost worthless even just a week before that."

Gordan made it back to the fence; he lay low in the weeds. "Kid, call me if that sedan comes out of here. I still need you to follow if you can. Thanks — and nice work!"

Gordan wormed back under the fence. Pulling a zip tie from his pocket, he tightened it through the fence and around the bottom of the post so that the fence would pass casual inspection.

• • •

Gordan low crawled to the heavier wood line and then waited and watched; after the next time that the two guards made it around the back of the main facility, he started to move back the way he had come.

• • •

Akihiko Watanabe looked down from the control room to three stories below him. With the black lights, on he could imagine that he was looking up into a starlit night; the bio-illuminate that the test had used glowed "danger-yellow" in a polka-dot pattern too numerous to count across the floor and up the walls by five or six feet.

"Oh, cheers, mate! You and your equipment have performed brilliantly!"

The engineer turned and smiled. "That's why we get paid the big bucks."

He reached down and pressed several buttons and then turned to behind them and spun a big red valve.

Hundreds of thousands of gallons of water began streaming out of nozzles in the ceiling and walls. The "stars" began to streak and then pool on the floor until they ran together into small streams and then disappeared into the large steel grates in the floor down below.

"Brilliant." Watanabe nodded his approval.

The engineer shut off the valve and pressed several other buttons.

"It's all as simple as that."

"I shall sing your praises to those who write the checks."

"That would be appreciated; do you have any other questions?"

Watanabe shook his head and then verbalized it: "No."

"I'm out of here then, sir. Thanks for your time." He rapped on his white hard hat in some kind of ritual that Watanabe was not familiar with and then turned and walked to the end of the control room. He turned when he got there, and, when he found that the doctor had not followed, he left the lights on and exited the door.

Watanabe followed but walked into his lab and office instead of heading up to the first floor to retrieve his driver, who was, he was sure, hanging out with like-minded mates in the barracks area.

He breathed deep the recycled air tainted with the smells of fresh paint and plastic; it was almost heady. This is where he belonged: Using his mind to travel into places others were unable or afraid to go. Nothing was more important than advancing his knowledge, pushing forever into the realms others felt belonged only to God.

He now just need to clean out Ft. Belvoir and retrieve his samples and serums that were locked up there. Watanabe ran his hand over the locked cooler that would soon hold all his work. It was nearly a piece of art, built from heavy glass and stainless steel, its top shelf nearly inaccessible to a man his height.

This was the perfect location for a man like him; no one asked him how he was accomplishing the goals that set before to him, and no one asked him how much money it would take to finish them. He turned and admired the area one last time before turning off the lights and heading up to the first floor.

One floor above, Louis Monreau looked down at his phone. "I gotta go — my master calls."

One of the men in the bunks turned and threw a pillow at Monreau as he turned to leave the sleeping quarters where he had been talking to his friend Allen Graham.

"Good — you women whispering over there were keeping me awake!"

"Beware the evil deer while you guard this hidden place!" Monreau jeered.

Hans sat up. "Do you feel that mad scientist staring at the back of your skull wondering what he will find when he cuts it open one day?"

"Fuck off," Monreau said as the door silently closed on good springs.

"Yeah, Dr. Frankenstein knows there is nothing in his head — no need to look." One of the others called out after him, but Louis could no longer hear in the sound-dampened hall.

• • •

Walter Schroeder sat still on the floor near the smaller of the two doors of his cell. Earlier he had felt vibrations; at first he thought it an earthquake but then changed his mind to maybe heavy equipment moving.

It had been followed closely by something like the close flyby of an F-16, with both noise and vibrations. Now he sat there, hand on the door, and it felt warm. He didn't have the slightest idea of what may be in store for him, but he was beginning to lose all hope of any rescue.

He closed his eyes and prayed for a miracle.

23

Today 0001 hrs. 9 hours ago
"JEEZUS, KID! I'M doing the best I can do without wrapping this truck around a tree or getting picked up by some local cop." Gordan put the phone onto the big center console as he drove.

"Adjust north up ahead, and then head east on Route 66. You'll make up time, I assure you."

"Yeah, roger that."

Lack of eating was a bit of a distraction for Gordan, but the lack of sleep was becoming a major factor. The best he had ever done before was three days without sleep, and he still performed well. But that had been several years ago, and, right now, he was not feeling all that well.

"Hey, Kid?"

"Go, Gordan." The Kid always liked to feel involved in the action side of the game.

"Count it down when I'm getting close; I'm afraid I'll ride right past them."

"One mile."

In the left lane of the two-lane highway, Gordan crisply passed two tractor trailers.

"One half mile — it looks like one more tractor trailer and then your target."

Gordan returned to the right lane and looked ahead as they approached an off-ramp for the town of Marshall.

"OK, Kid, eyes on target. But do me a favor: Don't go far... just in case."

"You'll ruin the image I have of you; books will need to be rewritten."

"Yuck it up — I'll remember."

He followed, allowing his speed to fall to nearly the same as the Mercedes', twenty car lengths ahead. Gordan's mind, while tired, continually tried to figure out this Rubic's cube of information, except this cube was missing a lot of colors.

He felt a bit drunk from everything during the last thirty-six hours; he had no idea what he should do next. Would Bulldog Mahoney help him with so little information?

Then the silver car ahead took an off ramp near a town called Centreville. Gordan was a little too close, and, as he came off the highway, he had to stop momentarily directly behind the Mercedes at the light at the intersection. It was poor work, probably sleep induced, but he could not allow that to cause a problem now.

Gordan called The Kid. "Still up there?"

"Sure. I was wondering if you were going to knock on their window."

"Yeah — I'm hitting this gas station here. Maybe let them get a mile ahead."

Gordan turned in and pulled up to some pumps; placing it in park, he sat idle for a moment.

When he no longer could see the Mercedes, he pulled out and took the same direction of travel.

"Call it out, Kid." Gordan yelled down at his phone; this made him nervous.

Gordan quickly realized that they were heading into a suburban area, where he guessed the doctor was currently living. The Kid called out turns, and Gordan stayed far enough back to not give away his presence.

The Kid called out the next turn. "This left is going to put you in some nice brick townhomes. It just circles around in about a mile or so, and I'm guessing you have reached your destination."

Gordan was still rolling dice in his head.

He approached the silver Mercedes, which was parked near the curb of one of the many identical-looking units.

Gordan's headlights panned across the front yards as he swung into a parking spot, the bright blue light finally stopping directly onto the big sedan, where Monreau was holding the rear driver's-side door open for the doctor.

Gordan watched; in his head, he watched the dice wobble and stop...he got snake eyes.

He exited the truck, flicking on the brights and off-road lights as he did, lighting the area before him like a white sun.

"Hey, Doctor Watanabe!" Gordan called out as his dark form surfaced from the blinding lights like a lion jumping through the campfire.

"What the..." Monreau got past his lips before Gordan hit him with a vicious elbow straight to the back of the ear. The pavement opened up, and Monreau folded down into the darkness.

Shock and awe.

Gordan grabbed Watanabe by the throat, his one over-sized hand easily wrapped around his neck pinky to thumb. Watanabe slapped at and pushed away at Gordan's chest for a moment, but then Gordan bent and used his entire body to throw Watanabe up and into the air. Gordan had always found that grown men often found being picked up and thrown like a bag of garbage...disconcerting.

Gordan threw him down onto the trunk of the car with enough force to remove all the air from his lungs.

Gordan knew that unless this man could produce and use a handgun, this was way over the top — exactly what he wanted.

He allowed Watanabe to roll off the trunk, landing in a thud onto the black, wet pavement. As Watanabe coughed and gasped for air, keys, a roll of bills, and a plastic key card fell from his pockets, and he reached out as if robbery was Gordan's motive.

Gordan picked up the much-smaller man with one hand and then slapped him hard several times, enough to bring a flow of blood from his nose.

"I hope you are beginning to understand that I can do whatever I wish with you."

Watanabe leaned out to look past Gordan. "Monreau?" he nearly whispered.

"If he wakes up, I'll kill him." Gordan shook Watanabe. "Are you paying attention?"

"Yes."

"My name is Gordan Hudde. I know what you are doing, and tomorrow, unless a better deal comes along, I'm blowing this entire thing wide open."

"I...I don't have anything to do with any of that."

Gordan back-handed Watanabe hard enough that it stood him up onto his tiptoes and spun him around like a limp pirouette; Watanabe fell to his knees.

"I'll be at my old workplace tomorrow at 0900 hrs. That's the CIA headquarters. Got that?"

"Yes, yes. Please don't hit me anymore."

"You go back and tell your friends."

"I will."

Gordan climbed into his truck and was gone; the entire event took only about two minutes.

Gordan forgot that his phone was still on and was startled when The Kid started talking.

"All this time, I've heard all about the sneaky surveillance/counter surveillance that you guys do out there, when all along it's just an episode of WWE!"

"Well, sometimes you just have to say, 'What the fuck?' and go for it; tonight was that time."

"What?"

"It's a movie reference; you've never seen *Risky Business*?"

Gordan could hear the keys tapping.

"Oh! An old movie."

"Kid, you've been hanging with the wrong crowd. Now, get me the hell to my hotel, would you?"

• • •

Tuesday 0700 hrs. 2 hours ago

Gordan parked his truck in short-term parking at Dulles airport and took a cab to CIA headquarters. The cab had to drop him off on Dolly Madison, well outside the campus grounds, and that was OK with Gordan — he wanted to be seen. The men at the main gate were unaccustomed to see a man walking toward them. There was a bit of excitement that an armed individual had walked right up to them. But, ultimately, Gordan was allowed to walk up to the main building after several tense minutes of phone calls.

He didn't want to be obvious but he allowed his eyes to wander, looking for anyone there who was going to intercept him and keep him from going into the building.

He was confused when it did not happen, and he stopped inside the main foyer, looking back to the windows, fully expecting someone to be charging him; there was no one. He stood and ran his hand down his beard.

"Gordan?" The Captain of the security force had come out to meet him.

"Hey, Zeke — long time. You keeping this place running smoothly?" He focused on the man in front of him. "Hey — a promotion. Nice!"

"Thanks, Gordan. You heading downstairs?"

"Nope, not today. I've got to see the Director."

"You on the list?" The Captain began walking over to the desk.

Gordan grabbed the biceps of his left arm as he turned. "I called late last night — I'm sure I'm not. But Stevens will see me."

This was not odd for Gordan Hudde, and the Captain knew of the special relationship that the two men were reported to have.

"Alright, Gordan. Maybe I'll see you on your way out."

Gordan was disappointed. He had misread the situation and obviously taken the incorrect action the night before.

He stopped at the Director's secretary's desk to announce himself.

"He's on the phone, Mr. Hudde, if you want to have a seat."

Gordan nodded and slipped into a chair, still deep in thought.

Gordan actually lost track of the time.

"Mr. Hudde," the secretary seemed to suddenly yell at him.

The inner office door was open, and the Director, a big grizzly bear of a man, was blocking the light from the windows from behind him, framing him in the door.

Gordan stood. "Director, thank you." He walked into the office and went directly to the window; he seemed lost in a daze.

John Stevens didn't sit down; this was odd behavior from his former top agent.

"Just what have you and The Kid been working on?" Stevens asked.

"What did he tell you? That chicken shit."

"No, he didn't tell me. I just need to know how much time he is wasting working for you."

Gordan turned back to the window. "Hey, Director — how many visits do you guys get from army MPs?"

Stevens lumbered over to the window and observed the two dark SUVs stopped way down at the main gate.

"This would be a first that I'm aware of; Gordan, you looked like hell before, but now you look happy. What the hell aren't you telling me?"

"Let me apologize in advance," Gordan said pulling his .45 semi-auto and pointing it directly dead center on Stevens's face.

"John, you need to tell me about any secret drugs you are working on."

"What are you talking about? Put that gun away before you get yourself killed."

Gordan stepped up. He pulled back on the hammer. "I'm not fucking around. I need to know *now*!"

Stevens's hands were up in a defensive posture. "We have just had a new "truth serum" designed, and that's all I can tell you."

Gordan was gritting his teeth. "I don't have much time, John. That's all you *can* tell me, or that's all there *is*?"

"That's all there is, Gordan; please, whatever there is, let me help."

"I believe you. Now put your hands into the air and call in your secretary."

"What?"

Gordan yelled, "just do it!"

"Frank! Frank! Open the door!" Stevens bellowed.

It must have been odd for the director to yell. Frank opened the door in a fraction of a second; he stood shocked at the sight.

"Frank!" Gordan yelled to snap him to attention.

"Frank, in exactly sixty seconds, I need you to set off the alarm. Do you understand me?"

Frank was confused; he looked at the Director standing there, with his hands seemingly nine feet in the air.

"Frank — just do what the man says, would you?"

"Yes." He turned to walk back outside.

Gordan yelled out, "Frank, close the door halfway."

The secretary sheepishly stepped back into the room to grab the door and pull it nearly closed.

"Good enough," Gordan said, and then he turned back to John Stevens. "I hope you forgive me if I live through this." He glanced down, obviously counting off the seconds, and then he stepped up and smacked Stevens in the nose with the butt of the handgun.

Stevens yelled out in surprise as well as pain. "What the fuck!"

"Sorry, sir." Gordan motioned with his fingers. "Give me your hands."

An alarm began screaming — a high-pitched *Whoop! Whoop!* — and a red-and-yellow light Gordan had never noticed before began acting like a strobe light in a night-club behind him, above the door.

Gordan screamed above the noise, "That's annoying!"

The big man brought his hands down before Gordan as if Gordan was going to tie them or cuff them.

"You're going to pay for this!" Blood was seeping into his grey mustache.

"Tell me about it. Now just go with it."

Gordan spun the gun around and placed it into the big hands of the director.

The director held the gun loosely his face contorted in confusion.

"You know that thing is loaded, right?" Gordan said.

Gordan put his hands into the air in submission and slowly dropped down onto his knees, finally dropping his head forward and placing both hands behind his head.

The Army men burst through the door.

24

Current time and date

GORDAN HUDDE LOOKED down into his lap at the zip ties that were secureing his wrists. He found it odd that the MPs had secured his hands in front of him. They also had treated him fairly well since the initial confrontation in Director Stevens's office.

The Colonel had mentioned Fort Belvoir — not an exceptional distance to travel, but during the morning commute, it might take a while. Gordan leaned against the window to catch any additional sleep he could.

When he awoke, they were slowing to go through the main gate at Belvoir. This base was open, as were most military bases during this time of satellite surveillance; there was little reason to maintain the cost of keeping a base closed when the internal activities were well known to almost all other countries.

The military SUVs made their way to the post commander's headquarters building. Gordan always felt it
odd that you could drive so long on some posts without seeing a single official-looking military vehicle like a
Humvee in camouflage.

One MP and the Colonel walked Gordan through the
building. There was the familiar hustle of the enlisted,
the non-interest of the civilian employees, and the high
polish of the floor and anything metal.

The trio slowed as they approached an attractive
sergeant seated at the desk outside an office door
with a large single star and "Brigadier General Emerson
Seibert" painted across the frosted glass.

"Go right in, Colonel. The General has been waiting."

The Colonel rapped on the door frame of the door
two times before entering first, with Gordan sand-
wiched between him and the lone MP.

Gordan watched the Colonel deliver a smart salute,
which was half-assed returned by the General.

Seibert step in and walked around Hudde, eyeing
him up and down; he appeared not to be impressed.

"Do you know who I am?" Seibert asked Hudde.

"I'm capable of reading the door." Gordan stood still,
standing tall with his shoulders back and head high.

"Why are you here, Mr. Hudde?"

Siebert was now standing directly in front of Gordan;
he was of similar height but easily seventy or eighty
pounds lighter. His uniform had no combat medals; he

had no special training patches or insignia. One man had spent his life training for the physical demands of combat and life in the trenches, the other for driving a desk. Gordan tilted his head as he glanced at the pistol flap on Seibert's belt, with the butt of a grip protruding to the rear.

Gordan studied Seibert for several more seconds, refusing to say a word. He then turned to glance at the Colonel and then behind him to nod at the MP.

"Colonel, please cut Mr. Gordan's ties, and you may wait outside, if you would."

"General?" The Colonel nearly swallowed his tongue.

Siebert sat on the corner of his desk, the only spot not covered with paperwork, the computer, or pictures that Hudde could not see. Hudde took a moment to attempt to read all the commendations and training certificates that Seibert had decorated his wall with.

"You will be on your best behavior — isn't that correct, Mr. Hudde?"

"Sure."

"But General — he just struck the CIA director!"

"You received a direct order, Colonel." Seibert waited.

The Colonel looked over at the MP Sergeant, who took out a folded blade and cut the plastic tie. The two men then exited and closed the door behind them.

Colonel Darby shared a confused look with the MP before he went to a window and stared out.

Gordan stretched his arms out and yawned. The general suddenly realized what a size and age difference there was and momentarily felt a bit alone. He shook it off and walked around Hudde again; he placed his hand directly on top of his holster flap for comfort.

Seibert stopped in front of Gordan. "Well, you got yourself noticed. Now, why don't we dispense with the charade, and you tell me what it is you think is going to happen now."

Gordan allowed himself one moment to grip his chin and pull down on his beard, something that he often did unconsciously when deep in thought.

"I just thought someone with my..." he shrugged his heavy shoulders "...skill set..." he liked that word "... should reach out and get a piece of retirement — you know: One way or the other."

Seibert was not amused. "Why don't you just explain what we would need you for?"

"Well, the way I see it, you can use a guy who does some work for you or the guy who just goes off and remains silent, never speaking about the horrors he knows about." Gordan furrowed his brows with the statement.

Seibert stood, walked around to the other side of the desk, and sat down in his plush leather chair. He pointed at a stiffer leather chair pushed up against the wall. Gordan slid it closer to the desk and sat.

Gordan leaned in to get closer to Seibert. "Unless, of course, I'm not asking the right person?" Gordan let that hang, but before Seibert tried to answer, he continued, "Or maybe I should be talking to Yvonne Lane over at the VA?"

Gordan could tell that that got under Seibert's skin.

Seibert blurted out, "She's not in charge!"

"So I sent a message to the right guy. As far as I'm concerned, there is 'Come work for us' money or 'Go away and be quiet' money. If I were you, I'd put me to work."

"Is that so?"

Gordan sat straight and said nothing.

"Just what do you think you can do for us?"

Gordan smiled. Seibert wanted to talk. "Oh, come on, General. You've been reading my jacket all morning."

Seibert nodded. "You were a good soldier. I see that, but your CIA years are empty."

"What does that tell you?"

Seibert nodded at the obvious answer.

"Why did you assault the CIA director?"

"I needed to know if he was in your circle. Now I know he is not."

"That seemed a bit of a desperate play. You could have just come here directly."

"I don't want to upset your operation, so, relax; I just want a piece of the money one way or the other. The CIA director has no clue what I was looking for. If you didn't have me picked up, Lane would have been next, then you, and then..."

Seibert interrupted him with a high-pitched laugh. "I'm afraid she would like it." He grinned at his own joke.

Gordan was serious. "Nobody ever has."

The serious look Hudde now had sent a shiver down Seibert's spine. From his nervousness, he began thinking out loud: "And if Lane or I wouldn't help you, then would you have the balls to go confront the Deputy Secretary of Defense?" He was shocked at the thought.

"If I had to."

"So what do you think you know that we should pay you for your silence?" Seibert asked.

A lot more than I did a half hour ago, Gordan thought, but he didn't let on one bit. "You're using veterans as lab rats. The good doctor not only is the genius behind your operation, but he gives good stock tips."

Seibert couldn't help but smile at the thought of the millions he was making and millions more he was going to.

Gordan didn't waste the moment. "I wish I was in on the ground floor of that."

A bit of fear flashed across Seibert's face. "How did you find all this out?"

I was just guessing and taking a chance. You have just confirmed it all. Gordan smiled. "I'm just that good, General. Listen — no one else knows. You couldn't have known, but you shouldn't have kidnapped my former Captain."

"I told Lane everything needs to be OK'd by me first!" he shook his head.

'Tell me this, Mr. Hudde. Why don't we just get rid of you as well? Maybe the good doctor needs another rat for his cages?"

"That's a good question. Allow me to answer with another question: If I know all that I obviously do, as well as other nuggets — like the secret location of your lab out in the country — how do you know that I haven't sent out several information packages to be opened if I don't make the Christmas party this year?"

Seibert studied Hudde for a few seconds. "That's what I would do."

Gordan looked down and then pointed. "Would you really shoot me with that pistol?" he asked.

"My father loved Patton. When I graduated West Point, he bought me a pair of these" he said, looking down at his holster. "I thought two would be too much." He made an awkward smile and continued, "Would I? Absolutely. Do I think I'm going to need to? No. Now I wear them whenever I'm on the post. This is my world, and no one ever challenges me here."

"Who challenges a General?" Gordan wanted to keep him talking.

"Oh, please, Mr. Hudde — you're one of them. Don't give me that 'confused' look. You know damn well that the military jocks look down their noses at officers like me. My entire career I've felt the looks, heard the mumbling as people speak in hushed tones about the REMF General."

"I didn't..." Gordan started but was cut off.

"I saw you do it when you came in here — checking out my uniform. This thing is a neon sign that announces my lack of combat skills. You looked and then turned up your nose. Tell me: You don't think I'm even a soldier, do you?"

Wow, touched a nerve.

Gordan frowned. "General, you know the military is filled with non-combat MOS's." Gordan smiled to himself "We need clerks, too!"

Seibert pointed at him. "That right there!" He walked in close to Gordan. "I don't deserve my rank?" He wagged a finger, waiting.

"I'm sorry, General. I just meant that every position is important."

Seibert began to pace, upset with his own outburst and yet angry at the man before him for reminding him of everything he was not.

"Mr. Hudde, my patience is wearing thin. Just what is it you're looking for?"

Gordan thought for a long moment. "One million dollars, and I will disappear from your radar; nobody ever needs to know anything. I think with the money you all are going to make, that's easy. Or you can hire me for a larger fee."

Seibert went back and took his seat behind the large oak desk. He took a few deep breaths to calm down.

Gordan stood and looked out the window. "I'd like to speak with the doctor before any deal."

"Why?"

Gordan didn't even turn to look at Seibert. "Take it or leave it."

"I can't make this call without consulting the others."

"Go ahead and consult. I'll wait."

Seibert dropped his head into his hands and rubbed his temples. "If only it were Friday."

"What's important about Friday?" Gordan asked.

"You see, Mr. Hudde, every Friday at 1840 hours promptly, I give a toast to a successful week at the offi-cers club."

Gordan's brow furrowed with questions.

Seibert brimmed with pride, excited to speak about something that he felt responsible for. "We have a wall filled with a pyramid of beer steins — one for every important officer on base. It's really rather impressive. Of course, mine is at the pinnacle, and the first beer, the first toast, is my responsibility; the men love it."

I'm sure they love you; I'm surprised you don't have a medal for that pinned on your chest. "Who does it in your absence?"

"I have never missed a Friday yet, and I certainly don't plan on missing one any time soon. Also, I'll have you know they grill the best rib-eye in a thousand miles — I personally guarantee it. Matter of fact, Meredith Ryan is scheduled to have dinner there this Friday; maybe we will decide your fate then."

"Sounds like a real swell time," Gordan said sarcastically. Seibert did not miss it.

The phone rang, and Seibert answered it as if he'd been expecting the call. He suddenly seemed calmer, and that added to Gordan's overall suspicions. "We will set you up with a meeting with the doctor. You're lucky he would agree to see you at all after what you did."

Seibert walked over and opened the door. He waved in the Colonel, and they exchanged some whispers before Seibert stepped back to his desk.

"Mr. Hudde may be staying here for a few days. Make sure he has a room at the old officers' barracks. He's a guest as long as he has the proper chaperone."

"Understood." But honestly, Gordan didn't think the Colonel understood it all himself. Something was up, but Gordan needed to allow it to play out now that he had played his hand.

They exchanged salutes, and Gordan was ushered out the door.

The Colonel rode in the front, and Gordan, now with his hands free, sat alone in the back seat of the GMC. He leaned forward so that he did not have to yell over the fan blowing out warm air.

"I'd appreciate my personal things back — my wallet, key fob, and cell phone at a minimum. It would be nice to have my jackets back, too."

Colonel Darby looked back over the seat, and Gordan sat back into his.

"Once we remove everything from your jackets, we will get it back to you. The rest — maybe later."

OK. They think I'm officially some kind of prisoner now.

Who was playing who now? Gordan knew that many conspiracies were held together very loosely and that criminal luck played as much a role in some successful plans as hard work and persistence.

He couldn't wait to find out just exactly what Doctor Watanabe was working on; his imagination was having a difficult time trying to figure out what the VA and the Department of Defense would be working on together.

Was Walter Schroeder still OK? Were there any others being held or used? Gordan had to remain patient even though it drove him crazy to have to wait and allow the current situation to play out.

They arrived at a barracks that may have held troops during World War II. They stopped, and Darby and the sergeant got out and looked back at Gordan until he got out and walked around the SUV to their side.

They walked up to the wood-and-cement stairwell and pointed out the chain and lock on the doors on the first and second floor.

They walked the length of the building and up the stairs on the opposite end, holding the door open for Hudde.

"I thought I had an appointment with the doctor?" Gordan asked as he came through the doorframe.

"Something has come up. It may well be tomorrow before we can make that happen," Darby said.

"That wasn't the deal I just made with Seibert."

"I don't know anything about that. What I do know is that you should be on your way to Leavenworth if not for the General, so maybe you should just relax until we come back for you."

"How about some chow, then?"

"I'll send in a pizza. Now please follow the sergeant up to the second floor, and understand: Our orders are not to allow you to escape, with all options at our disposal."

"I'm alright."

Gordan followed the sergeant up the old wooden staircase to an entire open floor plan. The skeletons of twenty bunk beds were pushed up against the opposite side of the open floor with twenty old lockers on the near end.

The square-jawed sergeant stopped near the top of the stairs and spoke for the first time. "We've turned the power on. You should have some hot water in an hour. I'll bring up the pizza when it arrives. If you come down the stairs, I will shoot you. If you try to leave here in any way, I will not hesitate."

Gordan stopped and looked back at the MP. He was going to say something smart-assed but decided against it.

"I've gotten very little sleep over the last few days; you have a boring time in store for you if you're guarding me."

The MP said nothing; he just turned and went down the stairs.

Gordan looked out of the window in the latrine and saw that the MP had taken up a place in front of the door while the Colonel walked back and drove off in the SUV they had arrived in. Within a minute, a second SUV drove up, and the MP jumped into the front passenger seat; there were going to be two-man teams babysitting.

Gordan looked for a mattress that looked like it had been made in this century and then turned it over to make sure it wasn't bug infested. He then did as he'd promised and slept.

He slept so hard and long that, when he woke up later, it was dark, and he was freezing. On a bunk next to him were a pillow, two Army-green woolen blankets, and a pizza box — cheese and pepperoni, just as cold as he was.

Gordan walked about in the dark and ate the pizza, all but two slices. Then he waited until a little warm water came out of the ancient pipes. He washed his face and rinsed out his mouth.

He lay back down, wondering if he was doing the correct thing. He fell asleep worrying about whatever was happening deep under the ground out in the country.

• • •

Emerson Seibert looked down at his .38 caliber revolver and its pearl grips. He always left it on the bathroom side of his bed on an old wooden nightstand. He brushed his teeth and thought that today had been a very successful day, much thanks to him.

Yvonne Lane had fucked up by picking an individual who was so active in veteran circles. Whether or not she could have possibly known that the guy had a friend who was formerly in the CIA, she should have checked with him. A man like Schroeder would most likely have some friends in high places somewhere; she had almost destroyed everything they had worked so hard for by taking action on her own, even after being told not to do so by Meredith Ryan.

Seibert knew Ryan would not be happy, and he fully planned on filling him in at dinner on Friday. Why not put the screws to Lane at the same time, telling the story of how he saved the day, further cementing his own status?

He spit into the sink and then used a cup to rinse.

He looked at his image in the mirror for a moment, turning his head first left and then right. Although he was not satisfied with the thin-necked, balding man looking back, he wished that one could see how well their brain functioned just by looking in a mirror. He smiled at the thought, and then frowned. Better that others could not see and get jealous. Let his enemies overestimate them-selves and underestimate him.

He had now taken the lemons that Lane had shit out and was making lemonade. The unimpressive fellow in the mirror smiled a happy, crooked smile back at him.

• • •

Yvonne Lane had felt cold enough to dig out her flannel pajamas. She was done with her evening rituals and had lain back onto her plush bed, closing her eyes with her arms folded across her ample chest, hugging a travel magazine close.

Until recently, she hadn't dared to dream of the successful outcome of her plans. She did this to ensure that she did not become complacent; she was almost certain now that this was going to be the ticket to a life lived any way that she wanted, without taking orders from anyone — especially men. Her 401(k) had nearly tripled in just the last week; she could hardly wait for the next announcements when the doctor finished with some of his other experiments.

Three years ago, a desperate doctor had approached her at a conference to talk about Alzheimer's and the possibility of medicinal therapy that could effectively stop the deadly disease.

His big fear was that the company that he worked for would be shutting off funding or, worse yet, going completely bankrupt and not only stopping his research but forcing him to lose everything he had worked for already. It was good instincts for him to search out the Veterans Administration with their task of dealing with many older veterans.

She had the foresight to put feelers out there in the areas of government that would be able, willing, or needy enough to play outside the rules.

Once the doctor was able to project about some of the other areas that his work may be able to affect, she realized how the Defense Department and Intelligence Departments may be interested in the work, and it was amazing how quickly the entire thing came together — all under the radar of every oversight agency.

The criminal elements, the things that she didn't dare to say out loud, even in the privacy of her own home — well, those things just happened.

It was like a witch's cauldron, where because of the items that they had thrown into it, other things had slithered out. They really had to have courage to carry on, and they had.

She couldn't help but to allow a small smile to creep into the corners of her mouth as she drifted off.

• • •

Meredith Ryan sat in his office chair at his quiet home in the Washington suburbs. His wife had just walked by and placed a small kiss on the top of his head as he typed a speech he would deliver to a Republican think tank Saturday afternoon in Cambridge, Massachusetts.

His mind, unlike Lane's or Seibert's, did not drift to the medical military testing out in the Washington countryside. Unlike the other two, he had many irons in the fire; they would not only set him up for an incredibly exciting and fulfilling retirement in the future but ensure the financial success of his children.

He had insider information regarding advancing missile technology, Navy ship plans, and the newest attack aircraft all destined for huge government contracts — and kickbacks enough to take care of him and his sons. If a contract with the Saudis was finally authorized, he thought that he might even purchase that yacht he and his wife had looked at last year while in Florida.

No, Ryan had no real concerns about his future finances. He typed away, humming to himself, desperately trying to write the type of paper that would get him a position at a law firm when his government "service" for his country was over. The kind of job that would keep the black-tie affairs scheduled long into the future. His wife often complained about those events, but she spent days afterwards gossiping on the phone with her friends, and he thought that, secretly, she enjoyed the attention.

• • •

An assortment of forty-eight male heads lay awake or tossed in a restless sleep on thin cots deep under the ground. Not knowing why they were being held or if any help would be coming was maddening. Some cried for loved ones whom they might never see again, while others gritted their teeth, realizing their worst fear, which was that they would never be allowed a fighting chance to regain their freedom.

25

FOOD AND SLEEP allowed for better decisions. Gordan looked out the second-floor window at the large black SUV idling in the cold morning air which was sweeping down from the north to meet the warmer waters surrounding this coastal area, and it was creating a thick, living fog. From his vantage point, Gordan watched it swirl, ebb, and flow around the black GMC. This would be a perfect time for him to disable the two men who were probably half asleep inside and to escape to rethink his strategy that had gotten him held captive in the heart of the beast.

But he kept coming back to the doctor. He had to know; he had to talk to the genius doctor. Everything somehow revolved around him, and Gordan needed his story to help him understand.

Gordan closed his eyes and turned back inside; staring out the window made him feel as if he needed cataract surgery.

He dropped into a pushup position and began knocking them out. His mind always counted out cadence; he could never get his brain to stop it, whether it was counting out pushups or jogging.

He jumped up and did some jumping jacks, while slowly spinning to take the room in again. When he stopped, he went to the latrine door — actually, they never had doors. Reaching up like a mountain climber and getting as good a grip he could on the top of the frame, he did some pullups.

After thirty minutes of exercise, he used one of the wool blankets like a monk's robe, attempting to stay warm in what had to be the low-forties or high-thirties temperature of the empty barracks; he continued to pace to help keep warm.

The MP Sergeant called out to him from the stairwell. Gordan's two jackets were dangling from his outstretched hands. "Let's go."

Gordan felt his phone and key fob in his pocket of the denim when he put the two on.

Maybe things were turning around?

The GMC stopped near the hospital, and the Sergeant turned in his seat.

"You need to be on your best behavior here, Sir. I don't need some kind of event today. Are we clear?"

"Crystal, Sergeant." Gordan smiled. "I just need to make a call before we go in."

The two MPs stayed close but turned their backs in a gesture of giving him some privacy.

"Hey, Jill."

"Holy shit, Gordan! Where are you? What the hell happened? Have you found Walter?" Jill Schroeder was nearly screaming into her phone.

Gordan knew his phone would most likely have been cloned; he would do the same to find out who knew what.

"Jill, I can't explain right now. I need you to forget the police department, OK?"

He could hear her breathing heavily, weighing his words.

"Jill, this is very important: For Walter to get home to you, you must forget about the police right now."

"Gordan, I don't understand…"

"I can't help you right now. I'm too busy. Just know that the police will not be able to help."

"I…just…don't…"

"Walter trusted me. You need to now."

She sounded like a little girl. "OK, I guess."

"Sit tight, eat, and rest. I'll call you in a couple of days at the latest."

"Gordan?" she whispered.

"I've got to go, Jill." Gordan prayed he could give her good news one day soon. At least anyone listening may give her some space if they had been worried that she knew anything.

He turned to the MPs. "Thanks. Let's go."

They weren't in the main hospital but a building next door. It was only three floors, and they were on the third. Gordan saw the doctor at his desk as they walked past the window to his office.

He had one of those foam collars on that they give to people with neck injuries. Gordan stopped himself from smiling. He scanned the floor for the Frenchman; he was nowhere to be found.

The MP rapped on the outside door of what looked like an empty lab. Gordan did not hear a response from inside, but they entered anyway.

Inside, the Sergeant called out to the doctor, who looked up from whatever he appeared to be reading.

"Doctor, we were told to drop off this person and to stand by outside. Please call out if you need anything."

They didn't wait. They just did an about-face and exited the room.

Gordan felt the unease and strode confidently toward the Doctor with his hand out to shake.

"Gordan Hudde. Sorry about that thing the other night."

Watanabe unconsciously touched his neck brace.

"Violence is an option for the uneducated."

"Spot on." Gordan pointed a thumb at his own chest. "High school diploma." He smiled and extended his right hand.

Watanabe reached out as if he was going to touch a snake and shook Gordan's hand using only his fingertips.

"Maybe you haven't heard, doc — we're going to be on the same team now. Maybe I'll pull security for you, and then you can deep-six that French fool."

"That French 'fool' and I have had to spend many hours together. He is from Paris; he is cultured and from culture. I abhor the thought of having a barbarian as a close aide." He closed his eyes and shook his head slightly.

"Whatever. The deal that was made is that you fill me in on what you have been doing here."

"As if you would understand." Watanabe looked back down at his tablet.

"I'll let you know when you lose me, doc, so talk slow. What were you doing for Biophaze?"

The doctor looked up at him in disbelief.

"Come on, doc. The sooner you start, the quicker we finish. Wow me with your brilliance"

The doctor gave in; he sat back on his stool and took a deep breath.

"As far as Alzheimer's is concerned, I have been experimenting with protein fragments, beta-amyloid enzymes, and tau proteins." He paused to allow Gordan to ask questions. When Gordan did not use the moment, he continued.

"I was attempting to find ways to switch on or off neurons that the disease had tampered with. We are talking about many years of research, so much information gathered and reviewed. I could not allow the company to fold and then to closet my information. I was so close."

Gordan sat across the desk in a hard wooden chair. "And the VA allowed you to continue your research?"

"Yes, in fact, while there is much research still to be completed, I demanded it must be continued. I have developed a serum that is best delivered through a patch. When applied against Alzheimer's in the earliest stages, it is highly effective and allows a person with the disease to stall the inevitable deterioration that affects those without the drug."

"Seriously?"

Watanabe was now highly engaged. "Oh, indeed." He paused. "It was the introduction of a synthetic opioid that started the successful trials."

"And your trials were conducted with the assistance of the Veterans Department and without..." Gordan searched for the proper words "...interference from other government agencies, like the FDA?"

The doctor just nodded. "I assume that everything was taken care of — yes."

"Does it really work?"

The doctor sat back up. "Oh, yes. Nearly one hundred percent, at least temporarily."

"So you need long-term human tests?"

"Yes, of course, that would be required, but short-term testing has been highly successful." The doctor locked eyes with Gordan, waiting for the next questions.

"And then what happened, doctor? What where you tasked to do next?"

The doctor sipped from a cup. He didn't pretend to care to ask Gordan if he wanted anything.

"It's an obvious question. I should have seen it coming, but I was so consumed with my own tests. If I had found a way to turn on or off certain neurons, neurons that have been mapped to control different functions, well, why not use the same process to change or control a person's behavior?"

Gordan sat back, and the doctor allowed him to ponder the information.

"So I could sneak into the Kremlin, dose someone, and have them open the safe for me without any need for special tools or torture?"

Watanabe smiled at his new pupil. "Yes — one of many potential uses. Imagine a missile flying over the troops at the North Korean border, and all the soldiers drop their weapons and walk away."

He smiled at this example.

Gordan's eyes narrowed. "No, our Defense guys would be more interested in getting them to turn on each other. How long would this work, and can you get someone to do something totally out of character?"

"You all think alike." Watanabe shook his head sadly. "From thirty to sixty minutes, and yes — if I know a man's weight, I can give you the correct dose to make that individual do anything you wish."

"But you wouldn't know every man's weight in your scenario, so what kind of success would you get?" Gordan studied the doctor. He loved having this discussion.

"Exactly why we have been testing: Too little, and we found individuals would be lethargic and some-time experience hallucinations that interfered with the new commands. Too much, and our test subjects froze with paranoia, and a few even developed severe schizophrenia."

"Either way, you would cause havoc with an enemy. How would this have been dispersed? I mean, how do you administer this drug to a mass of troopers?" Gordan was not shocked at this entire line of thought.

"It has been found to be equally effective ingested, inhaled, or from transdermal delivery."

"Really?"

"Oh, yes. It could be placed into an eye dropper, an inhaler, or even food or drink."

"What did the CIA want?"

Watanabe's eyes narrowed. "You are very well informed. They wanted only a better "truth serum" — nothing more."

Gordan sat back into the chair. "Oh, my God — what are you testing next?"

"Mass exposure and what delivery system is most effective."

"What will that consist of?" Gordan felt as if he was sounding a bit too concerned; he tried to allay that with a smile.

Watanabe did seem to notice. "Some non-lethal tests designed to gauge effectiveness of the dispersal method. We will replenish any test subject not able to continue the tests, and then we will need to use a final lethal test to properly measure the percentage of total effectiveness of the drug under less-than-perfect conditions."

"What would that mean?"

Watanabe looked up into the ceiling; he did not exhibit any emotion that Gordan could see except a certain level of excitement at imagining the results of a future test that he had devised.

"Based on the individual testing, to date, I imagine we would still have one man left standing at the end of the test."

Gordan shrugged his shoulders. "I don't follow."

"Imagine ten percent drop into a stupor, sixty-eight percent follow instructions to kill everyone, and the remaining twelve percent drop into a worthless schizophrenic state that does not allow them to defend themselves. So while the drugs may be imperfect and imperfectly delivered, I do think it will be a success. I am very excited to have those tests."

Gordan hoped he wasn't turning visibly pale from imagining these..."tests." "How soon will these final phases begin, doctor?"

Watanabe locked eyes with Gordan, suddenly exhibiting a confidence Gordan had not felt from him before. "I believe we will begin by this Saturday," he said.

Watanabe smiled. "I sense your condemnation. Tell me: What would be the difference between your General giving orders for a company of men to go off on a suicide mission and these men giving their lives for the future of your nation?"

Gordan looked down for a moment. "Americans don't believe in suicide missions. We leave our loved ones and go off to fight and win. Give me and my friends the weapons and support we need, and we have a chance. Nobody joins to die. It is your people who loved the *kamikaze*, not ours."

Watanabe slid off the stool and slapped the desk. "The two or three hundred men I will need will ultimately save more lives than thousands of fighting men! Do you have no grasp of history? Do you not understand your own country's history with biological weapons? Have you heard of the soldiers they marched into the desert and gave them sunglasses to watch a nuclear weapon test?"

Gordan nodded. "Operation 'plumbbob,' I think it was called."

"Did your country use the tests that the Germans allowed Josef Mengele, Viktor Brack, Rudolf Brandt, and Wolfram Sievers to conduct? Do any of those names ring a bell for you?"

Watanabe saw that they may have not; he reached for his pipe and began to use it to point at Gordan as he continued to make points.

"Your own CIA had a project called 'MK-Ultra.' Maybe you should research that before trying to judge me."

Gordan stared at Watanabe until the doctor turned his gaze away. "What do they call your tests, doctor?"

"MC-Zulu." He walked over to a refrigerator unit and opened the door. There were many vials and test tubes sitting in metal grates. Gordan looked over the shoulder of the smaller man.

"MC-Zulu 22." He pointed at a group of vials together. "It will go down as the most successful drug ever produced for your government." He turned and smiled up at Hudde.

"MC stands for…Mind Control … the Z?"

Watanabe closed the door carefully and then placed his hands into the deep front pockets of a cardigan sweater.

"Yes, 'Mind Control' …" he paused for effect, "… Zombies." He grinned. "Our attempt at injecting a little humor."

Gordan nodded. "Zombies. You're turning them into zombies."

"But, remember: Once perfected, it will be your enemies that your government would be using it on."

Gordan felt lightheaded. "And everyone understands that American veterans have died during your testing; you have briefed them all?"

"I've briefed the General, Yvonne Lane, and the Deputy Secretary of Defense, together and separately, especially as they have visited the new facility."

Gordan shook his head. "I bet." Gordan started walking to the door. Watanabe called out to him.

"I can't believe a man like you would judge me!" He sneered when he said 'you.'

Gordan stopped, placing his hand on the door-jamb while he pondered the disdain that he heard in Watanabe's voice.

Gordan turned so that he could look at the little man across the room. "I'll bite. What kind of man am I?" Gordan began walking back toward Watanabe.

"They said you are a hired killer — a man motivated by money and without morals."

Gordan nodded. "What I am is self-aware; I am also not delusional enough to judge myself as the 'good guy.' I have killed for country. Maybe that boils down to money if you count what my paychecks used to be." Gordan shrugged his massive shoulders and stepped into the doctor's personal space, looking down so that he could lock eyes with the little man. "I've also killed out of anger."

To his credit, Watanabe did not shrink from the bigger man "And now the barbarian does the only thing his little brain can come up with and threatens me. I'm sure the retribution would be swift and painful if you attempt anything."

"You know something, doc? I don't shrink from that description, but let me tell you what I am really thinking. If you were killing... let's say...*politicians* with your tests? Well, then I'd help you collect them myself; but you're using soldiers, my brothers in arms; you're killing my only family."

"And now that you are accepting a large sum of money, you are willing to be on the same team as I?" Watanabe smiled and folded his arms across his chest with what he believed was the winning comment.

Gordan nodded affirmatively. "I'll leave you with this, doc. I look around and see how things work; I've been involved in a lot of dirty, secret operations. I can't tell you who they may want me to kill for them today, but when this is over, I can guess who they will want me to kill last." Gordan allowed just a slight upturn at the corner of his mouth as he turned and headed back toward the door.

Once there, he stopped and looked back. "I'll see you again."

How the hell do I stop this by Saturday?

Gordan looked at the MPs in the hall to his left and right. "Back to the barracks?"

• • •

Allen Graham shifted in his seat and looked over at his friend Louis Monreau, who had been tasked with guarding the doctor over the past few weeks but had volunteered for this mission when it became active.

Looking into the rearview mirror, he could see the bearded Hun sitting in the back, keeping an eye on their captive, who still lay sleeping in a drug-induced stupor that was designed to last all the way to the facility in the Virginia countryside.

They worked well as a team, and Graham was happy to have a long list of successful missions accomplished to fill the doctor's test cells; in fact, they now had only one cell left to fill. Then he imagined he would be added to the security at the facility so that the guys could work two hours on and get eight hours off, an easy, well-paying job.

• • •

General Seibert felt much more comfortable giving orders to lower-ranking military individuals than dealing with civilians. One heard the order, snapped to attention, saluted, and then left to comply. The other felt comfortable arguing and asking questions, and Seibert couldn't pull rank.

Because he had the facilities, it had fallen on him to keep Watanabe housed and happy. Secretly, Seibert was going to be very relieved when the doctor would be lost in the woods and would be forced to call instead of these face-to-face moments that the doctor seemed to revel in.

The General focused on Watanabe's lips moving, but he was getting only every other word or so. Today, he just wasn't all that interested. He knew that Gordan Hudde was an issue, but he was trying to devise a plan in which he could first use Hudde and then rid himself of him at the same time.

The doctor's lips stopped moving, and Siebert blinked several times and cleared his throat when he realized that the doctor was waiting for a response.

"Doctor, I assure you that he will be taken care of. I am working on the plan even as we speak."

"He would be the perfect specimen for my experiments; I will not begin the final phases without him. I am sorry, General, but this is not negotiable."

Seibert suddenly realized that they were on the same page. "Oh, OK, doctor. You have convinced me. I will work on getting him to your facility to assist you in any way you desire."

"Another thing, General."

Seibert had begun to walk to the door, thinking the doctor would follow. "Yes?"

"I need to be present when he is informed that he will be a test subject." Watanabe rose and stepped to the door but did not open it during the silence as he waited for an answer.

"That is not wise, doctor. Something could go wrong, and there could be violence." He shook his head. "We can't afford to have anything happen to you."

"Of this, I will not be dissuaded, General. I want to see him at the very moment he understands his complete inability to escape, the moment he becomes a test animal."

"When I have the plan perfected, I will let you know. Until then, please ensure your office is properly transferred to the other facility, and wait for my call." The General opened the door and watched the doctor as he headed out, momentarily appeased, happy for the quiet.

• • •

The clock was ticking inside Gordan's head; it was as distinctive as his own heartbeat. Yet here he was, pacing back and forth inside the old barracks without a plan and without any pressure being placed on him by the opposing force.

Gordan always felt like he was a counter-puncher. He worked well under pressure, yet, here he was, wasting time, possibly allowing the enemy to get that much further out in front of him.

Wednesday night, another pizza and another cold restless sleep. He could easily escape, but then how would he dismantle the plans before the weekend? He was sure that he could get into and rile up someone in the Department of Defense, maybe the DIA. No way he could get the FBI to move quickly enough. No way he would get any of them wound up fast enough to act before Saturday. In fact, Gordan could see himself being held by any if not all of them while they checked out his story, keeping him from interfering well past the coming weekend.

Better for him to work from here. He decided to wait for tomorrow night before escaping and starting something on his own. That was part of the plan. Now, what exactly would he do if it came to that? One thing was certain: He would not allow any further testing to be completed by doctor Watanabe on any more of his fellow veterans. If nothing else, he would make sure of that.

26

Thursday

IT WAS AFTER lunch, and still, nothing had changed since the previous day. Hudde sat on the bunk going through a mental file of every action he had thought about over the last day and a half.

He heard a vehicle stop outside, and he rose to investigate. A smaller black SUV stopped out near the GMC with the MPs. A hulking, muscle-bound man got out from the passenger side of the Ford. His short-cropped hair made Hudde think of the Russian in one of those *Rocky* films. The driver was pale, with dark hair, much smaller, and carried himself lightly. "The dancer and the fighter" Hudde christened them.

There was a conversation with the MPs, who quickly placed the bigger vehicle into gear and sped off.

Hudde rolled his head and swung his shoulders to loosen up as he heard the door open, and then one man stomping up the old wooden stairs.

Both the dancer and the fighter came up onto the second floor and stopped for a moment to take in the ambiance.

"Gordan Hood," Fighter called to him. Hudde couldn't quite place the accent; Scandinavian maybe, not Russian.

Hudde answered in a rough Pashto, something he had picked up in the Middle East. "Nobody home — go away, American."

The Dancer stepped forward lightly. "You are being summoned. Do not run scared."

Dancer smacked Fighter on the hip; he turned and stomped over to the first stair, waiting. Hudde rose and walked slowly, following, watching, prepared to take action.

"The General wants to see you," Dancer said as he watched Hudde walk past him. Once Hudde was two steps down, two steps behind the Fighter, Dancer followed.

Hudde sped up to get right behind the big man, and Dancer smacked him on the head. "Keep your spacing, wise guy."

Fighter held the back passenger-side door for Hudde and he got in, folding his legs up so they could close the door. Dancer got in the driver's side, and Fighter slid into the passenger-side front seat.

Hudde started to slide over for some additional leg-room, but Dancer interrupted. "No. Stay right there. We're not going that far."

These guys were pretty good — relaxed outwardly but pretty disciplined and observant.

Once at headquarters, the three men repeated the walk Hudde and the Colonel had taken earlier, but this time there was no secretary, and they walked right into the General's office.

Seibert sat at his desk as if he imagined himself some kind of mob boss, his right hand fiddling with the holster flap — as if he'd ever use it. "We have decided to hire you, but we need a little test of your abilities and your dedication to our cause."

Hudde walked to the window and looked out at the empty parade field, grey clouds rolling overhead.

"What?"

"It seems your Captain friend's wife...Jill? Yeah. She didn't take your sound advice the other day, and she has herself a meeting with some detectives tomorrow."

Gordan shrugged. "So, by now you've gotten rid of the car, and I'm guessing you caught up to Walter before he got inside the VA hospital?"

"You are correct."

"Then she has nothing. Why make a second disap-pearance? You're just begging for a real investigation. A decent FBI agent might figure you guys out."

"Yes, Sir. Sound thinking, perhaps, except you are going to do it, and maybe a good FBI investigator will come looking for one Gordan Hudde. I'm afraid the only way you stay safe is to continue working for our little team." *Checkmate,* Seibert thought, and he smiled accordingly.

Hudde stood silent, looking through the General while he thought.

"Well?" the General asked impatiently.

"Oh, I'm sorry. Were you waiting for me? I told you that I'm 'in,' General. The guy tried to get me court-martialed. Do you think I owe him or his wife anything? I already saved his worthless ass once."

The General smiled, relieved that nothing negative was going to occur here on base — let alone in his own office.

"We expected as much."

Hudde pointed at Dancer-Fighter combo. "I don't need any babysitters for this. Just give me the keys."

"Nice try," Seibert said. "When you all get done, just head out to the hangar and wait for instructions." He nodded his head at the door, and the Fighter opened it, waiting for Hudde and his partner to exit.

• • •

Doctor Watanabe walked into his new lab; it was an amazing feeling to work with absolutely no financial restrictions and without any limits on how far he could push his experiments and studies.

He realized how happy he was to lose the constant observation of a bodyguard. After the incident the other night, Monreau had been miserable, and the other men ribbing him was not helping matters. Watanabe wanted to return to advancing science But so unlike him, the thing with that barbarian was holding him back. He kept thinking about ways to hurt the man, and he was resolute to see that situation to its ultimate end — to see the cell door close behind Gordan Hudde, to watch the confidence leave him, to see the life drain from him. Then and only then could he return to science.

He closed the solid glass door to his new refrigerator; even this seemingly simple thing was way more advanced than the others he had been using. This one was digital and exact, specifically the type of equipment one would expect in a facility with a scientist, a doctor, as famous as he.

He looked through the glass at the trays holding specimens and samples. The trays that held the vials of his versions of MC-Z from one to twenty-two were a simple way to see how he had advanced the science over the last two years. It was far more detailed in real life, but it was beautifully simple just to look over those vials and see the last several years of his life. It gave him shivers down his spine as he changed how his eyes focused from the vials inside the glass to his own brilliant reflection on the outside of it.

• • •

Hudde climbed into the rear passenger-side seat, his knees dug into the plastic of the front seat before him.

He prepared for the seat to naturally push back when the considerable weight of the Fighter got in and leaned back.

He wondered if he could reach between the seat and the window to draw the Fighter's weapon from his shoulder holster he was a fellow lefty. He knew there was no room whatsoever for even the Fighter to draw his weapon without him leaning over the center console; these vehicles just weren't built for someone of that size.

Gordan watched as Dancer slid easily into the driver's seat, his weapon momentarily in view on his belt under his right arm, a standard inside-the-pants holster.

If he reached for that and wasn't perfect, there would be an awkward fight, and Hudde was unsure of that outcome — so much so that he stopped thinking along those lines.

"So, how do you guys have this planned out?" Gordan hoped to get an idea from whatever they could tell him.

Dancer talked while watching the road. "There is a park across the street. It's a school night, getting cold, and near dinner, so the kiddies should all be indoors. We'll park there, and you run across the park and take care of it."

"Which one of you is going to give me your gun?"

"Don't be stupid. You don't need a gun to take care of the missus, and you don't want the mess anyway."

"Then what? Where will you take the body?" Hudde asked.

"I thought you were some super-smart secret agent." Dancer took his eyes off the road for a moment to look at

Gordan. "Make it look like a break-in or something — we don't care. Just make it quick." Dancer shook his head.

"Yah, maybe we get warm chow out in the hangar if we get back in time," Fighter said.

"OK. I give up." Gordan tapped the massive shoulder of the Fighter. "Finland?"

"The best country in ze world — Sweden," he replied, without trying to look back.

Gordan laughed. "That is arguable!"

"Not before me," the big man said without any sign of distress.

"Oh, that sounds like a challenge," Gordan said. "Maybe when this is over, we can find a ring to go a few rounds."

"I'd pay to see that," Dancer quipped.

"I'll crush you," Fighter dismissed the challenge. He sounded more excited about getting back in time for some hot chow.

They pulled into the park's small lot. Dancer had been right: Between the cool pre-winter air and the dinner hour, there was no sign of any children or parents around.

He placed the small SUV into park and sat still looking across the park kitty-corner. Gordan could see the Schroeder home with the little Japanese car, identifying that Jill was home.

"There you go, 'Secret Agent Man.' Get back here in fifteen minutes, or we are changing your status."

Gordan opened the door but leaned forward, "To what?"

"Enemy."

Gordan got out and stretched his cramped legs. He started two steps in the direction of the Schroeder home but stopped as if he'd just thought of something.

He tapped on the Fighter's window with his phone.

The window receded with a terrible whine. "Da?"

"Listen, I don't want to do something stupid like drop my phone in there." Gordan waved it about; he hit the top of the window frame and it dropped down between the fighters legs. "Whoops — ah, shit." Gordan started to lean in and reach between the big man's legs.

Fighter gave him a mighty shove, and Gordan popped back out the window, cupping his retrieved phone in his oversized hand. The big Swede then leaned over to try to find Hudde's phone.

"I think it slid under your seat," Hudde pointed out.

The Fighter leaned over as far as he could, his head nearly between his knees, hands and arms reaching under the seat.

Hudde quickly pulled out his wallet and held it out over the big broad back of the Fighter.

"Hey — hold this too, would you?" Gordan dangled his wallet before Dancer.

Dancer, almost out of reflex, reached out to take the wallet.

Hudde's massive right hand wrapped around the wrist of the Dancer before he could realize what had happened. Hudde used every ounce of strength to pull Dancer in his direction, up and out of the driver's seat, sliding him onto the broad back of the Fighter. Dancer screamed in pain as his shoulder was dislocated; Hudde didn't care.

Dancer now lay across the back of the Fighter, who had no room to move. Dancer's head was just outside the doorframe; Gordan raised his left hand high and, with as much force as he could muster, drove a hammer fist into the left ear of the Dancer.

The Dancer went limp. Hudde reached under his body, drawing the Dancer's own weapon from his belt. Then he quickly fired two shots into the back of the Fighter's head as he desperately attempted to sit up.

Gordan placed a finger on the neck of the Dancer; there was a pulse; Gordan twisted his neck, breaking it — no need to fire another shot.

This took just seconds; Hudde stood and looked at the warmly lit homes surrounding the small park. There were no faces pressed against the windows. Maybe the shot had been muffled enough to sound like a backfire from inside.

Gordan opened the passenger-side back door and pulled the body of the Dancer back through between the seat and onto the floor. He went over and got into the driver's seat; he found the correct button, and the window whined back up into the closed position. He placed the car in drive and headed down the street, parking near the Honda in the Schroeders' drive.

Jill Schroeder answered the door in an old sweatshirt and matching pants; while the outfit looked relaxed, her eyes showed a bit of panic.

She put her hand to her throat when she saw him. "Gordan — where have you been?"

Gordan placed a hand onto her shoulder. "Jill, there is too much to tell and too much I don't know yet. I need you to take a few deep breaths for me."

He waited until she realized that he was serious and did as he said.

"Good; I know that Walter has a few of those old, wool Army-green blankets somewhere in the house."

She nodded.

"I need you to get me one — two even better."

She furrowed her brows but then turned and disappeared into the back of the home.

Gordan reached over and turned off her outside lights.

She returned with a small pile of green and held them out for Gordan to see.

"Very good; now I can't answer any questions yet, but I need you to go into the back and pack for several nights away."

She looked at Gordan, and he could see her confusion. "Pretend that your life is in jeopardy and you must go into hiding. You won't need much. Go in the back, and pack a small bag."

He could see her chest begin to rise and fall, quick and shallow. "Jill, focus on what you must do right now."

Her eyes were a bit glazed over, but she nodded at him several times.

"Jill, I'm going outside for a moment. When I come back in, you will have a small bag with your toothbrush and several sets of underwear and socks, right?"

"Yes."

"OK. Be back here in five minutes."

Gordan turned and headed back to the SUV. He found the Fighter's phone and took it apart into three pieces, throwing them onto the back floor.

He found the Fighter's wallet and took out the two hundred thirty-seven dollars inside. Instead of fighting with the big, heavy, dead weight, he just covered the broad back with one of the blankets.

Then he kneeled into the back seat; the Dancer had no wallet but a money clip. He took the three hundred and twenty-six dollars; then he removed his phone and took it apart like his own, leaving it on the floor next to the Fighter's. Gordan then tucked the last blanket over the top of the body and closed the doors. He walked up to the front door and looked down at the SUV. He couldn't make out the bodies, and he knew they were there; he would not fear a trucker passing by and seeing something they shouldn't.

He opened the door and found Jill waiting with a small duffle.

"Very good. Now, do you have any cash available?"

"Well I can use the..."

"No, for the next few days, you will not use any cards or your phone. You will not reach out to friends or visit with relatives. You will not go see the police tomorrow."

"What?" she nearly screamed. "I have to."

Gordan reached out and grabbed her by the wrist. He led her to the window and pulled aside the drape so that she could see the SUV near her own Honda.

"Do you see that vehicle?"

She looked past him. "Yes."

"There are two men in there who were intending on seeing us both dead."

She jumped back from the window as if she'd been bitten by a snake. "Oh, my God! Oh, my God! what are we going to do?"

"Jill." Gordan tried to remain calm and steady. "They are never going to hurt anyone ever again."

"You mean?"

"Yes. Now listen closely. Not far from here, near the I-95, is a big mall with a Costco on the west side of the parking lot."

"Yes — I know the one."

"There are all kinds of hotels and motels in the area. Choose one. Don't tell me which, and go there. Pay up front for at least three nights. Pay cash for everything, eat takeout, and do not leave the room until Sunday. Are you getting this?"

She repeated it all back.

"Starting on Sunday, be at the Costco parking lot near lunch time. Park in with other traffic, but look out to the far reaches of the parking lot. When you see Walter or me, you'll know it's safe."

"You know where he is!"

"I think I do. Listen up now. Watch the news. If you do not hear from either of us by Monday, please go to the CIA headquarters and ask to see the director."

"I'm going to do what?"

"Use my name. They'll see you. Remember, this is probably a worst-case scenario."

"You are scaring me so much right now, Gordan." She looked up at the ceiling and took a deep breath.

"Is the place all locked up?"

"Yes."

"Leave your cell phone on the end table. Once I start to pull out in the SUV, get in your car, and disappear." He reached out and touched her shoulder. "Walter had one of those GPS map things. If you do as well, turn it off, and do not plug it back in until we see you Sunday afternoon."

She nodded and reached out, putting her phone down.

Gordan headed toward Dulles airport to get out of this death mobile, with its underwhelming performance, and get his truck back.

27

LOUIS MONREAU ENTERED the doctor's lab two floors underground with Hans and Allen in tow.

The doctor was a bit taken aback. He rose from his desk and walked toward the three men who were standing along a black-topped lab table.

Monreau placed his phone on the table before them. "General, we are all here."

Watanabe was still confused.

General Seibert's voice rose up off the table. "We haven't been able to get in touch with the men we sent out with Gordan Hudde. By now he should be asleep in one of your holding cells."

"Monreau says that your newest subject is secure."

Watanabe said, "Yes. Everything went as planned."

"Good. Take whatever manpower you need from the facility there, find him, and bring him back. When he knows what we have done, he will come peacefully. It's the way he's wired; he can't help himself."

"We'll bring him in," Monreau said into the phone.

"Good. I like your enthusiasm. Call me if you have any problems, otherwise, I will see you on Saturday, on time for your first big test." He disconnected from the call.

Watanabe realized how involved he was going to be in bringing in Gordan Hudde, and, while part of him was nervous, he was also excited knowing that this brigand would be brought to heel.

● ● ●

Gordan found a parking spot in a hotel parking lot that would get shade in the afternoon from a nearby tree. He backed the black SUV between the white lines. He took only the murder weapon that he had used and then left, locking the keys under the cooling body of the dancer along the floor. It was cool enough and the days grey enough that the car might sit there for weeks before anyone questioned it.

He walked up the access road to the airport and found his truck in short-term parking. He understood that he would need some firepower if he planned on storming the hangar out in the wilderness area west of there.

Gordan turned South, thinking that he could buy something more suitable for a real firefight from an acquaintance from his CIA days. Then he thought better of assuming that the man was still in business and pulled off into a strip plaza parking lot.

He sat for nearly fifteen minutes, looking at the three components of his phone, wondering if he should find a place to pick up some "go" phones like he used to carry before becoming a homeowner civilian in Georgia.

Gordan shook his head and then put the pieces together; once powered up, several messages showed missed calls over the last half hour. Gordan was trying to decide if he should return the unknown-number call when his phone rang in his hand. He nearly jumped out of his skin, and he realized just how tight he was feeling.

Gordan answered the phone on speaker; he left it in his lap, keeping his head on a swivel in case anyone was moving in on his location.

"Go."

"Congratulations on your recently gained freedom."

Gordan recognized the caller. "What can I do for you, General Seibert?"

"You should understand that I am a chess player, Mr. Hudde. You do not have me at a disadvantage." Seibert sounded very confident; Gordan began looking around, feeling that he must have missed a tail.

"That's odd, General. I got the feeling that your entire plan was beginning to come undone."

The General chuckled. "Far from it. Now you need to go meet with the good doctor and a few of his friends to discuss what will be required of you next."

It was Gordan's turn to chuckle. "Fat chance I go any-where near your facility out in the woods. No — it's just the opposite. I'm heading home for a shower and some sleep. Any of your clowns who come sniffing around will be returned in a box."

"Mr. Hudde, that is just not who you are. I know you think you are heroic, and I am telling you that we know you would more than likely try to save your friend. You did save his wife, at least for the moment, did you not?"

"What I'll probably do is just call my contacts in the FBI and send them; it's not my problem, really."

Gordan could not discern any nervousness in the General's voice. "What you will do is go meet my people; you don't want us killing our other captives."

"Who else you got up there?"

"Mr. Hudde, there is a parking garage under con-struction near the VA hospital where you first met the doctor."

Gordan thought he remembered it. "So?"

"So be there, unarmed, in an hour, and the doctor will fill you in. Anything other than this, and additional, unnecessary deaths will be on your head; of this I assure you."

The call was terminated. Gordan took apart his phone back into the three pieces and put them back into his pocket.

Gordan drove from the parking lot onto the road. He was only twenty minutes out, and he guessed that the doctor and whoever else he had with him was already on site.

Gordan drove past the construction site by a block, to the east; the garage was going up in the center of a horseshoe-shaped ring of business buildings. The VA hospital was two blocks south and east. Gordan parked there, looking across where Walter Schroeder's car once sat near a fast-food joint. Gordan's truck clock showed 2110 hrs. Business hours were over for almost all businesses, and he knew nearly all those buildings would be empty except for security guards and cleaning crews.

He walked slowly back to the garage, ever vigilant for anyone tailing him, always reminding himself to look up. He knew he had more than enough time, and he was determined to find a way to get the information that had been teased by Seibert without getting himself caught again.

The building site was typical. It was ringed by a flimsy hurricane fence. There was enough unpaved area around the growing garage that, without rain, it would be a dusty, dirty job site; with rain, it would be a muddy mess. Two large, green steel trash bins were off to one side of the site, where it would be easy to back a truck in to haul them off.

The garage was six stories high. The first four floors appeared to be completed, while the top two floors were obviously still under construction as they were walled off by bright-orange two-by-four constructed rails.

The exit looked nearly complete, although the booths for payment did not have the bright-orange arms to deter people from driving through. There were several large speed bumps that looked like they needed to be shaved down a bit just past the booths.

Gordan allowed his eyes to follow the construction crane that loomed above; he did not see anything out of place but felt eyes on him.

Gordan sprinted across the open ground into the first floor of the garage. The smell of concrete and dirt filled his nostrils. It was not unlike what his own home smelled like when it was being constructed.

The stairwell in the northeast corner had no doors yet. This floor was devoid of any other humans, so Gordan climbed the stairs.

At each floor, he dissected the open floor with the handgun he had taken from the Dancer. Each floor was as empty as the last until he looked around the fifth floor. There, he could look up through the ramp and see the large silver Mercedes trunk and rear-left tire sticking out from behind a stack of pallets up on the final floor.

Gordan walked silently up to the next floor. He set each foot down toe first and then slowly allowed the rest of his weight to shift until his entire body weight was fully on the floor. He knew that no one would hear him coming even if they were standing just outside the final stairwell door. Two pallets stood leaning against the door frame, and Gordan paused there, trying to see past them, into the twenty percent of the open floor that he could see.

"Please join us, Gordan. No need to lurk there in the shadows." It was the British accent of doctor Watanabe.

Left-handed, Gordan pulled the handgun up to "cut" the corner, moving slowly around until he could see the good doctor down the barrel of the gun.

Watanabe took a radio off of the sedan's roof. "Let him know that you are here."

A red dot danced on the wall to Gordan's left, and another was flicking over his hands before him and then onto his chest. Gordan rolled back onto his heels and then stood up, leaning on the other side of the pallets against the cool concrete block wall.

The doctor called out again. "Do us a favor, and come out to talk with us. Don't worry — we have no desire to shoot you."

"I told the General I was on my way home; you don't have anything that interests me!"

"Oh, Mr. Hudde. You have no idea what we have. Why don't you speed this up and call your girlfriend for us?"

"I don't have a girlfriend, doctor. I live alone. Try again."

Gordan looked over the railing to see if this was a diversion to have someone come up from under him.

Louis Monreau called out with his distinctive French accent, "Oh, you should brag about having such a fine woman, Hudde. I can tell you that the Indian bitch from

Georgia really wanted to fight before she went down. Maybe we call the boys and let them play until we get back. You know the satellite TV isn't up and running yet, so there is not so much to do."

Gordan completed putting his phone back together; the light given off from the small screen seemed intense after the relative darkness. He scrolled down until he saw her name: Valerie Baker. He allowed the phone to dial.

Gordan yelled out while he waited. "How the hell did you come up with that tenuous connection?"

Gordan heard the first ring from the phone. There was no tune or funny sound — just a simple ring.

Monreau yelled back, "When your friend Walter wanted to speak to you, you called back using her phone. Since then, she is the only other person you have called from your own phone."

Gordan hung his head, thinking about how a few simple phone calls had put Valerie Baker at risk. His head went back up when he heard the ring coming from somewhere out on the open sixth floor.

After Watanabe was sure Gordan had heard the ringing, he answered.

"I'm sorry. Valerie can't come to the phone right now."

"What do you want?" Gordan said through gritted teeth.

"Come on out," Watanabe said. "I promise that the girl will not be a part of my tests."

Gordan set the handgun on the top of the wooden pallet and stepped slowly out into the night sky, hands held high.

Monreau reached into his pocket and slid a not-very-well-named set of brass knuckles on over his fingers — they were shiny and made of a highly polished steel. Then he pulled his glove back over to hide them; he squeezed his hand closed into a fist and watched with satisfaction as the fine leather stretched across the rectangular shape underneath.

• • •

Valerie Baker was standing on the opposite wall, under the TV and on the hinged side of the door, in case anyone came through.

"Why?" she screamed at the top of her lungs at the ceiling, where she knew a CCTV camera was looking down at her.

She had to know why this was happening to her; she felt it would help her to find some kind of peace under the strange circumstances.

At first, she imagined that she'd been dropped into some pervert's elaborate basement for some kind of sick sexual satisfaction, but now she no longer believed that.

If she'd been imprisoned for violating some law, well, then she would know what she had done to get there.

Crazy people.

Her mind had begun to repeat that over and over. She knew what that meant: Crazy people don't know why they are locked up.

She shook the thought from her head, at least temporarily. It was ridiculous.

You finally did something. You wigged out, and they threw you in here, for everyone else's protection.

"Bullshit," she yelled out.

She still had her boot laces. There was a blanket. What kind of mental institution would allow that?

Where you gonna hang yourself?

She looked up; there was no way the tallest person in the world could get to that height.

Valerie shook it all from her thoughts. It just couldn't be.

Well, then...why?

She slid into the corner and covered herself with the blanket, rocking herself to sleep, keeping warm and keeping possible prying eyes off of her at the same time.

• • •

Gordan stepped out into the breeze, taking in the entire site first and then narrowing his field of vision.

The little red dots continued to dance across his chest.

"Don't make us kill you here," Watanabe called over to him.

Gordan looked at the small tent set up at the higher end of the parking floor. He looked at the pile of sand and the pallets of rebar; a forklift was parked there, too. A small trailer was set up, probably where the boss sat and drank coffee while the worker bees took care of the hard labor.

The crane rose up from that end on the northwest corner; it seemed to travel upward another four or five stories above them.

Near the nose of the Mercedes, four men were standing. Gordan recognized Monreau and Watanabe but not the additional muscle. Allen and Hans were standing on either side of Watanabe in the "ready" stance, unsure if they were going to have to fight or shoot. With those four and the two dots — and maybe a driver for the snipers — Gordan guessed his current odds at seven to one.

Gordan walked around the hole for the ramp that he imagined, once completed, would have a railing. The three bodyguards stepped forward as Gordan approached so that Watanabe was "safer."

Gordan stopped about ten feet away. "So you make a call right now, and let her go."

Watanabe laughed. It was high pitched and sounded quite feminine.

"Mr. Hudde, I never said I would let her go — just that I would not use her as a lab rat." He smiled from behind the heaviest of the men.

Gordan looked at Monreau on his right, the heavier dark man in the middle, and another thin, quick-looking fellow on his left.

Watanabe continued, "What I think I will do is to put her in a room with you after I dose you with MC-Z22. Then I will tell you to kill her. See if all that training can overcome my drugs."

Hudde was going over all the different scenarios for stopping the three men in front of him, hopefully ending with him behind the engine of the sedan as cover from one shooter and with the pallets protecting him from the other.

Then he thought about Valerie and another woman who had entered his life, only to find danger — or worse.

He tossed all his plans and charged forward, too fast for the snipers. He caught the largest of them flat footed and drove an elbow into his face; it was not good enough to put the man down.

Gordan kicked at Watanabe, his toes touching the little man's sternum just as the quick Monreau struck him in the jaw, snapping his neck, and putting Hudde to sleep long enough that he didn't remember going to the ground.

The three men encircled Hudde and began kicking him. As he regained consciousness, he tried to grab a leg and then rolled left and right, trying desperately to protect himself. Monroe hit him again in the temple, and Gordan fell unconscious.

Watanabe called out on the radio, "You men may come down now. Please drive up here and pick up Mr. Hudde. I don't think he is going to be much of a problem for now, and I don't need his blood in my trunk."

Gordan rolled into a ball and moved only enough to attempt to protect his kidneys and head. If this was going to be a final moment, it was not going to be a proud one. An old wound above his right eye had been torn open, and the jagged cut was pouring blood.

"Hey! Hey! That is enough," Watanabe yelled at his three men. "I want him alive for my tests! Now search him for anything, and let's get back."

Monreau felt around the jacket pockets and held up the key fob, with one house key on it, and Gordan's wallet. Monreau held the items out to Watanabe, who placed them into his own jacket's left pocket. Then he climbed into the passenger seat of the silver sedan. Monreau walked back and spit on Gordan as the other two went to their ride. "*Je te tuerai,*" he said as he walked away.

Hans smiled a big bloody smile at the Frenchman Graham as Monreau slid into the driver's seat and they began to move; he looked out his window and saw Hudde trying to sit upright.

"That bloke's going to be pissing blood for a week." He turned back and smiled again.

Gordan rose to his feet. The world went in and out of focus as he swayed uneasily on his feet, watching the silver sedan's roof slip silently under the concrete. The first thing he laid eyes on was the forklift.

He stumbled the two dozen feet to the forklift, traveling in a serpentine movement, due to his equilibrium — not the fear of a potential shooter. Jumping into the seat, he turned the key and put it into gear. The forklift moved forward, sliding the pallet in front of it with a large pile of rebar. He kept his foot on the floor, making the propane gas engine purr while he pulled back on one of the mechanical arms.

The lift began tilting back toward him, but that's not what Gordan was trying to do. He turned the wheel to follow the Mercedes into the concrete depths. He lifted up on another lever, watching the pallet rise up. Then the forklift approached the down ramp, gaining speed.

Suddenly a new idea formulated in his head, and he turned the wheel enough to go past the down ramp in the direction of the stairwell he had come out of.

Gordan pictured the Mercedes coming out of the ramp below only to find the way blocked; he knew he could not slow them down otherwise.

The forklift bounced toward the bright-orange two-by-four railing encompassing the wall-less floor. Gordan steered it toward the middle, where he had seen the payment booths below.

As the pallet full of rebar crashed through the worthless railing, Gordan dove off of the driver's seat, rolling in the direction of the stairwell. The bright yellow forklift disappeared over the edge.

He may have passed out for a second or two because he did not hear the crash.

Gordan stumbled into the stairwell and grabbed the handgun he had left on the pallet earlier. He did his best to run down the six flights, keeping his mind on coming out of the doors at the bottom. He was prepared to begin shooting at the men who would be trying to clear the way.

Except that isn't what happened. Gordan stumbled at the end of the last steps, his forward momentum sending him tumbling, trying to regain his balance and his footing.

He failed; falling and sliding forward, peeling skin off the palms of his hand as he slid to a stop. Blood pooled under his face as he lay once again momentarily unconscious. The handgun had slid forward, stopping near the back tire of the motionless Mercedes.

28

GENERAL SEIBERT CLOSED up shop for the night. The Sergeant in charge jumped to attention and saluted smartly as he passed.

The Captain who drove his staff car saluted as he approached. Seibert flipped a terrible salute in return and then stepped aside, waiting for the back door to be opened.

"Late night for you, General," the Captain noted.

Seibert paused before ducking into the Ford. "I just need to have the old desk cleared for tomorrow night. I haven't missed a Friday night yet. I'm not ruining a perfect record this late in my career." Then he disappeared into the back of the car.

The Captain climbed into the front and turned the six cylinders over; he turned a knob, and the headlights cut out a large wedge of darkness before them.

Seibert looked at his phone. He had a desire to call, but they had a plan, and he decided he would allow it to play out. After all, he had told the men to call him if they ran into any problems. Seibert was not going to allow insecurities to weaken him at this point. He was going to go home, have a drink, and relax in his favorite chair. He stuffed the phone back into his leather satchel, rested his head on the raised headrest, and closed his eyes. Everything was going as planned.

In fact, he had already begun to lay the groundwork for the next part of his plan. He had reached out to a Colonel in the Chemical Defense offices at the Pentagon. He smiled to himself; they could not ignore his requests for review. The drugs, after all, already existed; this was no "what if" scenario.

So, ultimately, they had to work with him — at a minimum, to learn how to protect our own forces. But he was confident that they would pick the "team" up for offensive weapons systems as well.

They would pay the doctor a figure so substantial that it would be ridiculous, and they would pay Seibert to stay on to wrangle the doctor for the US government. In uniform or as a civilian, he would be the doctor whisperer. Now the general grinned at his own genius. He guessed this would take him to retirement in most likely the easiest job he had ever performed.

He just needed everything to go as planned through Saturday, and then all the pieces would be there, in place, just waiting to work as he had planned. Even Ryan over at Defense had agreed that the military would go along with the operation once the results were in. If you were confident in the results, then it was always better to beg for forgiveness than ask for permission in the armed forces.

All the years he had worried that he would be discovered as a fraud were now behind him. He let out an audible sigh. From here on out, his life would be on Easy Street, and he would retire immediately when he was offered the new position. Being a wealthy civilian contractor would change his life, and he knew it. Yes, sir — he was going to be on Easy Street from here on out, and there was no looking back.

• • •

Gordan regained consciousness like a sub breaching. He rolled up onto his feet, albeit on very unsteady legs, and stumbled over to pick up the 9mm. When you've been "out," you never know whether it had been several seconds or hours.

Gordan stretched out to his full height and took several deep breaths as he tried to believe the image before him.

It's better to be lucky than good.

The forklift had come down almost dead center on the Mercedes. It had landed sideways, and some of the rebar had spread out in a haphazard pattern in front of the vehicle.

The top of the roll cage was dug into the roof, and he couldn't quite make out that there once had been a human driving. The roof was crushed down to where it was touching the seat bottom. Glancing into the now-teardrop-shaped rear passenger window, where Hudde knew Watanabe had been sitting, he could make out the left shoulder of the doctor, and he could follow most of his left side. But his head had been crushed downward and backward, possibly now resting in the trunk by the heavy back end of the forklift. The other side of the Mercedes was crushed even lower, and the frame of the car bent upward in the middle, causing the front and back wheels to actually lift slightly up off the pavement.

Gordan's arm barely fit into the crushed window. He felt around and reached into Watanabe's front-left jacket pocket, removing everything. He laid out the contents onto the concave roof for further inspection. Hudde put his own key fob and phone back into his pocket. He looked at the items that were left — a magnetic card with several small keys attached. He turned it over and found nothing interesting on the card, which made it very interesting, Hudde added it to his own pocket.

Gordan went back into the stairwell, sitting on the third step up; he ignored the "Missed Call" icon and con-tacted Bulldog Mahoney.

"Bulldog, I need your FBI friends to close down a crime scene. I can't fill you in right now, but I can if you can also meet me out at the following address." Hudde texted the info and then stopped even breathing while he listened.

Gordan heard a vehicle drive up and doors close.

He set the phone down and frog-marched over to one of the exit booths still standing guard after the violence of the crashing forklift.

Gordan peeked through the glass window of the small structure; he could see two men approaching from a white panel van. They were both armed, but they were preoccupied with the amazing sight before them. It appeared as if neither of them had ever seen a flying forklift land on a car. Gordan shot them both center mass and then once to the head as he ran past them.

He never slowed down. Charging up he threw open the doors at the back of the van, sweeping it with the muzzle of his gun. The van was empty; there had been no driver for the snipers.

Gordan went back and collected his phone.

"I need a few days where this doesn't get out, Bulldog; do you think you can do it?"

"What the fuck is going on there?" Bulldog asked.

"A bunch of foreign-born terrorists is what it looks like to me."

"But...it's not; is that what you're saying?" Bulldog was confused.

"If you make it out to the country address, then armor up. These assholes aren't playing."

"Roger that."

Gordan walked back to his truck. He used the fishing tacklebox filled with medical supplies to superglue his forehead back together and then put several butterfly Band-Aids to ensure that held up. Then he put on a bigger patch.

Good as new!

He pulled out his seat and looked at the ammo he always had stored under there. He discovered a terrible flaw in his planning for disaster. If he lost his .45, then packing the back seat with extra .45 ammo didn't help; especially when he had stolen a 9mm handgun.

Back in his own truck, he set his jaw and started heading west out to the hangar. Somebody was going to have a bad Friday morning.

29

THE AGENT IN charge dragged Mahoney around to the same stairwell Gordan had stumbled out of forty-five minutes earlier. Mahoney was dressed in jeans and a dark jacket; the agent was layered in full urban tactical gear.

"Mahoney — just look at this." He pointed back at the pile of steel and blood behind him. "We all know you have more knowledge about this thing, so you'd better start giving me something, or I'm dragging you in as an accessory. There are at least five or six bodies over there, and they appeared to be heavily armed!"

Mahoney smiled. "'Five or six'?"

The agent took a deep breath and looked up as he pointed at the crane overhead "We're trying to get someone to use that thing to lift the forklift. Maybe we can be sure then."

Mahoney nodded. "Why don't you give me two shooters to check on a lead, and then you guys can catch up later if it pans out."

"I can't leave this crime scene."

"Yeah — that's why I said 'shooters.'" He pointed at a Virginia state-y walking in their direction. "You'd better shut this place down, brother." And he started out to his car.

• • •

Gordan took the east turn onto the dirt road that would take him to the secret structure deep in the woods. He paused to shake out his hands; two times he had had to slow down to make sure he wasn't pulled over by some local cop while he sped there.

Now he turned off his lights and crept forward, keeping himself between the ditches and keeping the noise level at a minimum.

He had contemplated for the entire hour and still wasn't sold on any plan. He couldn't wait and hope for reinforcements via Bulldog. Besides, the Famous But Incompetent would encircle the area, put up tents, and sell hotdogs and lemonade to the media for a week before they decided on a course of action.

No, if he had friends, another woman he liked, trapped in that facility, then tonight they all go home. He had been toying with reaching out to the guard at the

gate in an attempt to get these foreigners to give up and
go home, but he knew that it was a pipe dream and not
a viable option. The fact that Seibert was using foreign-
born talent off the post was enough proof for Hudde
that this entire operation, so far, was not approved
officially.

Gordan hated to use his phone in the case someone
was still listening, but his curiosity was too much.

"Hey, Kid. Do me another favor and search for high-
ranking government officials who've made large investments over the last two years in the company Biophaze.
Look closely at the Department of Justice; I'm sure
there's at least one. Thanks."

Gordan hung up just as he reached the left turnoff to
the toolshed. If he continued around the corner to the
right another half mile, he would run into the gate and
small guard shack.

Gordan went left and backed into the foliage near
the shed, much as he had done previously. He ensured
that he did not touch the brakes except briefly when he
placed it into park. Gordan stepped up onto the deuce
truck and opened the door. Somebody had modernized
it with bucket seats and a more modern-looking dash.
Hudde liked the look; he also appreciated the key.

Hudde walked back down the road and hung to the
left side of the road, picking his way until he could make
out the guard shack. The small light above the lone

sentry ensured that his night vision was ruined and that, most likely, he was unable to see out into the night.

Typical of this time of year, the cold, moist air was touching the warmer, damp ground, causing fog to rise up. It swirled and moved with a mind of its own as it came down the open road to settle in the open field behind the guard.

Gordan tried to determine the math of how many men would be required to secure a place like this. They were using three men around the clock — one in the shack and two that seemed to rove together. Would they use two or three sets? Gordan would want three, so that they would be fresher. That's nine men for perimeter. Now, for the interior. This was a total guess on Gordan's part but there had to be a minimum of, say, eight more men. So, if he planned for seventeen to twenty-five men, he wouldn't be too upset if he was one or two off in either direction.

Gordan knew that he had only eleven rounds at his disposal.

Out in front of him, he could see the two roving guards begin to emerge from the thickening mist. At that moment, Hudde decided on his plan, and he scurried back to the big green deuce back at the equipment shed.

He said a silent prayer after he turned the key and then pressed the start button. Within a moment, the familiar whine of a big diesel created a warmth in Hudde's heart.

He put it into gear and began heading out. As he approached the turn, which was more relaxed heading to the guard shack than if you came from the street, he punched it. Picking up speed, he rounded the corner, the tires sliding in the dirt as he pushed for fourth gear.

His prayers were answered because the two roving guards were still leaning onto the guard shack, shooting the shit with the gatekeeper.

Gordan pointed the two tons of steel at the center of the shack and turned on the headlights before impact. He saw the guard inside the shack briefly hold up his hand in front of his face; then he leaned over to protect himself in case something made it up through the windshield.

The big truck bounced, and sparks flew from steel-on steel contact; the fence held onto the big I-beam bumper, and a sixty-foot section dragged behind. Hudde hit the brakes and jumped out after placing the rig into neutral, allowing it to stop wherever it wanted to.

Hudde charged back at the gate with the 9mm at the ready; the gun was not necessary. One man had been crushed at the gate, and it appeared that another had been struck solidly by the front of the truck and thrown fifty feet off to the left.

That man was still breathing until Hudde put him out of his misery with the heel of his boot; there would be no heroic action by a man Hudde had given mercy to tonight. There would be no testimony from any man he found here tonight. They were holding his people as lab rats, and now they would die like vermin. He would not allow anyone injured to gather their strength to kill when no one was paying attention and maybe lie in wait out here until Gordan returned from the hangar.

Gordan scanned around and found an AK-47 with a folding stock lying off to the side; he still hadn't found a third guard, and he began to worry. He walked silently around the back of the deuce and found a body and fencing wound up into the back wheels; he would never threaten anyone.

Hudde walked up to the edge of the turn to the south that he knew would bring the hangar into view.

There it stood, like a small mountain peak growing up out of the primordial mists. Hudde threw caution to the wind and just ran as fast as he could to the front corner of the steel building.

The steel was cold on his back as he stood catching his breath and keeping an eye left and right. There was no sign of any activity; he walked across the huge aircraft door in the direction of the tiny glowing light near the single, seemingly tiny man-door.

Hudde fished into his pocket and came out with the doctor's magnetic card. If this didn't pan out, he felt he had the ultimate can opener parked behind him a hundred yards back.

There was a familiar clunking noise as the lock released. Gordan eased into the space behind using the AK-47 to sweep in front of him. Directly to his front, just a dozen steps away was a cement structure; Hudde quickly ran there for cover. There was a small light overhead. Hudde peeked around the corner, and the darkness was broken up by lights to the right, where some vehicles were parked. There was what appeared to be a large freight elevator standing alone, and one more small light further to the back of the structure. Hudde could not make out what that was from this distance.

The structure he was standing behind turned out to hold a steel door with another card reader on the side. Obviously, everything here was underground; nothing was above ground except these entrances and parking.

Hudde picked slowly through the assortment of vehicles until he could charge quickly across less dead space to the elevator. It also had a card reader and a key. Hudde passed the card, and the cage lock released. He ignored it and went to the side of this structure to look back deeper into the darkness and the single light there.

It was another door standing alone, like the one behind him.

They have to have emergency exits. No one uses the staircases — especially the back one. It must be two hundred yards to the vehicles.

Hudde waited and listened; he could hear nothing. He made another dash across the asphalt to the door, standing at the rear of the building. He kneeled and allowed his heartbeat to slow.

He waved the card and gained access. It looked like the top floor of a stairwell in any concrete building. Light-grey concrete and dark-green steel railings; three black "no slip" strips went across the entire five-foot-long step.

Hudde eased over the center of the railing and looked down — five or six flights at a minimum. He slid along the outside wall and then stepped forward at the landing to scan with the muzzle of the AK. There was no activity inside the stairwell, and Hudde made it to the first door.

He did not need the magnetic card to gain entry here. He stepped silently into the brighter lights of a long hall-way. There were three doors that Hudde could discern on each side of the hall, with no apparent pattern.

The first door was on Hudde's left; he listened and didn't hear anything. He opened the door without need of the key and conducted a visual scan. It was storage of some kind; farther down, there were swinging doors heading farther into the building.

Hudde passed by all kinds of boxes marked as flour and other dry-goods. Halfway down, Hudde could make out what appeared to be a large walk-in cooler. In the room to his right, Hudde could hear some noises: water running, metal pans clanking together.

Hudde tapped the door enough so that he could get his fingers on the edge and pull back to peek inside. It was a kitchen, complete with large stainless-steel pots and pans hanging over large stainless-steel prep tables. Someone was washing dishes to the left. Hudde fell back and headed to the door he'd come in from; he wasn't going to kill the cook.

He checked the hall and then crab-walked to the first door on the right. He entered, and the lights all came on automatically. It was a well-equipped gym, with no occupants; the wall was mirrored to ensure that strict adherence to proper form was practiced — or maybe just for vanity.

Hudde guessed that the next door on the opposite side led to the kitchen that he had just observed, so he walked to the next door on the same side.

Now he heard voices or music.

He took a couple of deep breaths and closed his eyes; at the ready, he raised the muzzle and got into a shooter's crouch. Grasping the lever, he pulled down and leaned in.

• • •

Bulldog Mahoney couldn't wait any longer. He didn't look for the agent in charge; he just stepped under the crime tape and headed for his car. The FBI had gotten the contractor out of bed and demanded that he get down there to fire up the portable light towers and operate the crane.

The crime-scene nerds were beginning to swarm, setting small reflectors up at every important spot and then scanning to get a 3D image for some future court proceeding.

All incredibly high tech, but Mahoney didn't need all that to figure out what had happened here; he just needed to talk to Gordan Hudde.

He slammed the door shut to his Dodge Charger and allowed the over rotation from too much gas clean the tread of his tires from any mud that the site had packed in. He pushed the car through its paces; he didn't fear the police. He understood that he was at least an hour behind, but this confiscated car was the closest thing to a time machine; he would do his best to catch up.

• • •

Hudde froze; he was standing in a long, barracks-like room. There were a dozen bunks along the inside wall and ten more on the opposite side. The voices he'd heard turned out to be coming from a TV further to the right; he heard shower noises from a room to the left.

The problem was that three bunks were filled with sleeping bodies.

Hudde waited for two long, slow breaths to ensure that the three were actually asleep and then slowly walked in the direction of the noise. He crept to the edge of the room and then began shuffling his feet as he cut the corner.

He stopped momentarily as his front sight stopped upon a shaggy blond head sticking up from a plush chair. Hudde crouched even lower and shuffled a bit further; a second head stuck up from a sofa, a large-screen TV holding their attention. Hudde paused, holding his front sight on the second target.

"*Was zum Teufel!*" someone screamed out from behind Hudde.

Hudde squeezed off two rounds, the AK-47 rising more than he wanted. The first shot stuck dead-center mass on the sofa, and the man fell forward. The blonde stood and turned in surprise, taking three rounds: the first in the abdomen, the second in the chest, and the last in the chin.

Hudde didn't even watch the man fall. He had already turned to engage movement at the bunk beds.

He had killed two men scrambling from their bunks before the third realized that he would not get his locker opened fast enough, and he screamed something in French as he was put down; Hudde found the cordite smell to be comforting.

Hudde shuffled his feet in the direction of where he had heard the shower and whoever had yelled out in German. He got his back to the sinks and kept the muzzle pointed toward the next room over.

He first observed bathroom stalls. He couldn't see feet under the walls; each of the four doors was open, and none were swinging. A foyer opened up to a large, open shower room; at the end of the bathroom wall was obviously the third door at the end of this hall. Hudde could make out wet footprints out that door.

Hudde went to the door, pulled it open, and pointed both ways with the barrel before stepping out into the hallway. The wet footprints led back toward the barracks door. Hudde quickly doubled back and went through the bathroom. He kneeled and looked around into the barracks. He could see feet under the open door of one of the large wall lockers. He put three rounds into that door, and a man in only a towel took two steps backwards, firing off a round into the ceiling from an AR-style rifle.

Hudde fired two more, and one of the bunkbed mattresses burst into cotton chunks as the bullets tore through it on the way to the dead man.

There was no longer silence; Hudde's ears had a continuous, high-pitched tone ripping through them that impeded his ability to trust his hearing.

There was a noise that broke through the steady monotone whine; he went into the hall to find that the elevator had just moved. According to the light overhead, it was moving to the ground floor. Hudde ran to the door at the end of the hall and charged up the steps.

He knew he would exit in front of the vehicles between them and the only exit.

He stopped at the steel door for a moment and waited until he heard the mechanism used to swing that giant door skyward began to clank.

Hudde opened the door to find a car sitting at the door, waiting for it to get high enough to escape. He fired half a dozen rounds into the driver's-side door, hitting the glass with the last shot. The driver stomped on the gas, and the tires squealed, burning rubber while the hood pressed up against the steel door. Finally, the front began to slide under the door.

The steel screamed out — a high-pitched wail that broke through Hudde's tinnitus — and the car rocketed out from under the door, leaving a lot of paint behind. Hudde ran and ducked at the last second, firing off every round he had left. The car never changed course. It just crashed into the wood line dead ahead.

Hudde caught up and looked in. The driver had probably been dead while the vehicle was still inside the hangar, and Hudde had probably fired off the last ten rounds for no reason. He threw the empty AK into the woods and walked back into the now totally open hangar. He disappeared into the first stairwell, hoping the second floor was much less exciting.

While the element of surprise was obviously gone, Hudde still stealthily crept down the steel stairwell. He passed the first floor and stepped toe to heel, now using the 9mm to point the way.

He opened the second-floor steel door slowly; there was nothing inside except grey doors both left and right, with no apparent intervals, down a bright-white hallway.

The first door on the left opened into a bathroom, but, unlike the one above, it had three stalls for showers along with three bathroom stalls. The wall directly behind was mirrored with multiple sinks.

Hudde crouched and peeked around the small open archway that led down another hallway with four doors spaced about ten feet apart. Directly above him, there was a barracks-like sleeping quarters set up for many men. Hudde opened the first door and found a small bed along with a refrigerator that would have looked at home in any dorm room across America. A bookshelf and small desk with all the connections needed for a computer sat empty.

Gordan began to speed up his search; none of these rooms seemed occupied. At the last, he found another door to the hallway. Once in the hall, Gordan could see two doors missed on the right side. He opened the first and found the lab with all the new stainless-steel equipment, computers, chalkboards, and lab desks.

Looking back, he could see a glass-enclosed large office at the very back of this lab. He needed the magnetic key to gain entry; it had one small lab desk as well as a very modern glass-and-steel business desk. There were two dozen scientific journals and other study materials on a shelf behind the desk, right next to a large stainless-steel-and-glass refrigerator.

Oh, you liked shiny things — didn't you, doctor? Gordan didn't need to open the door, as it was glass, but he tried the key that was hanging off the magnetic card, just for curiosity's sake. It turned.

There were dozens of numbered vials, duplicates of many, all neatly stacked and in order, from the MC-Z-22 the doctor had bragged about to the MC-Z-01 near the bottom of the shelf. There were other items, with totally different nomenclatures. Gordan wondered what the hell they did.

He noticed a small silver ring set into the wall, and he pushed it, stepping back, waiting for something to happen. The ring popped out and now stood at a forty-five degree angle to the floor.

He pushed to see if the wall panel slid inward but was rewarded when he grasped the ring and pulled. The panel swiveled at the center, allowing a man of Watanabe's size to walk through. Gordan had to turn sideways to get inside.

It was a bedroom, much more luxurious than the others across the hall; he also had a small bathroom all his own. There was clothing and some personal things strewn about but no photos. There was nothing that would help you find the man that was going to live here.

Gordan exited the lab, never letting his guard down, although he was beginning to believe that he was all alone — at least on this floor. The other doors opened to other things he imagined were important for science and medical research. There was no need for him to enter and search. He just had to step, in allowing the lights to come on automatically and him to search visually.

There was one grey door at the end of the hall on the left wall. Standing near the door, Gordan knew this was the entrance to the steel stairwell that he had used earlier to search the first floor.

Hudde paused and listened. When he heard nothing, he opened the last grey door and stepped into the darkness. He closed his eyes to quickly bring back his night vision, but when he opened them, he found that a red light glowed everywhere down a long, narrow hallway. He began walking and could see what appeared to be a service desk of some kind with many monitors, buttons, and levers.

He looked until he found what appeared to be a power switch; he said a small prayer and hit the green button. Behind the previously dark glass in front of him, lights began blinking on in consecutive sequencing.

"What the fuck?" Gordan couldn't believe the size of the room below. Just above him, the three monitors went from dark to lit. One by one, Gordan began to see what could only be described as cells begin to light up. There seemed to be a five-second delay as the screens changed from one cell to the next.

In some of the images, there seemed to be an individual sleeping; in others, people were sitting or looking up in the direction of the cameras.

Gordan stepped forward when he recognized Walter Schroeder, who was standing and scratching his head. Then that screen switched to another, and Gordan's jaw dropped. Valerie Baker was sitting on a metal bunk; then the video feed switched, and Gordan yelled out.

"No!"

He looked at the panel and tried to get the video feed to stop, but he was afraid to hit any other button or switch. Instead, he tried to decide how he might release the locks to all the doors he could see below — all fifty of them.

On the far right-hand side of the desk, a small screen offered one through fifty, in order. It was a touch screen, and when Gordan touched a number, it became highlighted in a green square. At the bottom of the screen was the ALL option. Gordan touched this, and all the numbers now were highlighted. Gordan pulled down on the lever adjacent, and then he looked below.

All the doors below, marked #1 to #50 opened in unison; faces appeared in the door frames. Gordan looked left and right and then ran down to the doorway at the end of the catwalk. Inside this door, the catwalk continued further into the ground; there was a ladder that disappeared into the darkness below.

Gordan stuffed the handgun into his belt and swung out onto the ladder, descending into relative darkness. The ladder ended, and Gordan found himself in an electrical/equipment room. There was a single door with a large mechanism at the center and something like an old ship's helm. He grasped it and began to turn it.

30

BULLDOG MAHONEY MADE the left-hand turn onto the dirt road and realized that he'd better slow down before he needed to be extracted from a crash. Unlike fog on the coast, this was a thick, ground-based mist that seemed to end five feet above the ground. His Charger cut through it like a knife, but his headlights, unfortunately, did not — in fact, they made it worse.

He crept up to the road that split off to the left and hit his brakes. Behind him, the mist lit up like a movie screen painted in blood. He put the car in park and shut it off, getting out of the car in darkness.

Mahoney closed his eyes and listened. Besides woodland creatures and a slight breeze blowing through the top of the trees, he heard nothing but the big engine beginning to cool. He walked in front of his car and around an easy arc to the right; he just had a feeling that there was open space ahead. He walked back to the Charger and leaned in to get out the M4 rifle, several extra magazines, and the body armor Hudde had suggested.

The noise of the Velcro separating was a hundred times magnified standing alone in the slowly rising tide of this fog. As a right-hander, he hugged the left side of the dirt road and walked forward without the car. His front sight scanned ahead, panning left to right.

A piece of aluminum caught Mahoney's eye, and he crossed the road to see that it was part of a chain-link hurricane fence that was lying twisted off the side of the road. Mahoney followed until the fence twisted itself upright and continued off into the woods, standing the way it should. He walked carefully back to the road, stepping between strands of razor wire, and found the flattened gate along with splintered wood and sheet metal.

A body lay just a bit farther off to the left, and Mahoney knelt to check for a pulse. The body was cold, and he could feel no heartbeat.

As he continued forward, a familiar old beast appeared from the primordial mist. Mahoney followed a length of fence to its back wheels, where he encountered the next body.

He shook his head. *What the fuck has Hudde gotten into this time, and could I be too late?*

He fought the urge to run and crouched to continue forward. An open field opened up before him, with

the large steel hangar holding the ground ahead, chal-
lenging him to keep coming. The fog moved with every
breath of wind, and his eyes watered as he tried desperately to keep them focused; his brain kept screaming
about movement as light played tricks in the diamond-
encrusted blanket of moisture.

He walked carefully up to the car wedged between
the trees. He glanced inside to make sure there were
no threats; the man inside was certainly not one. He did
not touch the car, something he had learned quickly in
Afghanistan; he just knelt beside it, using it as cover. He
sat, looking into the ominous cavern of the open hangar door; he could see there was some lighting inside
but no sign of movement or human activity. He had no
idea what he might be walking into, and he weighed his
options.

• • •

Some kind of seal released, and the heavy steel door
swung inward. Gordan stepped out onto the floor, with
forty-nine other people.

He could see confusion on the faces of several
nearby men. Across the vast room, several men were
already attempting to open the doors there. Gordan
smiled at how these people almost immediately began
to work together to get out of their predicament. If this

had been an attack on politicians, Gordan felt that they would be holding a vote to see who was in charge.

Gordan began walking in the direction of the other side of the room. He whistled a brief, three-burst whistle. When everyone turned, he put up his left hand and spun it in a small circle multiple times. Every grunt knew this to be the sign to rally-up.

"Hudde! Thank God! What is going on?" Walter Schroeder turned from greeting Andrew James to walk over and hug him before he could say anything.

Gordan strained to look past all the faces that had begun to gather around. Back at cell forty-nine, Gordan made out the face of Valerie Baker peeking out. *A wise thing to do*, he thought.

"I'm here to get you all out. Please stand by. I'll be right back. I need to know if there are any injuries and what they are. Will anyone need assistance walking out of here?

A few murmurs were heard: "Hell, no." But Gordan left them to figure it out.

He approached the cell, where he saw her. "Valerie Baker — it's Gordan Hudde."

She stepped back out, her brows furrowed in thought. "Why...what the hell am I doing here? What the hell are you doing here?"

"It's a long story, and I'll fill you in, but I need to know: Are you alright? Did they hurt you?"

"Scared." She paused and stepped out into the large room "Angry, confused...but I'm alright, I guess. Nobody touched me; they just dumped me in this room, and I didn't know why." She looked at him and reached up, touching his face. "Are *you* alright?"

"I don't know. Some people would argue." Then he smiled at her, giving off confidence. "OK, then. Let's get out of here. Follow me." Gordan turned and headed in the direction of the other forty-eight men.

"SITREP anyone?" Gordan called out as he entered the group.

Schroeder stepped up. "We have a head count of fifty altogether — forty-nine men, all veterans." He paused to look around. "And everyone is walking out on their own power."

"I have never served?" Valerie wondered out loud as many of the men turned to look at her.

One of the men stepped up and looked at Hudde. "Who the hell are you is a good first question."

Hudde nodded at him and turned to point at the last cell at the end of the room. "That's me, back there — number fifty. And she's here because I got away from them." He stood tall and looked around at his platoon. "Who's ready to get the hell out of here?"

"*Oohrah!*" James yelled out. "But we've already been trying; we're all locked in." He pointed over his shoulder at the door with his thumb.

"I've got something for that Jarhead." Gordan patted him on the shoulder and smiled. "Now, listen up. Outside this door is another, leading into a stairway. At the sixth door going up, you will find yourself in a large steel hangar. Everyone got that?"

Everyone was nodding and paying close attention.

"I will head up the other stairwell on the opposite end of the facility and make sure we're clear. You should know that we are about five floors underground right now. Just give me a few extra minutes before you exit that last door."

He pulled the handgun from behind him and held it high.

"I only have this one right now; I'm giving it to the Captain here to lead you guys out."

Hudde walked up to Schroeder and handed him the handgun while placing his other hand flat on his back.

"Remember, Captain — give me five minutes before you exit the stairwell. And, if you need to, make your shots count. That's all we got."

He turned to Valerie and whispered, "Give the captain a few feet of space and then follow. Make sure the man behind you knows you're moving, and I'll see you up top."

He swiped the card at the door, and it hissed and popped open. He peeked out into the long, narrow hallway; there was nothing except grey concrete. Hudde guessed that they hadn't wasted money to beautify the floor designated for the lab rats.

He turned to the left and popped open the stairwell stepping briefly inside.

"It looks all clear, but go slow and keep noise as low as possible."

Schroeder nodded. "Roger that."

Hudde sprinted down the hall, getting to the stairwell door on that end. When he turned, he could see that the men were still filing out and into the stairwell at the opposite end.

He swiped the card and listened; he didn't hear anything. He quickly went up the stairs two at a time until he reached the first floor. He went back onto the floor, working as quickly and quietly as possible — now he was unarmed.

He slipped into the shower room and slowly made his way into the barracks area. There was no movement, and nothing had changed: Six dead bodies. He went to the one open wall locker where the one tango had been trying to get a weapon into play before Hudde had gotten his sights on him.

He stepped past the body and found exactly what he was looking for: The dead man's AR-15. Hudde saw that there were two magazines on a shelf. He cleared and checked the rifle, pulling the trigger to hear a distinctive *Click!* Then he slammed home a full magazine. Pulling back on the charging handle, he ensured the weapon was not on "safe" and then used it to point the way out.

He charged back out and into the stairwell bounding up the stairs until he got to the top door. As silently as possible, he stepped back out into the night air. The fog was heavier outside, but, oddly, it swept past the open hangar door as if there were some kind of ancient treaty that did not allow it to come inside.

Gordan stepped out fully into the hangar and around the concrete frame of the door, using it as cover and concealment from anyone approaching from outside. He looked back into the darkness and saw that the survivors were still inside their own stairwell.

He refocused on the outside and the surrounding area, looking for possible reinforcements for the guards. There was nothing but an eerie silence as he stepped outside and looked around the side of the hangar. Hudde came back in and began walking across the vast, open hangar door when two short whistles came from the tree line near the crashed car.

He dropped and pointed the AR in that direction, waiting.

"Hudde, it's Bulldog!" came a loud whisper from the darkness.

Hudde waited for Bulldog to step out into view before he placed his weapon on "safe" and stood up.

Bulldog walked up and shook Hudde's hand. "Man, did I have you there!"

"Fuck you, Bulldog. My ears are still ringing from firing off a dozen rounds in the bathroom downstairs."

"No shit? You get yourself in a firefight in there?" He began looking past Hudde, trying to see what was inside.

He suddenly raised his rifle and pointed it inside. "We got company!"

Gordan turned and looked inside the hangar; he placed his hand onto the barrel of the M4, pushing it toward the ground.

"Don't you recognize "Captain Court Martial," Bulldog?" Hudde said.

"What the fuck? How many people are in there?"

"Well, I would have been number fifty." Gordan put his hand on Bulldog's back. "Come on inside. Let's figure out what we do from here. I think this place is secure."

Gordan rallied everyone up near the few vehicles parked there. "Stay alert, everyone. I think the place is clear, but you never know — I didn't check every closet. Everyone: This is a friend. You can call him 'Bulldog.'"

Everyone said, "Hello," and then someone said, "Is there anyone else?"

Bulldog stepped up; there was no need to ask for quiet. Everyone seemed to be practicing proper noise discipline.

"I know some FBI folks. I'll get a fire lit and make sure you all get out of here, make sure you get some medical attention, take statements, get some hot chow."

"Just where is 'here'?"

"We're near Fort Valley, Virginia, about an hour and twenty minutes from Washington, DC, actually," Bulldog pointed out. He then got out his phone and began pressing buttons. When it appeared that someone had answered, he held up his hand in the "one moment" sign and stepped away from the small crowd.

Gordan found Valerie and asked her to follow him back to the side of the elevator doors.

"I've got a feeling that these men will be tied up for weeks with the government. They will be looked after, but there will also be lots of questions and concerns."

"So?" Valerie bit her lower lip and raised her eyebrows.

"You don't need to get drawn into all that if you don't want to..."

"What are you suggesting?"

"My truck's parked a couple hundred yards straight through the woods in that direction, if you're up to it. I could get you out of the bureaucratic clusterfuck that this is going to become."

She looked back at the huddled mass of men out front as she thought. "Do you think it would be OK?" she asked.

"I've never been one to ask permission. Here's the catch: I've got some more work to do, and I just got an idea" He stepped in close and whispered, "I need some help. It would just be some driving, and that's all. You can read a map, can't you?"

"Just what is your work, Gordan Hudde?" Her eyes narrowed, and she stepped in close to him. "Why was I here?"

"If you come with me, I can fill you in on everything. Right now, I just don't have time; wait here a moment and think about it."

Hudde ran back down to the stairwell and disappeared back down into the ground. Valerie leaned against the wall and watched the men as they held some kind of conversation with the man that Hudde had introduced as "Bulldog." She felt somehow connected to all of them, even though this was the first time she had ever seen any of them.

She had gotten a lot of sleep and actually eaten fairly well while she was there. She was really physically no worse for wear and knew she didn't need medical attention — maybe a shower. Her brother was in the Marines. She knew the "hurry up and wait" stuff that he always bitched about and weighed those thoughts as she waited.

She heard the door close behind her, and she turned to see Hudde walking with purpose in her direction. He looked beaten to a pulp, but he walked upright, and those deep-set green eyes still gave off an energy of their own. She didn't really know this man at all, but he was obviously a lot more than the wealthy man she had once sold some property to.

Before he could speak, she said, "Let's go."

He almost smiled and changed direction to meet up with Bulldog.

Hudde pulled him aside. "This is going to be a cluster-fuck — you know that."

"Yeah — I was thinking the same thing."

"Listen: The woman's got nothing to with all this. I'm taking her with me."

"And what?" Bulldog asked.

"And I still need time before all this makes the paper or any big waves in Washington."

Bulldog made a face like he smelled something rotten. "Brother, I still have no idea what is going on; you think the FBI is going to ride in here and figure anything out soon?" He chuckled low. "But then, maybe you want to fill me in?"

"I'll give you the *Reader's Digest* version, Bulldog."

"Sure — go ahead."

"Scientist working for failing drug company gets a small group of American B-list government hacks to fund his research through some illegal activities, most likely embezzling and or misappropriating from our Uncle Sam. At a certain point in all of it, said scientist needs human lab rats to advance his studies." He pointed at the group of men sitting and standing around.

"Jesus Christ."

"I doubt he would approve."

They stood in silence for about thirty long seconds. "OK, Bulldog. I appreciate everything you're doing, but I gotta go."

"Wait — how did you get in there?"

Hudde flipped him the card. "Maybe they don't need to find this; you decide. Don't worry. I'll be around when it's time to come clean. Somehow, though, I don't think there will ever be a congressional hearing on this one."

Bulldog grinned and shook his head. "No, I don't think so."

Hudde turned to Valerie. "Are you ready?"

"Yes."

Hudde led out into the mist. It quickly curled and closed behind him. She took off after him, happy that she had on some sneakers when she had been taken and not coming home from work, with heels on.

They crossed the open area, and Gordan swore.

"What's the matter?" she whispered.

"I'm in too much of a hurry. I forgot that I don't have anything to cut the fence. We'll have to go back down to the road."

They followed the fence downhill toward the access road. They walked near a body, and Valerie let out a gasp.

"Sorry. I should have warned you. There may be a few more."

"Who did this, Gordan?"

He kept walking until the grass and weeds gave way to the dirt and gravel. The damage to the gate, fence, and guardhouse lay like a graveyard.

"Gordan, did you and Bulldog do all of this?"

Gordan stopped and took a breath. "They told me that they had you. They mocked the American servicemen they were holding in there." He took her by the shoulders and looked down into her eyes. "It doesn't matter what anyone else thinks. I wasn't going to let them hurt you, and I couldn't leave my brothers." He looked past her at the bodies in the dark. "I did this, and I'm not done." He stopped and locked eyes with her. "The people in charge are all out there, living their lives, while you were going to die down in there — all to advance their own prosperity or egos."

She swallowed hard and set her jaw. She stared back at him, trying to match his intensity. "I want to help."

He didn't say a word; he just turned and walked out past where the gate would have stopped them.

31

GORDAN DROVE IN silence. Valerie sat back and closed her eyes, but she did not sleep.

She sat up straighter and spoke while looking out her window, "I get that we were going to be the test subjects for some mad experiments, but I need to understand... I mean...why *me*? I can't see how *I* could have anything to do with any of this."

She tapped her chest with her right hand lightly. "What does a realtor in Georgia have to offer?"

"You were leverage against me — that's all."

"You told them about me? Why?"

"No." He shook his head sadly "No, what happened was that I called Walter Schroeder on your phone that day we had lunch together, and, a week ago, I called from my own phone to make sure you still wanted dinner. Remember?"

"Two phone calls, and that's it?"

"I'm sorry; I have no one else they could get with any kind of personal relationship that they could use for leverage. They already had Schroeder and forty-seven other ex-soldiers, but..." He shrugged his shoulders. "I'm sorry. They felt like they needed someone special."

"That's... sad."

She returned to silence for what seemed to Gordan a long time. He didn't look at her except for the occasional reflection that floated, ghost-like, across the inside of the windshield via a trick of lighting.

Finally, she reached out and grabbed the large right arm holding the truck's steering wheel.

"Gordan, there is no way you could have known anything about all this. I'm angry about it, I'm still frightened of what it all may lead to, yet I just can't see how to transfer that anger to you."

"Thank you. I'm grateful you feel that way." He finally broke his gaze from the road so that he could glance at her; she smiled. "I mean, not being frightened — the 'angry' part."

She nodded at him. "That doctor was positive that he was going to help Alzheimer's patients? I'm horrified that there is a part of me that feels a bit relieved, because my mother was just diagnosed with early-stage Alzheimer's. God, I'm a monster to have to fight the desire to be happy about it."

He reached out and squeezed her hand. "No, no. I don't think you are. There is a drug that the company he worked for will be selling — I'm sure of it."

"A cure?"

"I don't know for sure, but he was excited about the results."

"Why everything else, then? If he was so brilliant, why does all this feel so evil?"

"Again, I don't know. But if I had to guess I would suggest that it's a rogue operation. Understand that, if they were successful, there was a good chance that they would get official sanctioning at some point, and then they would have the full backing of the entire US government."

"Do you really think so?"

"I'm not a planner...I'm the guy who gets things done. I'm a disrupter. I have a history of making good decisions based on limited information in dangerous and volatile situations. This is not my strong suit."

He thought a moment more before continuing. "Here is what I'm sure of: If the government was *already* behind them, you and I would both be dead. Also, each of the security guys I got a good look at or heard speak was foreign born."

"Was?"

"I don't have a 'team.' I have a few people I trust who can help under certain circumstances...only in movies can you knock out people and carry out a successful mission."

"I'm sure that I can speak on behalf of all those men back there — and probably on behalf of their family members, too. Thank you. I'm not going to ask you how you freed me. I'm just going to say 'Thank you.'" She sighed and closed her eyes. "I wonder." She shuddered. "Why was he testing only on veterans? You know — other than me?"

"The chemicals he was testing were to be used on enemy troopers. He said he needed to make sure it would work on men from similar backgrounds. He had an entire spiel about why what he was doing was OK. He told me all about the 'evil' experiments that the Nazis did during the war that, ultimately, were used for good by the Allies later. He also was well versed on many of the operations that the US government had carried out on military troopers."

She looked shocked. "Like what?"

"It's all out there now — online, I mean. There were some especially bad ones involving radiation poisoning and nuclear testing. At one point, the Army gave a bunch of troopers sunglasses and marched them out into the desert to watch an atomic bomb go off."

"What? That's fucking crazy and evil!" Several minutes of silence went by.

"Gordan?"

He looked quickly at her. "Yeah?"

"We aren't driving south. Where the hell are we going?"

• • •

Bulldog Mahoney waved at the first dark SUVs with a flashlight as they headed up the foggy dirt road. The back window rolled down, and the head of the FBI Terrorist Task Force, Gary Reeves, came into view.

"Good morning, Gary." Mahoney leaned in on the doorframe.

"Bulldog, it's already become a very busy and scary night. If you talked me into getting all this support out in the middle of nowhere on no notice for nothing, I swear you'll be taking a cruise in the middle of the Atlantic by morning."

Mahoney understood the veiled threat at being placed on an interrogation ship in international waters; he had witnessed those interrogations himself just a few years before.

Bulldog smiled and looked back at the growing caravan of equipment that was building up behind this lead vehicle. "Not sure how you guys feel about evidence gathering, but me, personally — this is where I would stop."

"Right here in the middle of nowhere?"

"I know you may be worried about getting your shoes dirty, but maybe you should walk the rest of the way in with me."

He waited a heartbeat and then turned and began walking. The access road to the dead end where the utility shed was located was on the left, and Bulldog pointed it out as they passed.

Bulldog heard the quickening pace of Reeves and the sound of a hard-soled shoe on gravel and sand.

"Just who the hell is your contact, and what the fuck are we all doing out here? You know there are two dozen agents, two busses we commandeered from a high school, and everything we have for crime-scene tech and biological threats. All this was based on your insistence. I'm serious — if you don't deliver, you're done."

"Thanks for the vote of confidence. Now, if you would just look ahead, you'll see the beginning of some kind of battle that took place here. I did check for pulses on — well, on what ended up being the dead — so I've walked all around here and touched a few things. I know I stepped on some blood back there." He pointed off to his left, where the gate guard had been crushed by the incoming deuce-and-a-half.

The scene was starting to show itself to Reeves; he called for two of his tactical team members to approach.

Mahoney put his hands up, palms forward. "Hey, guys. I think we're clear here; I've been wandering around nearly two hours now."

The fog still ebbed and flowed, especially visible in the more-open area that they now found themselves in.

Reeves stepped up to stand side by side with Mahoney, looking at the truck and then past it, as the trees to their right began to fall away and open up.

"Tough to find anything right now, even with lights. This shit won't burn off until noon, I'll bet." He turned to his two shooters. "Stay with us."

Mahoney nodded and continued around the truck, where they then could see the hangar standing out alone. It looked wrong in this environment.

"What the hell is that?" Reeves followed.

Mahoney stopped as they approached the large, closed hangar door.

"It was cool and wet." He gestured with his hand at the surrounding area. "So I allowed the victims to shut the door." He turned to the two men dressed in all black M4s held high; their Kevlar helmets made them look a bit like pawns on a chessboard. "Last I checked, nothing but friendlies, boys. So go easy."

He turned and kicked two times hard on the giant door, paused, and then kicked it three times again. Gears began to turn, chains ran round, and the giant door began to rise.

Inside, the surviving forty-eight people sat on the asphalt in a fairly well organized platoon-sized forma-tion as Mahoney had instructed them to do once he gave the signal to open the door.

"What the fuck?" Reeves was looking around like a tourist on Broadway in New York City.

"Crazy, isn't it? These are all victims, maybe poten-tial witnesses, who, until a little earlier tonight, were all being held down below — or so they tell me." He stepped back and smiled. "So, have I disappointed you yet?"

Reeves was on his phone, barking orders. First, he needed the surrounding open fields to be swept for evidence by agents; then he wanted tents set up for interviews. He called for food and coffee to be delivered and for an ambulance to be there on standby. And, most of all, he wanted access to whatever lay beneath them.

Reeves turned his gaze back on Mahoney. "I'm not fucking around. I need the name of that informant, and I need them here now."

"Maybe later; for now, you all have a lot of work to do." Mahoney started walking away. As he walked, he stuck his hands into his pocket and found the key card.

"I wasn't asking you, Mahoney!" Reeves stepped after him.

Mahoney didn't stop walking. When he approached the destroyed guard shack, he took out the magnetic key card and wiped it off the best he could with the end of his shirt. He flipped it off into the high grass just as some of the FBI people began filing into the open space.

• • •

Hudde leaned into the driver's-side window of his own truck. "You sure you understand? I'm guessing 0330 hours, at the latest. If I don't meet up with you by sunrise, you need to head back to your home. OK?"

Valerie reached out the window and touched his shoulder. "Gordan, I said I can read a map, and what is it — like, twenty miles? I'll be there."

"If I do this right, I'll be cutting across the golf course." He leaned in further and pointed at a spot on the map, which was unfolded across the large center console. "About here."

"Gordan, where are you going from here?" She glanced around the quiet homes along the street near the Potomac River, not far from Mount Vernon.

He smiled and winked. "I need to borrow a boat. See you soon."

"Wait, Gordan!" she whispered louder than before.

He stepped back. "Everything OK?"

She reached out and pulled him close by the neck of his dark hoodie. "Thank you," she said and kissed him on the corner of his mouth. "Whatever you're doing, please be safe."

His brow furrowed for a moment, and then he grinned as he stepped away. "Don't worry."

She turned the truck around as he disappeared between homes across the street, and she headed out the way they had come in. Near the Richmond Highway, she spotted a 7-Eleven and turned in to get some coffee and some snacks. She was grabbing a few things when she stopped herself and shook her head; she had picked up enough for two.

Heading south from there, the road she was looking for came up way too fast, and she nearly spilled her coffee as she ate one of those spongy, cellophane-wrapped treats with one hand and steered with a knee.

Gunston Road was dead quiet at this time of the morning, and she rolled slowly past the golf course that Gordan had pointed out. She yanked the wheel at the last second and pulled into the entrance. It was blocked by a black metal gate, but there was more than enough room for his truck to sit off the road. She shook her head. *That won't be acceptable.* She went back in the direction that she had come.

She knew that she had seen a larger driveway a couple hundred yards down the street, but, then, she had been focusing on the left side of the road. A nice little church sat off the tree-lined road. She pulled in and backed in near some trees. She actually could see down to the access road for the golf course from here, and she thought it would keep a local cop from asking her why a truck with Georgia plates was parked on the side of the road. She felt Gordan would approve, and that made her happy.

Then she remembered the impulse that she had to kiss him, and she began to question what her reasoning for that was. *Maybe I was just thankful to be alive and was merely showing him.*

She shook her head "No." *That wasn't it, I never thought hard about whether I liked him or not because we haven't even gone on a date yet. That would be stupid. I am a strong, independent woman. It's not like I was going to reward him with sex for saving me — was I?*

She laughed out loud. *Isn't this thinking something like a schoolgirl? He's a crazy man who had killed people today! How can these thoughts be creeping into my head? But he couldn't be crazy if he had helped the sheriff last year and was still friends with ex-military guys and an FBI agent — that "Bulldog" guy?*

She looked at the dash clock, and it said 0130 hours. She didn't know if she could take two more hours of this internal conversation with herself.

• • •

In the third back yard, Hudde found exactly what he was looking for — a canoe. It was tipped over, and the paddles were tucked up and underneath.

The sound of the river flowing would mask any noise he was making, however, the small dog next door yapping furiously from inside a back porch was going to wake someone eventually.

Hudde righted the canoe and slid it into the water of the Potomac, heading downstream. He kept it close to the shore, crossing the point where Dogue Creek met with the larger river. His first destination was just a couple thousand feet away to the south as the lazy bend in the Potomac led the larger river off to the east in an easy bend heading toward the coast.

Fort Belvoir appeared on a map to stick out like a small, rounded peninsula, due to its being surrounded on three sides with water. He needed to fight Dogue Creek trying to push him further out into the center of the river, and he rowed hard until he found a spot on the easternmost point of Fort Belvoir to step back onto land. He pulled the canoe onto land behind him, partially hidden by a large fallen log and heavy overgrowth.

Hudde crept through a small stand of trees and knelt at the last trunk before an open, well-kept grassy area.

There was the stately O-club. The back patio was brick and wood, which was all painted white, and the weather had not yet made them remove the patio furniture. The glass doors and windows were obviously meant to impress on the officers and guests inside of the loveliness of the grounds as they met the Potomac as it headed off to the Atlantic.

"No shit," he said under his breath, but he wasn't all that surprised. It was more like happy; it wasn't like an enemy had ever come up the river to stage an attack since it had been built in the fifties.

Twenty-five minutes later, he was pushing the canoe back into the water. He paddled hard until he reached the mouth of Gunston Cove, where he pushed the canoe hard into the cove. Driving the paddle deep was straining his shoulders and pulling on something that hurt in his chest on his right side — most likely something that had happened while the Watanabe boys were kicking the shit out of him. He pushed the small craft against the current, alternating strokes, keeping the nose pointing west-southwest; he figured he had close to a mile to go.

Each time he reached out to take the next deep stroke, he wondered if he had separated a rib.

• • •

Valerie would have fallen asleep, except Hudde's phone kept vibrating, and the light seemed bright in the darkness of the truck's cab. She turned the phone over and set it onto the floor of the passenger side, where she could try to forget about it. She leaned back and closed her eyes. It was nearing three a.m., and she figured she would just need to wait ...

A knock on the window made her jump, and she let out an audible yelp. It took her eyes a moment to adjust, and then she could make out Hudde standing outside the door. She opened the door and stepped out into the night air.

"Sorry — I was just nodding off." She stretched and then bent to touch her toes. "Everything go OK?"

"So well that it scares me. Are you ready to go?"

She nodded and walked around to the passenger door; she used the black rail to step up inside.

"I grabbed you some coffee and a snack. Of course, the coffee is cold."

He nodded and peeled the white plastic lid off the cup, drinking it down in one gulp.

"Oh, yeah. That'll help. Let's get some heat going. I'm freezing." He started the truck and headed out. "Listen,

Valerie. I was going to try to drive you back to Georgia this morning, but I had another idea. Is it OK if we get a hotel for a night so that I can get some work done tomorrow?

He raised his eyebrows, waiting for a response "I need some real food, maybe a couple dozen aspirin, a shower, and some sleep."

She could see this was important. "OK. I need the same things, maybe a clean set of clothes."

"Good idea." They drove past the hotel that Hudde had been thinking of to a twenty-four-hour superstore, where Hudde pulled into the parking lot.

She looked at him a bit sheepishly. "I don't have any money, Gordan. They didn't let me take my purse when I answered the door." She tried to smile at her own joke.

He sat back in the seat. "Come to think of it, I lost my wallet somewhere, too." He looked at her very seriously. "Want to see one of my secrets?"

"What?"

He reached into the center console and pulled out a small folding knife. "Hand me your floor mat, would you?"

She started to reach down when she saw the phone. "Oh, I forgot — your phone's been ringing." She held it up and handed it to him.

He stole a quick look. "It's Bulldog. The FBI is up his ass. He can wait."

He took the carpeted floor mat from her and began to pull at and then cut the stitching along one side.

When it was a large-enough tear, he pulled it open eight inches; he reached inside, pulling out a clear plastic bag with cash in it.

"Two grand for an emergency." He smiled at her and fanned the bills.

"Must be nice." She smiled and followed him out of the truck and into the store.

He waited for her to catch up. "When someone tries to give you lemons, take their cash."

"Oh, is that how that saying goes?"

"Yeah. I think Sun Tzu said it."

He grabbed a cart, and the two shopped for under-garments, and they both bought jogging suits. They picked out toothbrushes and then walked into the gro-cery area.

"How about some sandwich meats and a beer; that and a hot shower sound so good right now." Gordan said.

"It does. I try to stay away from bread, but what the hell? It does sound good right now." She put her hand on the back of his arm as he pushed the shopping cart. "Hell of a first date."

He looked down and smiled a sad smile. "Were we going to have a date?"

She allowed a small smile. "I'll admit I liked teasing you, I guess. But, yeah — we were going to have a date. I just liked making you sweat a little."

"I've been thinking about you more than I should, I guess." The corner of his mouth went up just a little.

"Oh, yeah? That's interesting, Mr. Hudde. Like what?"

"Like how your skin would feel, what you would taste like, how it would feel to run my hands through your hair."

"Oh, my!" She took a half step away from him. "You make a girl blush. You don't hold things back, do you?"

"I'm sorry. I'm not all that good about this kind of stuff. Tell me: Should I keep thoughts like that to myself?"

She stepped back close and took his arm, guiding him into the correct shopping aisle. "Honestly... I would be upset to find out you *weren't* thinking those things." She gave a sheepish little smile. "Don't tell anyone, or I may lose my 'woman's card.' OK?"

"OK — it's a deal."

• • •

Gary Reeves allowed his arm to drop down to his side, the voice on the other end of the phone falling away. He hung his head and rubbed his temples, cursing under his breath.

He returned the phone to his ear. "What do you mean, 'It doesn't exist'? You need to explain!"

He listened and then exhaled deeply. "Alright. I'll make the calls and try to find out."

He looked up as one of his agents who were conducting interviews approached. She was, obviously, not dressed appropriately for the wet fields; her black slacks sopped from the knees down to the ground.

"Sir, we need to get that tent up and heated. These men are cold, and we're all out of emergency blankets. If we could get some hot chow here, it would help, too."

He took another deep breath and counted to ten before he spoke. *No shit, Sherlock.*

He ran his hand over his scalp, wondering as he did how much hair was coming out.

"The tents and space heaters are en route, and I just can't do anything about food until the morning. Do you have anything useful to report?"

If she'd heard the sarcasm, she didn't show it. "From what we've heard so far, they were all being held against their wills in cells deep underground here. The stories are strikingly familiar; it can't be a coincidence that all these men are veterans with almost no family. I think only a couple have any missing-person reports filed as of this moment — from what information we currently have."

He nodded. That was useful information. "OK. We can't keep them here under these circumstances. Let's prepare to move them to Quantico. We can use the agents-in-training to set up tents and whatever other grunt work needs to be done."

"Yes, Sir." She turned and started picking through the high weeds.

"Agent?" Reeves called out.

"Yes, Sir?"

"I hate to admit that I have no idea what's happening here." He shook his head. That had sounded even worse out loud. "We have to keep a tight lid on this until we figure it out."

She nodded. "Understood."

"I'm glad something is," he said under his breath.

He dialed his CIA-agent contact. "Mahoney!" He stopped himself from sounding panicked and lowered his voice. "If you aren't front and center within an hour..." He was about to threaten, but he knew that the man didn't work for him. "We'll be at Quantico just after first light." Then he hung up.

He walked the fence until he was at the farthest reaches of this "nonexistent" facility's grounds. Even with the odd acoustics of the woods, no one would overhear him for the call he dreaded.

He contacted the director of the FBI first. It was always better to follow the chain of command. It was never good, with an obviously big issue, to call with minimal facts. If he couldn't answer any questions that he had while he stood here on the scene of "...something big...," he just knew that his bosses would not be happy with his ignorance. It was not going to go over well.

Fifteen minutes later, he was still trying to explain himself to a sleepy director.

"Of course, we can gain entry — that's not the problem. I'm telling you the place doesn't exist."

He listened and nodded to no one. "Yes, of course, I've thought of that, and our live satellite feeds don't show anything," He listened again. "Yes, I called, and they say it is some kind of software that has been downloaded."

"Of course, all of our feeds need to be investigated, but it doesn't answer the problem of whether we should bust down doors without a warrant for a location that doesn't exist."

"Of course, that would be helpful, but our CIA agent has disappeared and has not returned my calls."

Reeves closed his eyes while he listened to the obvious questions and practiced his deep breathing.

"So far, none of the bodies have been identified, so I can't say one way or another. Yes, of course."

Reeves looked up into the slowly lightening sky. "Sir how could I possibly know if the two crime scenes are in any way related?"

The call ended, and he realized that he hadn't gotten an answer on whether he should wait for a warrant.

He called his agent inside the hangar. "Yea — do it. Bust them down. Let's get in there."

• • •

Gordan took a big bite from the sandwich he had made with the groceries they had brought into the twin-bed hotel room. He took a swig of the domestic beer and closed his eyes, enjoying the tastes.

He opened his eyes when he heard Valerie opening packages that they had just bought.

"I need a hot shower more than a meal," she said as she took her things into the crook of her arm and went into the bathroom. He noticed that she didn't quite close the door all the way behind her.

"OK." Gordan finished the beer and opened another. He figured a sandwich and two beers would satisfy him, but then he got up and made another sandwich and opened a third beer.

He was exhausted, and, yet, he had to shake thoughts from his mind when he saw the half-open bathroom door and heard the shower running. The thought of a wet and soapy beautiful woman so close was difficult to shake. He went over to the bed that he would use and turned on the TV. Maybe some world tragedy could cleanse his mind.

Fifteen minutes later, the water stopped running, and ten minutes after that, the bathroom door opened, allowing the steam to fully escape. Valerie Baker emerged, wearing the hotel robe she'd stepped into. She bent at the waist, twisting her long, black hair into a towel before standing quickly.

"It's not my practice to stay in a hotel and shower with a man on my first date," she quipped.

Hudde was snoring, lying on his back; he was obviously exhausted. A half-eaten sandwich and an open beer sitting on the nightstand next to him was proof of this.

She opened her own beer and ate his sandwich while mindlessly watching the early-morning newscaster talk about yesterday's news and speculating about today's potential.

She turned off the lights and pulled back the covers. "Goodnight, Gordan Hudde," she said as she closed her own eyes.

32

THE EARLY-MORNING SUN had begun to burn off the mist from the open area around the hangar. Gary Reeves stepped out into it from the fluorescent fake lighting in the command van.

The steam from his coffee was now thicker than the mist hanging over this wooded area. That meant that the crime scene had lost some of its horror-movie mystique, yet it brought no answers to the questions he had hours ago.

According to his people, there was no building out here in the wilderness. That screamed "Government" to Reeves, yet no one had taken ownership; he had heard nothing but denials so far.

He ran a hand over his head. How would this affect his next position if he failed to figure this out to the satisfaction of the director? He had ten dead men at this scene and six from the parking garage downtown. They could be entirely separate incidents with absolutely nothing tying them together. But he didn't think that, because both scenes had been called in by the same man, and now Bulldog Mahoney was suddenly silent.

That fucker is really leaving me out to hang, Reeves thought.

He called his agent-in-charge back at Quantico. They had settled in and gotten food and medical attention for the forty-eight men. More detailed interviews were underway, but still no information had come to light that would solve this problem.

He sipped his coffee and watched the lab teams swarm the hillside and walk in and out of the hangar. Another team set up lasers to determine the location of the shooter who'd seemed to have shot up the car in the woods from just inside the hangar.

Who was involved? What was the purpose of this place, and who owned it? He was not going to get any sleep until he could tell his bosses the answer to those obvious questions.

He shivered. A night out here, and you may as well be fully submerged; the wet and cold cut right to the bone.

Maybe I'm just getting too old for this shit.

"Anything, boss?" his Lieutenant asked as he came back into the heart of the command vehicle.

"I just can't shake the feeling that that building out there" — he pointed in the right direction — "is something our government would build. I don't know what it's for, but it doesn't look like something one of the cartels would need — and would they be able to conceal the site from our own satellite feeds?"

The Lieutenant nodded. "Then, maybe a foreign entity? After all Mahoney is somehow involved. If the CIA is somehow in the loop...."

Reeves rubbed the bridge of his nose and closed his eyes. "Really? We would allow ISIS or Russia — or anyone, for that matter — to build something this elaborate an hour from Washington, D.C.?"

Reeves flopped down into one of the chairs, allowing himself to go limp. "I should have taken that transfer last year and left this fiasco for you to handle."

"Excuse me, but...fuck you very much."

"Yeah — you're right. Fuck me." Reeves got back up and went to the window to look at the steel monstrosity.

• • •

"Oh, fuck." Gordan struggled to sit up. "I'm not a doctor, but my diagnosis is that I got the shit kicked out of me."

Valerie sat in a desk chair, with the curtains pulled back just enough to look out. "I didn't wake you, did I?"

He looked over at the clock. "No. Five hours was more than enough. I just need to get a hot shower and get moving again, or I might not be able to finish this."

He stopped and turned to look at her. He didn't feel odd standing there in his boxers with a t-shirt, but he suddenly noticed a lot of leg sticking out from the white, fluffy-looking robe.

"Nice 'get-away sticks,' Valerie." He smiled.

She stuck her right leg straight out in front of her and pointed her toe. Her calf tightened, and the muscles in her thigh created clean lines of distinction between different muscle groups.

He whistled his approval. "Any dancer would be proud to have those."

"Thank you. A different time, a different circumstance, and I think I would appreciate that more." She smiled up at him.

He smiled back at her during a brief and somewhat-awkward silence. Then he turned to the bags on the table. "I'll turn the shower cold before I'm done." He picked up the packages that he had purchased at the big box store and shuffled into the bathroom, closing the door.

He came out twenty minutes later. She was fully dressed and ready to go; he was now in jeans but shirt-less.

"God, Gordan — you really should get to a doctor." Valerie stood and walked over, getting behind him as he raised his arms to push them through a new t-shirt.

She placed her hand on the large purple area under his arm that had spread the size of a bowling ball under his left arm. There was something similar on the right side, but smaller.

"They would just tape me up. Nothing they can do unless the ribs are broken, and I don't think they are."

She allowed her hand to slowly trace up and around his back to the dimpled pale holes from bullets long removed to a jagged scar from some shrapnel near his hip.

"You've lived a hard life."

"I've been lucky. Many people around me — not so much. Now *you're* near me, Valerie, and this is not over by any means. I don't want to be sitting near you in a hospital bed."

"What do you mean? The FBI is involved. What more do you have to do, and does that have something to do with whatever I helped you with last night?"

"Yes to everything." He pulled the t-shirt down and sat gingerly on the edge of the bed that she had slept in.

"After everything I have been through over the years, I just can't rule out that the government may just want to eliminate everyone involved and pretend that this entire thing didn't happen. Except to take control over everything that the research had uncovered up until last night, that is."

"They'd *do* that?" She allowed her hand to touch his shoulder as she walked past him to sit back down into the chair. Her brows furrowed as she recoiled from the thought.

"How do you stop that from happening?" she asked.

He studied her face; she looked fresh and beautiful even after the events of the last forty-eight hours, her hair pulled back into a high ponytail. If nothing else, he didn't want to lose her friendship. He'd enjoyed sharing a meal with her, so he searched for words that wouldn't sound so harsh.

"I take away anyone they would want to protect."

"What does that mean?" She pulled her legs, now encased in a jogging suit, up under her tight posterior.

"In the beginning, I had to wonder if the government was involved in this. But events and people have me about ninety-nine percent sure that this whole thing is a rouge operation. It's probably unknown to the central government, however, important people in the government are involved."

"OK — like the president or something?"

"No — no one that important, but people who are high up. You never know what relationship they have that would cause others to rush to defend them, and then you and I would be threats."

She placed her hand to her throat. "You're scaring me, Gordan, and I've been pretty scared enough the last few days."

"Listen, Valerie. You are neck deep in this with or without me now. I can lie to you, if you wish, but it won't change our circumstances one way or the other."

"No — I don't ever want that!" She sat up and uncurled her legs from under her. She set her jaw and locked eyes with Gordan. "Go ahead."

"There are people out there — important and powerful people — who identified me as a threat and you as leverage. People like them have gotten to where they are..." he paused, looking for the right way to explain, "they're like mobsters. There always is another guy who owes them a favor. The best way to be sure is if they are out of the picture, and then nobody owes them a thing. Maybe then it would increase both our chances of survival. Unless, of course, someone wants revenge, but the caliber of everyone so far...I don't know — I just don't think so."

"You've doubted our chances to live through *this* the entire last ten hours we've been together?" She leaned forward.

He nodded. "If our government is all in agreement that someone must go, trust me — they're gone. It is always just a matter of when and where."

"But look what you did back there!"

"They'd send one guy, then two, then a team, and finally they'd send a bomb and blame a gas leak; it's inevitable."

"Oh, my God!" She stood up and started to look out the curtain and then suddenly stiffened, standing upright, closing the curtain and taking a step back. "What are we going to do?"

"I'm thinking. I'm close to a plan, but I'm not sure how it ends right just yet. But last night was a good start."

"It was?"

He nodded. "Yes, and I think I can make it even better. Then, I think we are close to becoming... safer."

"'Safer'? That's not so comforting to hear right now. How long before you *know* for sure?"

"Honestly?"

She stared right into his green eyes and nodded.

"We won't be sure for some time — six months, a year, or even more."

"You're serious?"

"Yes. Here's what's comforting: While these people are all important muckety-mucks, I really don't believe they're doing what they have been doing officially. If it's true that they went rogue, many would rather lose them than have someone like me out there."

She frowned a little but decided to ignore the "someone like me" phrase. "What does that mean for us, and what can I do to help?"

"I'm going to ask you to stay here and hide; it's the best thing for you right now." He dug through the bags, pulled out a go-phone, handed it to her, and took out one for himself. He paused for a moment. "It means Uncle Sam won't come looking for us, which may be the best news."

To her, the knife was in his hand like magic. He cut the phones out of the plastic and handed one to her.

"The only call you make is to me in an emergency or 911. If I don't call you back by Sunday afternoon at two, I need you to go to the Costco parking lot I marked on the map; be there by three." He handed her all the cash that he had left over from the truck mat.

She held the cash out in front of her. "Won't you need some?"

"I've got three other floor mats." He smiled, and it seemed somehow reassuring to her.

"Don't worry. I'll be back." He pulled the tags off the new hoodie and slipped it on. He reached down and placed his old clothes in one of the store bags. Gordan held up his old denim jacket; it looked huge to Valerie.

"It looks OK, right?" He looked past the jacket to meet her gaze.

"Its fine. Nothing a wash won't fix later."

"Good, it has sentimental value. I'm throwing these things out on my way." Gordan slipped the denim over the dark-blue hoodie; he grimaced as he stretched out his arms to get the coat to fit right over his shoulders.

This close, she realized how wide he was across the chest, and she stepped in and hugged him hard.

"Hey — go easy," he said but he held her just as tight for a moment; she was soft in all the right places, and her hair smelled good.

"Thank you." She stepped back and straightened the oversized sweatshirt she had picked out.

"Don't worry; I'll be back before midnight, even earlier, if everything works out. Um, I paid for tonight actually this morning, so you're good. Just get room service and relax. Remember, you have my number, but only for an emergency."

She nodded. "I get it. Be safe."

• • •

Gordan just needed to move; he started the truck and headed out in the direction of north DC, with the intention to make some calls of his own on his new phone.

He found a parking lot that was busy with business people just about lunch time on a Friday afternoon. He punched in the correct numbers and got transferred to The Kid, deep underground at CIA headquarters.

"Bulldog says he's going to kill you himself if you don't surface soon," Kid Mykhaylychenko said into his end.

"Every fucking time, Kid! Someday, you're going to have to tell me how you know it's me after a phone switch."

"Not unless torture is involved." Gordan could almost hear the grin that he knew The Kid must have had on his face. "The director might want a shot at you, too. I'm supposed to rat you out if I hear from you."

"Trust me — he doesn't want to know. Listen; any luck with the mystery investor I asked you to look for?"

"Yeah...he tried to hide the investments, but he ended up making them through an online firm."

"Good. Send me the info, and I've got another request."

"Of course, you do."

"I need to know where one Yvonne Lane, the Chief of staff of Veterans Affairs is at all times for the rest of today. Nobody can know but me, Kid, so cover your tracks."

The Kid laughed. "I always do that, Gordan. You'd better watch your back. It's like a pissed-off hive of bees around here, and, somehow, I think it has to be something you've been involved in."

"Thanks, Kid. If the director pushes, tell him I'll be in soon. If Bulldog cries to you, tell him he better stay low until I surface — and maybe tell him 'Thanks.' He helped a lot."

"Will do. I'll text the info to your new phone. Maybe don't switch them out today — you know, just in case I'm not following."

• • •

Four floors above The Kid, John Stevens leaned back in his plush desk chair and closed his eyes to listen to the nuanced rant of the FBI director, Madeline Hunter.

It wasn't unheard of to have the directors of the FBI and CIA meeting or having conversations. After all, they both answered to the President, collected information to protect America, and were required to rub elbows with the same people at Washington functions.

It *was* odd, however, to have the FBI director accusing the CIA director of conducting operations without giving her some kind of heads-up about something big going on.

Stevens lost track of a few minutes as he allowed his mind to wander. Then he lost patience when she accused him of being a racist. She was one of the earliest selections of the administration, and everyone knew why she had been selected early and very visibly — except no one was willing to say it.

Stevens also knew that he would not ask to continue as the CIA director after the election, and he pondered just hanging up on this silly bitch.

"Director Hunter?" he interrupted her pontification.

"Yes. Are you prepared to give me the information I need?"

"What you need to do is take a breath and stop accusing me of something you obviously know nothing of. I have already informed you that there is no operation, so I can't tell you what you want to hear."

"You can't speak to me that way! You're a sexist homophobe — do you know that?"

"I will repeat: I do not know anything about the location you have spoken about near Fort Valley, and my agent has still not reported in. I can't share what I do not know — it is just that simple."

"I'll be asking for the President to intervene, and, if necessary, the Senate will convene a hearing — trust me on this."

"Now you threaten me? Have you ever run an investigation, let alone an entire department? Ma'am, I respectfully suggest you hang up…"

Madeline Hunter interrupted: "That is not acceptable language, and I don't have to listen to you speak like a caveman. You have not heard the end of this!"

"What?!" Stevens was confused more than angry. After all he really *didn't* have any operation going on currently — he was telling the truth.

"'Ma'am…'" she said, and Stevens could hear her shaking with rage or frustration "…is sexist and offensive, and I will not be spoken to this way."

Stevens knew that she'd hung up but couldn't help but to tell her she was delusional.

"I've lived too long." Stevens said to his secretary as he headed out of his office and walked to the elevator to descend into the below-ground floors. The stainless-steel doors slid open, and he walked down to the correct door, accessing it with his ID card.

He entered the relative darkness and dry, cool air that circulated to help keep the computer equipment running at peak performance.

"Mykhaylychenko!" Stevens yelled, knowing the soundproofing on the floor, ceiling, and walls would muffle his voice.

"Sir?" The Kid looked past the array of six screens in front of him. He thought if the director came to him, he *had* to be in trouble.

Stevens walked up and looked down at the computer genius. "I have just gotten off the phone with the FBI director....Why are you smiling?"

"She...um..."

"Just say it."

"She has a reputation." Mykhaylychenko couldn't help it; he looked down in an attempt to hide a grin.

"Look up at me," Stevens said.

Mykhaylychenko complied. "Sir?" He tried to look as serious as he could.

"Bulldog is not responding to me. Do you know where he is?"

Mykhaylychenko furrowed his brow, and his tongue flicked out to wet his lips. "Sir, do you really want to know where he is?" He raised his left eyebrow at the end to accentuate the question.

Now Stevens paused and thought for a second. Then he nodded, accepting that he needed to change his question. "Is Bulldog OK?"

"Yes, Sir."

"And Gordan Hudde?"

"Good enough to use the phone, but that's all I can tell you at the moment." The Kid studied his director in an attempt to determine if he was answering the questions correctly.

Stevens closed his eyes and rubbed his temples for a moment.

"Director, I believe that Hudde will come here when he is done."

"You do? That's comforting until you say 'when he's done.' Then I'm…frankly… scared shitless, I think. Would you be led to believe it would be soon?"

Mykhaylychenko shook his head and shrugged his shoulders. "I can never figure those guys out, but I would guess so."

Stevens frowned. "I'm not sure I want to know anything anymore. You ever go fly fishing, Kid?"

'Can't say I've ever been."

"Me, neither, but I'm going to learn. It's better than golf, because at least you're getting dinner while you're practicing." He turned and stormed toward the door.

33

GORDAN WATCHED AS Chief of Staff of Veterans Affairs Yvonne Lane strode confidently down the sidewalk. With a quick glance, one may have observed her dowdy apparel and lack of makeup. Gordan knew that she was hiding a secret life — possibly of yoga and exercise. Her skirt of modest length was tight enough to show a taut backside, and her toned calf ended in sensible shoes.

He had followed her from the VA in Washington to this plaza, where upscale boutiques and coffee shops lined the streets. She appeared to be heading into a wine store filled with labels that Gordan was sure would be totally foreign to him. Nothing like the real moonshine he sometimes shared with a friend in Georgia.

It was easy to follow most people; they seldom paid that much attention to their surroundings, and, if they were important enough, they paid others to perform the security for them. Lane was not one of those, but neither was she too concerned with her surroundings.

Gordan held up his hand and made a fist, tightening the tight leather gloves over his knuckles. He slipped out of his truck, pressing the fob inside his pocket to set the alarm.

He didn't look like someone making six figures working and living in this area. Any area that shows an accumulation of wealth also brought out panhandlers, shoplifters, and other swindlers that the wealthy were so used to that they often didn't see them or at least pretended not to.

Gordan walked into the café between the liquor store and Lane's car, a sporty Audi, and stood in line, never allowing his eyes to drift from the front windows.

He made it to the front of the line and felt compelled to purchase a five-dollar regular coffee. Before it arrived, Lane drifted by the painted window. Hudde left the counter and fell into step directly behind her; they needed to walk past a half-dozen vehicles before she stepped to the driver's-side door of her own car.

Gordan stepped into her, using his weight to pin her against her car. Her body stiffened, and he felt her strength as she pushed back against him immediately, as if it were second nature. She tried to turn and throw an elbow, and Gordan grabbed her arm and before she could scream. He whispered into her ear, "We need to talk about Dr. Watanabe."

He felt her body relax, and she leaned back into her car, her ass momentarily resting on the upper part of the door's frame. Gordan never released her right arm, and, in a movement that could have almost been sensual, he allowed his soft leather glove to slide down her arm, past her elbow, and down her forearm, following her arm into her purse to her hand, now tightly gripping a small J-frame snub-nosed .38 caliber revolver right next to a bottle of wine.

"Nicely done, Ms. Lane. I appreciate your choice in handguns. You don't mind if I hold your purse, now — do you?"

She locked eyes with him, nearly his own height. "What are you going to do?"

"I just need to talk to you. Please unlock the vehicle, and get in the passenger side. If you do as I say, my plan was for you to be fine when I leave your car."

She kept her eyes locked on his, studying him. She slowly brought her left hand up to her chest, and she uncurled her fingers, showing her own key fob.

"That's right," Gordan said.

She depressed a button two times, and both doors made a familiar *Thunk!* noise. Gordan took the purse and slid into the driver's seat.

Lane opened the passenger side door, pulled up her skirt a bit, and slid slowly into the seat.

"Now what?" She looked over at him while she started biting her lower lip and running her tongue over it. She took a deep breath and looked up into the uphol-stery. "What do you know about Dr. Watanabe?"

Gordan turned his right wrist over and looked at his watch. "We have a few minutes to waste." He pulled the wine bottle from her purse and read the label. "This expensive stuff?"

"No, not really."

"I never liked wine; it gives me a headache, no matter how much I drink."

She closed her eyes, now taking deep breaths.

"What do you think you're going to make on the Biophaze stock?" Gordan asked.

Her eyes narrowed.

"Yeah — I know everything."

"Then you know what I've made on the stock."

"I know what you've made so far. I'm just wondering how long you plan to hold it and what you think it will be worth when you sell."

"If everything the doctor says is possible, maybe sixty to eighty million." She looked into his eyes with a new strength, as if maybe she had his angle. "I'll give you half when I sell if you just let me go." She raised one eyebrow.

"Tempting. In fact, you just gave me an idea. But, no thanks, just the same. Don't worry. I'm really planning on us both walking our own separate ways today, unlike the good doctor after our last meeting."

"Why — what happened to the doctor?"

"The doctor, it seems," he paused for effect "was looking forward to killing me — right after he'd conducted some experiments on me, that is." Gordan gave a sheepish smile. "I didn't take to that. I'm sure you can imagine that I voted against that plan."

She was staring at him. "What happened to the doctor?"

"It was an accident; I mean, I couldn't do that again if you gave me a hundred chances." He shook his head.

"What did you do to the doctor?" Her voice rose and became shrill. She lost all her fear of him and leaned in close, waiting for an answer.

"I dropped a forklift on him and his 'muscle.' It was really very messy — I am sure you can imagine."

She sat back as if he had pushed her, her breathing once again rapid and shallow. "He's dead? You killed him? Are you sure?"

"It's not like I checked his pulse or anything, but his head was in the trunk while his body was in the back seat."

She closed her eyes and shook her head. "No! No! No! — you couldn't have done that!"

"Oh, sure, like I said — I couldn't duplicate that feat if I tried. I can go you one better, though. Right after that, I went out to the country and freed something near fifty people from some underground freak show."

He spun the cylinder on the little revolver and allowed it to slam back into the frame. "It's just too small for my hand."

"I'm going to throw up."

He held her purse out for her. "In here. Go back to that deep-breathing thing." He glanced at his watch again. "It's almost time...I need you to place a call for me." He held her phone out in his gloved hand.

"Who am I calling?"

"I need you to call your *compadre*."

"Who?"

"What if I were to tell you to call your friend in the Justice Department who has been ignoring and burying the Attorney General reports about the VA scandals?"

"You want me to call Stephen Reynolds?" She turned the phone over to start dialing.

"No, I don't want you to call Reynolds. I was just checking. I need you to call General Seibert."

She glanced down at her phone. "He won't answer."

"Why is that?"

She shook her head "Some bullshit military thing he does every Friday night. He thinks that he's some Viking warrior giving a toast in a longhouse for his men. He's tried to get me to go several times — 'best steak in a thousand miles' — he keeps saying." She looked at Gordan out of the corner of her eye, arching her back and sliding a bit forward in her seat, causing her skirt to slide further up her toned legs. "I think he just wants to get me drunk."

Gordan didn't mind looking, and he nodded his approval. "I bet he does, but I don't get the feeling you like men all that much." Gordan shrugged his shoulders.

"Whatever; to each his own. Now, what I need you to do is call the Officers Club and ask them to take the phone to him. Don't worry — it's cordless. I checked."

Her brows furrowed, and she relaxed, allowing her shoulders to roll forward a bit and accentuating her breasts a lot less.

Gordan showed her the number. "Identify yourself; tell whomever answers who you are and what position you hold. Tell them that, right after the toast, they are to give the phone to the general — it's an emergency."

Her right eyebrow arched even further, but she dialed without verbalizing her question.

"My name is Yvonne Lane. Can you hear me?" Unintelligible. "I am the current Chief of Staff of Veterans Affairs, and I have an emergency that needs the General. Can you bring the phone to him? Yes, I'll hold." She held her hand over the microphone and looked at Gordan. "He's giving his weekly toast right now."

Now both her eyebrows went up as Gordan reached over and took the phone from her.

He pushed the speaker button and held the phone out chest high.

Voices and fine china clinking came across the speaker, and then he could overhear the bartender identifying the caller.

"Lane — are you close by? You can still make dinner." General Seibert was robust in his element; you could hear the energy he got from being in his environment, the joy in his voice.

"Hey — sorry if this disappoints you, General, but it's me: Gordan Hudde."

"Wait. Didn't you meet..."

"Oh, sure, he extended an invitation. But you will understand I had plans and had to decline."

There were several seconds of silence.

They could still hear some background noises, but the General did not speak.

"General Seibert, are you still there?"

"Yes." The voice sounded a bit flat, and the joy from just moments ago was now gone.

Hudde looked at Lane. His eyebrows furrowed, and his head cocked to the side. "General, are you wearing your sidearm?"

"Yes." The same flat response. Gordan couldn't believe it.

"General, are you eating with the Deputy Secretary of Defense?"

"Yes." It was now barely audible.

Gordan sat up as if he needed to look more authoritarian for this next part. "General, when I count to three, you will set the phone down on the table, draw your service revolver, and shoot Meredith Ryan."

Lane let out a small gasp; Gordan reached out with his free hand and placed it over her mouth.

He continued, "Then you will place the barrel of the gun in your mouth and pull the trigger. Do you understand?"

"Yes."

Gordan glanced over at the larger-than-ever eyes of Lane bulging over his palm. He slowly removed it, and she remained quiet.

"One...two...three." He held the phone out, waiting.

They heard the phone being set down, and then there was nothing but background noise, voices, and sounds of a mess hall until the loud report of a shot. Then there were screams, maybe a table being overturned, and then another shot rang out. Hudde looked at Lane, who was white as a sheet, hyperventilating again.

Hudde shrugged his shoulders. "Holy Shit!" He reached out and placed his right hand on Lane's shoulder, telling her to calm down and catch her breath. She closed her eyes and began getting her breathing under control.

She looked at Hudde with wide eyes and began to explain why she was involved in this operation. How difficult her life had been and the sexism that she had overcome to be in the position she was currently in.

"Ms. Lane, I believe you have had it tough — I really do. Nothing like killing off some of my friends to get rich and get even."

She stiffened up, feeling something cool on her throat. A liquid rolled down her neck and between her cleavage. Maybe, if a little of it made it that far, it would pool in her belly button.

"Oh, no!" she gasped.

"That's right. I broke into the Officers Club at Ft. Belvoir and poured a good shot of Watanabe's concoction into Seibert's famous mug on display for all to see. The thing is…" he showed her a small brown, empty vial from his hand on her shoulder "…I just don't know how much of this stuff you need to put a person under, but I just used all I had left." He sighed audibly. "Oh, well. The other half seemed to work on the General."

Her eyes went even wider with the knowledge that formula MC-Z-22 had just been poured down her shirt. "Please," she begged, but her eyes were already beginning to glaze over, and she began to look sleepy.

Gordan studied her like he guessed that Watanabe would have; her breathing quickly came back to normal, and her face grew slack.

"Lane."

"Yes," she answered without any feeling.

"When I count to three, you will take your purse and walk out to the intersection. The next police car you see, I want you to shoot at it with your handgun."

She didn't flinch.

"Then I want you to drop the gun and remove all your clothing. If you feel like you need to go the bathroom, you will do it right there. Then I want you to pretend that you're a big cat. Do you understand?"

"Yes."

He looked into those glassy dark eyes, and, when he was satisfied that it was time, he counted out, "One...two...three."

She took her purse and exited the car. Gordan got out and walked back to his truck. He wondered if he had given her too much; he tried to remember the side effects. Then he shrugged his shoulders and started the truck. He backed out just as he heard the gunshot. Car tires squealed, and pedestrians screamed. When he got a look at her up at the corner, Gordan nodded his appreciation. She did look pretty good naked. "Whoa," he said out loud. He was a bit shocked; he hadn't realized she had needed to move her bowels.

He shook his head before turning in the direction of the hotel. The cops were handling the crazy naked woman very carefully as he drove by. Suddenly sirens were everywhere. He rolled up the windows, turned up the stereo, and headed to the hotel.

• • •

Robert "Bobby" Reynolds was a self-made billionaire, a business tycoon in the mold of the giants during the industrial age. At sixty-three years old, he hadn't slowed down one bit. He was an alpha male in a world full of alpha males; he pulled himself from the indoor pool at his estate after swimming laps for the last half hour.

Bobby was a barrel-chested, silver-haired force of nature. He grabbed a towel and walked to the glass-and-iron table that was holding his morning grapefruit and a dish of the vitamins that now made up his morning ritual.

His hands were dry enough to pick up the electronic pad nearby to check the stock market, and he began thinking about selling or buying the next phase of his empire.

There was the *Click! Clack!* of heels on tile, and he turned his head until he could take in the vision of his third wife. Half his age, she would turn heads in her tennis outfit with her long, lean legs, shiny with lotion, sticking out of a ridiculously short skirt.

"Honey, I'm going to shower at the club and do some shopping with the girls after tennis today. Be home for dinner."

"Sure, darling. I'll be a little later; I think I may try to see my son on the way home."

"Oh, why don't you have Stephen come over and have dinner with us?" She winked and sashayed away, that skirt nearly showing underwear — or maybe the lack thereof — with each directional change of her hips.

"Oh, he's way too busy these days in the Justice Department." *Besides, he'd be flirting with you the entire time, and I couldn't stand watching you enjoy it so much.* "I just wanted to talk to him about his portfolio and make sure he's following through with his plans for the future."

"Jesus, Bobby — he's nearly forty. It's no wonder he's so gun shy around you."

"Why don't you just try to keep your charges under ten thousand today? That would feel satisfying."

She made a "pouty" face and pulled her ponytail through the back of her visor so that it bounced in sync with her ass; she turned and caught him looking.

"That would make me so sad! You want your baby happy, don't you?"

"I'm an idiot," he said out loud. She smiled and *clickety-clacked* out of the pool room.

• • •

Stephen Reynolds was also wet. He stepped out of the shower and wiped the huge mirror with his hand; unlike his father, he was lean, like a dancer. He was proud of the discipline he showed to maintain his single-digit body-fat content. He wrapped a towel around his waist and admired himself from several different angles. He didn't think forty would be any different than thirty-nine had been, and thirty-nine so far had been spectacular.

He hadn't really wanted to go to Ivy league schools, and he really didn't know what he wanted to do other than bed hot women, drink a bit too much, and drive fast cars. But Dad had pushed him into law school.

His dad was always pushing him further and faster; Stephen figured out over the last few years that his father was living through him vicariously, as did fathers who desired their sons to excel in sports.

His father had figured out later in life that being a business icon was not as powerful as being a senator or other, higher government official, and Bobby wanted this for his son. Bobby didn't care what the son wanted.

"Hate" would be too harsh a word for Stephen to use with regard to his dad. Maybe "scorn"?

He leaned into the mirror to inspect his teeth; they were way whiter than any natural teeth in man's history. He smiled and then winked at the perfect image: "How about it, then?"

He set his jaw and turned his head left and then right trying to figure out if he needed to see the barber.

Since the day his father had seen to it that this job in the Justice Department was offered to him, he had responsibilities that he never had before. But like he always did, Stephen had begun to plan on his own, and when something had come his way — even though it was a shortcut to prosperity that his father would disapprove of — he had jumped at the chance. Maybe it was *because* his father would disapprove of it that he accepted the risk.

He had weighed the risks, and he figured that, from where he was standing, no one would ever want to admit that the Justice Department was responsible in any way with the activities that had been ascribed to him. And if the government was willing to find a way to hide an important person's mistakes — crimes even — they would certainly do it to save face.

Even if he wasn't considered to be "important" enough, his father would make sure he was protected; it happened all the time during his life, and as long as the old man was alive...he figured it was a lock... *unless I kill someone maybe?*

Yeah, well. That didn't happen — not yet, anyway.

He pushed up on his nose to make sure no hair was growing out; he was good.

Maybe he'd keep his old man happy and stay working for the government until he knew if he wanted to run for an office himself. Maybe he'd just keep looking for ways to make as much money as possible with all the connections, and just vacation for the next twenty years. After all, if you're rich enough, even as an old man, you can make it with the hottest young ladies. Hell, his father was proof of that.

He laughed out loud and walked into his vast bedroom.

"What's so funny, Stevie?" Gordan Hudde said from the comfort of a large chair near the window. Hudde was wearing his skull balaclava, the image smiling grotesquely at Reynolds and adding to the fright of having a person in his room.

"Fuck! I nearly had a heart attack, you son of a bitch!" He spun around and slapped his thigh. "Fucking-A! Who the fuck are you, and what the fuck are you doing in my house?"

"Sorry about the fright. I let myself in. Stephen?" He paused. "I actually wanted to talk business today."

Reynolds stomped over to his phone, picking it up to dial. "Then you call my office — and take off the ridiculous mask, unless you're here to rob me."

"You may have something I want, but you'll just give it to me. I won't rob you. I came here with bad news about your Biophaze investment."

Reynolds held the phone at stomach level. He stared at Hudde, who remained seated.

"I'll bet even your dad won't be able to protect you on this one."

"What are you talking about?"

"I'm talking about the investigations that *aren't* happening because you shelved them over at Justice. Come on — you know the ones. I'm talking about dead veterans. I'm talking about embarrassment that gets a fuckstick like you removed from your dad's will. That hot step-mom — is she number three or number four? — will be happy, I suppose."

"Wait. I don't understand…"

"That's right. You're not the sharpest tool in the shed, are you?" Hudde stood. "Your old man must cry himself to sleep at night. You've been hiding Inspector General reports and delaying the congressional requests for information. You know why they wanted you to do this, don't you?"

"Well, I..."

"They have been using veterans as lab rats, Stephen — my fellow soldiers, men I lived and fought with, men who survived the horrors of war only to be killed in a lab experiment."

"Well I..."

Gordan crouched as he punched him hard in the liver. Reynolds stumbled backwards and fell onto a small table; the lamp fell off, and the bulb broke. Gordan was on him before he could roll over. Yanking the towel from his waist, Hudde wrapped it around his head. Picking up the lighter man, he spun him and threw him from the towel like a rock from a sling.

The now-naked Reynolds crashed into a dresser, the items on the top scattering. Reynolds lay across the top, gasping for breath. "I'll pay!" he choked out.

Hudde gritted his teeth and wrapped an extra-large right hand around the neck of Reynolds. He leaned in and whispered, "Why shouldn't I break your neck? Why should you live?"

Hudde squeezed, making it impossible for Reynolds to talk, let alone breathe. His eyes began to bulge, and the perfect tan began to fade from his face.

Hudde released Reynolds just as he went to sleep. Hudde pushed him off the dresser, allowing the limp body to slap onto the tiled floor; a small, bright-white piece of enamel skidded out from under his face.

When Reynolds woke up, he immediately began saying, "Don't kill me," repeating it over and over, now sobbing.

Gordan stepped up and tapped the crying man on the top of the head with the toe of his boot. "Get up, and put some clothes on. I'm tired of looking at you."

"I didn't know everything. Please — I'll make it all right! I promise! Just don't hurt me anymore." Reynolds scrambled to find some pants; he ended up putting on some monogramed pajamas.

Hudde sneered, "Really?" He pointed at the gold-embroidered "SR" on the top of his right thigh on the otherwise royal-blue bottoms.

Stephen Reynolds had never been treated this way, and he pleaded like his life depended on it — which it might very well have — for Hudde to allow him to live.

Hudde stood and told Reynolds to sit in the chair he'd formerly occupied. "I came here with two options for you, Stephen, and killing you was one. Are you saying you want what is behind door number two?"

All the color drained from Reynolds's face when Hudde mentioned death. "Yes, anything — I promise."

"You *promise*?" Hudde scoffed. "According to your own father, you've never followed through on a promise yet."

"Anything, mister — I swear it."

"Stand the fuck up!"

"Please, mister."

"Do you understand that if you fuck this up in any way, if you fail, if you run, I will hunt you down and kill you?"

"Yes, yes. I promise."

"Then raise your right hand."

Reynolds sniffed hard a couple of times and looked confused, but he raised his right hand slowly, until it was near head level. He rolled his shoulders away from Hudde, as if Hudde were going to hit him.

"Do you swear that you will make good on this promise?"

"Yes."

"Do you love your country?"

Reynolds was now very confused. "Well...sure, I guess."

"Good enough." Hudde reached into his denim jacket's deep inner pocket.

Reynolds flinched and stepped back, but Hudde merely pulled out some papers.

"Sign right here." Hudde held the papers out and pulled a pen from his pocket, holding it out for Reynolds to take possession.

"Wait — what is this?"

"Really?" Hudde reached up and grasped the man by the back of the neck, forcing him to bend down over the paperwork.

"No, no — I'll do it." Reynolds signed with a flourish and stepped back, dropping the pen as if he had just touched a snake.

Hudde grabbed Reynolds by the shoulder and pulled him close; Hudde's eyes flashed green under the grinning skull.

"Congratulations, trainee. I suggest you tell your friends and say goodbye at work. You report to Fort Benning Monday morning at 0230hrs. You're going to train to be an infantryman."

"What? You can't be serious. I'm thirty-nine years old. I can't join the Army!"

"Don't sell yourself short, Stephen. You look to be in great shape. It seems that has been the one thing you've really been good at. I know all the right people, and we're all ready for you."

Stephen Reynolds went over and sat gingerly on the edge of his bed. He touched his abdomen where Hudde had struck him. "I think something is broken. We're still fighting in the Middle East, aren't we?"

The mask loomed over Reynolds. "It's time for you to serve your country, even if it kills you. But understand: You *will* die if you do not fight for your country!"

Reynolds wrapped his arms around his stomach and rocked back and forth. Hudde was not sure if it was pain or the realization of what was in store for him.

"That's not all, Stevie. Next, you need to sell all your stock in Biophaze and donate it all to this veterans support group."

"Are you fucking out of your mind? Do you understand how much money that is?"

"Actually, I know *exactly* how much money that is, and I *am* kind of out of my mind. I can't wait to find you when you run. Dying in Afghanistan won't look so bad then."

"Fuck me." Reynolds lay back on his bed.

"Yeah, fuck you. I've got dead friends — don't get me angry."

"This isn't angry yet? Fuck! Alright — it'll get done." He rolled off the bed and sat on the floor. "Oh, Christ — where the hell is Fort Benning?"

"Oh, they're going to love you." Hudde went over to the door and then stopped and turned. "Maybe you should start checking on your co-conspirators in this. I think getting in touch with them — or maybe I should say *trying* to — will convince you to see it through to the end. I'll bet even your dad will be proud when this is over for you."

34

ON SUNDAY, WINTER reached out and squeezed the East Coast, reminding them of the weather they were going to get for the next four to six months. An icy wind crossed the mall parking lot, making a white plastic bag dance through the cars. It picked the bag straight up into the air twenty feet before dashing it back down to earth, where it scurried for safety under some parked cars.

Gordan Hudde and Valerie Baker sat in his truck overlooking the stores. The mall was busy — it was the weekend, and there were many eager Christmas shoppers out, getting it done well before the real rush. They sat in relative silence, looking about, waiting to see if Walter Schroeder was released by the FBI so that he could meet his wife.

"There she is." Gordan pointed out the small Japanese car as it approached a parking spot half a dozen rows away from them.

"What if he doesn't show?" Valerie asked, concerned about the mental well-being of Jill Schroeder.

"My guy says that they sped up the processing for him. He'll be followed, but I'm not worried. For now, it will just be observe and report; I'm not going anywhere."

The two shared a weak smile and then continued to keep watch. Gordan fiddled with the heat and fan, trying to keep the windows defrosted while not making it too hot inside.

Twenty minutes later, Gordan watched Jill Schroeder's head rotate and swivel all around; she suddenly stiffened and sat up straighter. Gordan followed her gaze to a yellow cab and a passenger who got out and closed the door.

Walter Schroeder looked well. This was good because his wife hit him running, like a safety coming hard at a receiver reaching high and crossing the middle of the field.

Gordan glanced over to tell Valerie, but she was wiping tears from her eyes, and he knew she had seen the same thing he had.

"Do you want to come?" He reached out for the door handle.

"No. I'll stay here in the warmth." She paused and then reached out and touched his shoulder just as he cracked open the door. "You did a good thing, Gordan."

"You sure?"

"I really am now."

He slid out of the seat, closing the door behind him. He smiled at Valerie before he turned to cut off the Schroeders, who were heading toward their car.

"Hudde!" Walter saw him first and stopped short of their car.

"Walter, you're looking good; Jill, you look better." He smiled at the two of them and extended a hand that Walter swatted away as he took Hudde into his arms in a hug. Gordan raised his eyebrows in surprise, looking over Walter's shoulder at Jill. "I rather be hugging your wife, man," he said, but he squeezed him hard in return.

"I don't know how you did this, Gordan, but I'll gladly hug you," Jill said, and she pushed her husband aside to wrap her arms around Gordan's chest. "Thank you for everything you've done."

"Listen, I don't want to interfere with you guys getting home. I just wanted to touch base with Walter for a second, OK? If you don't mind, go ahead and get warm in the car. I'll be done with him in a second." She nodded at him while sniffling; he was unsure whether it was due to the cold or the emotion of the moment.

Gordan put an arm around Walter's shoulders; they turned away from the wind and put their heads closer together so that they could speak easier, without raising their voices.

"I had to tell them everything, Gordan. They couldn't stop asking questions about you. I'm sorry if that gets you into any hot water."

"It's OK, Walter. I just wanted to make sure you made it back and to see if they told you anything of interest."

"Like what?" Walter asked.

"Well, did they ever feel the need to threaten you for some violation of laws, or did they make you feel as if you owed them? Maybe they said you need to come back?" Gordan shrugged his shoulders.

Walter laughed. "They did suggest that you and I had interfered with government investigations and could be brought back to face charges at a later date, especially if they felt I'd held anything back. Before I left, they made me sign some confidentiality forms."

Gordan stood up and looked around before grinning. "Too late, friend, they're probably taking photos right now and preparing a file."

"Fuck 'em."

"Agreed. Now go home. Call me if anything else pops up or if they pay you a visit. Understand that, for a while, at least, they will be listening to every call and reading every email."

"I got it. Thank you, Gordan." Walter held out his hand, and Gordan shook it without hesitation.

"Take care of yourself, Walter." Walter slapped him on the shoulder as he turned back to his truck.

• • •

Deep under the White House is a secret meeting room nicknamed "The Tomb." The Tomb was airtight and, for breathable air, depended air scrubbers that were designed for our submarines operating underwater for weeks at a time.

There was a non-stop hum, and most people who had ever made it into this room were not sure whether it was anti-surveillance equipment or the air conditioning.

Presently, it was filled with an assortment of the nation's security directors, the president's closest advisor, and members of Homeland Security.

The president entered, and the heavy door was closed behind him. For a moment, there was complete silence as he looked around, seeming to get eye contact with every individual before he stated that they could all be seated.

The president picked up a three-ring binder and took a few deep breaths before he spoke.

"Director Hunter."

Madeline Hunter said, "Sir," acknowledging that she was in the hot seat.

"Your report is beyond disturbing. Is it accurate?"

"Sir, in the short time we have had to conduct an investigation — and I assure everyone in this room that this is preliminary — it is accurate." She did not appear to be at ease in her seat.

The president lowered his head and rubbed his temples, where his hair was the whitest.

"This begs an important question for the men and women in this room." He stood now and slammed his palm onto the stainless-steel tabletop. "How the fuck does this happen anywhere in America — let alone right here?"

No one dared make eye contact now.

"What the fuck were your guys doing out there?" The president pointed at Hunter.

CIA director Stevens noted that she didn't protest his use of "guys" in his question.

"Or you." The president pointed at the director of Homeland Security. "Or you, too." Now he pointed at Stevens.

Stevens did not hang his head but tried not to look as ashamed as the others appeared.

The president stormed back to his seat at the head of the table. He reached down to grasp a folder marked "Eyes Only."

He waved the folder in the air. "Is this accurate? Is there anyone here who is going to dispute what this former CIA agent says happened or is happening?"

His stare was not returned by anyone.

"Holy Christ." The president shook his head. "Stevens!"

Stevens stood. "Mr. President."

"I know it's early, but you people have reviewed the work of this Dr. Watanabe, and they say his stuff works?"

"Sir, if Watanabe's own logs are accurate. Honestly, from what former Agent Hudde has testified to, it appears it all works as advertised."

"My suggestion would be to lose the former agent and anyone who can talk about this entire fiasco and put our own scientists to work testing and perfecting what this Watanabe has already worked on." Everyone turned to look at the voice from the other end of the table.

The president looked over and down at the speaker. "Director of National Intelligence...isn't that right? How many times did you brief me on this operation?" He paused as he walked to the man. "That's right — *zero* times. So why don't you just sit there and listen? Maybe offer *zero* interruptions."

Stevens cleared his throat. "Sir, if I may — there's more..."

• • •

Gordan Hudde's truck cut through the familiar streets of Otter, Georgia, and he suddenly was comforted by the thought that this was home.

Valerie Baker stirred in the big passenger bucket seat. "Oh, it's good to see Main Street. It seems like I've been gone for months, even though I know it's been only days."

"It gets harder when you realize that no one else will ever be able to know what has happened to you, and when you're surrounded by people, even friends and family, it feels odd that you can still feel alone." Gordan wondered if he should have left her to find that out herself.

She sat silently, looking out her side of the truck. "I can see that." Gordan pulled up the driveway to her small house.

"Gordan?"

"Yeah?"

"We're friends now — right? I mean, we've been through this together, so, if nothing else, we do share that?"

"Almost like brothers-in-arms, I guess." He smiled at her, not knowing where she was going with this line of thinking.

"I've spent a lot of time putting on a tough face and being my own woman, making a good place to live in this town."

"Sure — I've noticed."

"Would I ruin it if I asked to spend some time at your place? I just suddenly feel incredibly unsafe just looking at my own home. They took me right off my own front steps — right there." She pointed.

"With one condition..."

She bit her lower lip, waiting for it.

"...you can't offer any decorating tips."

She smiled with relief and nodded. "I promise. Come in with me while I get a few things?"

"Sure."

They walked up the rest of the way to her front porch. She stopped at the top step. "Fuck — it makes me mad, but this is giving me the creeps."

"You know there are some things that could be done to your home to help you feel safe — some motion floodlights, more secure windows and doors." He took her hand, pushed her fingers in, and had her index finger point out until her hand formed a gun. "You could get some training from someone who knows a thing or two."

She was on the top step, and he was standing on the ground. She smiled down at him. "If only I knew someone like that? Thank you, Gordan. I just can't afford all that right now."

"You never know when you may get a windfall and come into some extra cash."

• • •

"Two million dollars apiece?" The president was taken back.

Director Stevens went on. "The funds that the deceased made from the Biophaze stock purchases will cover way more than that."

The DNI cleared his throat.

The president looked at him for a moment without the disdain that he had shown the man before.

Stevens continued. "If this two million dollars is offered free and clear of all taxes to each of the detainees and to the surviving family members of those slain at the hands of Watanabe and this operation, and if all the offenses committed by individuals from the administration to the bureaucrats in the Veterans Administration are addressed, he assures you that he will do everything he can to keep this report out of any press — foreign or domestic."

Individuals were glancing about the room as Gordan Hudde's demands ricocheted off the walls in silence.

Stevens tapped on the table. "If I may offer my own evaluation."

The president stopped looking at the DNI to look back at Stevens. "Oh, by all means."

"Confiscation of the ill-gotten gains from the sale of the Biophaze stock will cover all the victims easily. Gordan Hudde — dragged into this as a civilian — deserves a share as much as anyone else. Hudde is one of the most patriotic men I have ever served with. He loves this country. He's no fool; he knows that, on a whim, someone here could come after him."

Stevens looked around the room, looking for the person who could not lock eyes with him.

"If you do — if someone here does some math formula that equals an assassination attempt on Hudde — well, I assure you that those people will not end up happy."

The DNI stood. "Are you threatening *us*?" he stretched out his arms to encompass the entire room.

The Secretary of Defense seemed to agree. "We thought we were working with Watanabe and Biophaze. I would not agree to pay a ransom to this...brigand."

Stevens smiled. "He was one of your boys first, you know — before we stole him out from under you."

"A head case and troublemaker, if I read the file correctly before coming over here." He smiled first, and then it turned into a wide grin, without showing any teeth.

Stevens smiled back. "Of course, the one charge that had been filed against him was from a man saved by Hudde from certain death this weekend. So we should check to see what his former commanding officer thinks now."

Stevens scanned the rest of the room and nodded at the president. "I am, of course, not suggesting a threat; I'm discussing the talent of a man I know." Stevens pointed directly at the DNI. "Know this: Hudde will not disappear in a foreign country. He will disappear right here, in the country he loves." He nodded at anyone willing to look at him now, and he walked to the center of the table.

"I don't know how men like this operate so well... in the harshest environments, places that we send them to, and, I might add, I have had the pleasure to know a few men like Gordan Hudde. I'll testify to anyone who will listen: He's either the luckiest son of a bitch to walk the earth, or he's the sneakiest, meanest one to ever walk the earth. Either way, you can decide for yourself on the day you meet him. Of this, I am sure: If you intend to try to have him sanctioned or hurt any of his friends, well, then, the day you meet him — it will be your last."

Stevens walked back to his seat in utter silence. "The Tomb" was never a more apt description.

Finally the President sat hard into his own chair and let out a gasp. "Everyone out!"

As Stevens was on the far side of the room, he was nearly last in line to exit the smaller-than-normal door.

The president called him out. "Stevens, close the door, and come back over here."

Stevens complied. "Sir?"

"You're right about what's right. Damn the money — that's nothing. We can give them more if you think it's the right thing to do."

Stevens nodded.

"Is your man as good as you say he is?"

"Better than that — trust me."

The president looked Stevens in the eye and then glanced around the room as if someone else were present. "Has he ever been to North Korea?"

• • •

Andrew James looked across the cheap card table he used as a kitchen table. The sharp-dressed female attorney looked out of place in this environment, but, to her credit, she seemed not to notice it one bit.

She looked James directly in the eye and pushed her IPad containing the document across the short distance between them.

"This is the release form we spoke about. You can take all the time you need to read it, and then, if you agree, you place your right thumb onto the pad in the place indicated, sign it, and the check is yours."

Andrew liked her smile. She didn't make him feel as if she were selling him something, and he felt in control.

"What's your deal, then?" Andrew asked the stone-faced man in black who had stood silently the entire time.

"He's my driver and security. His services were offered via the FBI to help me visit the other victims and make them all identical offers. He is sworn to secrecy." The pretty attorney looked down at her own phone; she was just answering his question — and nothing more.

"So everyone is being made the same offer of three-point-six million dollars?" Andrew slid the pad over and began to pick it up to look it over.

She nodded. "The same exact offer. Everyone must recognize that the government had no knowledge of this foreign operation and that, once it uncovered this terrorist attack, it acted in everyone's best interest. They have extracted enough funds from the terrorists' operation to offer this financial reward to help you and the others get past this outrageous illegal action against American citizens. We, the United States government, would like to continue to investigate under the umbrella of secrecy, and all of you, of course, do not hold our government responsible in any way. It's that simple. It's up to each of you, but there are no negotiations, and, after this meeting, there will be no further offers. Everyone must decide to take it or leave it."

She put her phone into her briefcase and folded her hands before her, waiting patiently.

Andrew felt that if he asked any further questions, this was the same answer he would receive.

He looked down at the spot where he needed to place his thumb, lined his right thumb up, and set it down directly in the center of the square.

"Mr. Andrew James is moving out!" He flashed a brilliant smile, and she nodded her approval in return.

• • •

From his kitchen, Gordan looked over the counter to make eye contact with Valerie while he spoke to her. "No, seriously — I bought the couch based on how well I thought I could sleep on it if I needed to, so these arrangements have been fine."

"Maybe I should be a 'big' girl and face moving back to my own home."

"Or, there is the other option." Gordan smiled. "Popcorn's done; lots of butter."

"Absolutely, and let me guess what the other option is: We share the bedroom for a while."

"It's a big bed. There must be lots of room in there." He walked back into the living area, a large bowl of popcorn in his hands. He stuck his tongue out and got a piece and sucked it inside his mouth before putting the bowl into her lap.

"So let me review my options." She could see her own reflection in the large-screen TV, and she felt like an attorney giving closing arguments. "Option Number One, we'll call it: I go back to my normal existence back at my own home, or, Option Number Two: I start sleeping with you?"

Gordan looked her up and down, and then his phone rang. He walked over and picked it up, looking at the small screen in his palm.

"May it go on the record that I have never said a word about 'sleeping.' Sorry — I need to get this."

He walked back to the kitchen and spoke in hushed tones. She could see his body posture change as he stood straighter, and she heard a couple of "Sirs."

He walked around the bar stools at the end of the kitchen counter. She knew it was serious — maybe even bad — but there was something about Gordan. She could feel the energy beginning to build; she could see him taking a few deeper breaths.

"Is something the matter, Gordan?"

He stood looking at her but obviously thinking about something else.

"I have some good news for you. Remember those security upgrades we spoke about? Now you can do them all."

"How? I will not allow you to just give me the money. I'm just not built that way."

"My Uncle Sam is sending someone, as we speak, to offer you a confidentiality agreement and to entice you into signing a release... a three-point-six-million-dollar check."

She jumped up from the sofa, forgetting the popcorn and knocking the bowl over. "What? Are you kidding me?"

He was happy that the government was taking this option. He felt it was a positive outcome for her — maybe the best that any of the people touched by this series of events could hope for. But she looked at him and realized that there was more. "But that's not all; what else do they want?"

"That's all for you. You just have to promise never to talk about it, I'm sure; for me, they've come up with some work I could do to 'fix' what they think I owe them now."

"Are you going to do it, whatever it is? I won't take the money if that's the deal and you don't want to do it." She walked up and placed her hand flat on the center of his chest.

"I already said, 'Yes,' and they have a helicopter coming in from Benning to take me to Bragg. I need to meet them down below in my meadow in a little bit."

"Really?" She paused to look out his back-patio window. "That's kind of sexy."

"Try to remember that, then. Maybe, on my return, I'll fast rope onto your roof."

The end.

Gordan Hudde will return.

Please come visit me at: www.markhudsonofficialsite.com/
Or: www.facebook.com/markhudsonauthor/
I can be found at Amazon, Barnes and Noble, and other locations that sell eBooks: amazon.com/author/hudsonmark
Smashwords: www.smashwords.com/profile/view/sp4x2

• • •

Mark Hudson is owner/operator of
ONE FLYER PUBLISHING.

What is being said about Gordan Hudde novels?

A Deep Purple Hue-
"With an extraordinary conspiracy story, this book is perfect for fans of 24 as Hudde reminds me of a bearded Bauer - he doesn't always play by the rules and never bows to authority." -The Book Magnet.

"The perfect conspiracy, well-suited characters, a beginning that hooks you right away..." - Serious Reading.

An Angry Orange Sky-
"With plenty of shocks and surprises, An Angry Orange Sky does not disappoint and I have no doubt that we will be hearing a lot more from Gordan Hudde, at least I certainly hope so!"- The Book Magnet.

"...Hudson expertly narrates what a single man driven by determination and courage can do to counter the evil forces around him." - Serious Reading. "This violent, cinematic second entry in the Gordon Hudde Novel Series shows promise, with its surprisingly original plot, and despite a dauntingly large cast of characters..." - BookLife Prize in Fiction.

A Hint of Silver-
"...Graphic and violent, the gritty manuscript powers along relentlessly... it's hard not to root for a hero like Hudde." - BookLife Prize in Fiction.

Words being used by other reviewers-
"Addictive, interesting, dark, disturbing, brutal, brooding, and exciting."

One reviewer said: "This novel would make a great movie!"

A Retail Investigator
Many 5 star reviews!
"The book clearly outlines the excitement, risk, and exasperation that is part of the deal being in the investigation business. The stories narrated are fun to read and extremely informative for anyone who is currently serving or interested in anything related to the investigation industry." - Serious Reading.

*Don't forget to leave **your own review** at
the location you purchased this book!*